PENGUIN MODERN CLASSICS

Fakira

ANNA BHAU SATHE was an illustrious Indian Dalit author, folk poet, staunch humanist and social reformer from India. National integration, a unified and glorified Maharashtra, identity politics, class and caste struggle, eradication of caste, women's and tribal issues were some of the broad areas his pen covered. Despite lacking any formal education, Sathe, the man of letters, produced thirty-five novels including *Fakira* (1959), which is presently in its forty-sixth edition and received the 'Best Novel Award' from the Government of Maharashtra. Many of Anna Bhau's works have been translated in world languages. His novels *Chitra, Fakira*, short story *Sultan, Khaprya Chor* (A Black Thief) have been translated in Russian, Polish, Czech and many Indian languages.

DR BALIRAM GAIKWAD is presently working as Registrar (I/C) of University of Mumbai and has served as Vice Principal and Head, Department of English at N.G. Acharya and D.K. Marathe College Chembur, Mumbai, for twenty two years. A Fulbright Post-Doctoral Fellow at the University of Florida, he has twenty-two years of teaching experience in English Literature at the undergraduate and fifteen years at the post-graduate level. He also guides PhD scholars at the University of Mumbai. Dr Gaikwad authored two scholarly volumes, *Representation of Femininity Society, Identity and Literature and Socio-Political and Cultural Discourse: Women, Literature and Struggle*. Along with an extensive research experience in Dalit literature, he has delivered many guest lectures in United States of America and has been active both on social and academic fronts.

ANNA BHAU SATHE

Fakira

Translated from the Marathi by
Baliram N. Gaikwad

PENGUIN BOOKS
An imprint of Penguin Random House

PENGUIN BOOKS

USA | Canada | UK | Ireland | Australia
New Zealand | India | South Africa | China

Penguin Books is part of the Penguin Random House group of companies whose addresses can be found at global.penguinrandomhouse.com

Published by Penguin Random House India Pvt. Ltd
4th Floor, Capital Tower 1, MG Road,
Gurugram 122 002, Haryana, India

First published in Penguin Books by Penguin Random House India 2021

10 9 8 7 6 5 4 3 2 1

ISBN 9780143455295

Typeset in Sabon by Manipal Technologies Limited, Manipal
Printed at Replika Press Pvt. Ltd, India

www.penguin.co.in

This book is dedicated to the mightiest pen of
Dr Babasaheb Ambedkar

Foreword

Photograph by Faye V. Harrison, 2001

I am honoured to have been invited to write the foreword to this translation of Anna Bhau Sathe's most celebrated novel, *Fakira* (1959). Dr Baliram N. Gaikwad, who translated the book from Marathi to English, is a colleague who has inspired me to learn more about Dalits in India, and the literature and scholarship they themselves have produced in dialogue with the texts that others have written about them. In the context of comparative literatures, the creative writing of Dalit literary artists can perhaps be seen to resonate with certain aspects of the cultural production of downtrodden people in other parts of the world. Indeed, the pursuit of overlapping and convergent themes led Dr Gaikwad to learn more about Native American (for example, the Ojibwe of Northern Ontario, Canada) and African–American literature, particularly the writings of Indigenous and Black women, including Ruby Slipperjack, Maya Angelou, and Zora Neale Hurston. He has brought his interpretations of these bodies of creative work into his analysis of the issues that Dalit women (for example, Urmila Pawar) address in their autobiographical writing. Dalit Literature, however, as a contribution to world literature should be appreciated in its own right and not only for its comparative significance. Over the years, problems of comparison, relationality, and intersectionality (particularly with class, gender, and religion) have arisen in my encounters with questions concerning Dalits and caste. These issues nuanced my thinking about Sathe's poignant novel and how it is situated within the wider streams of creativity, cultural critique, and knowing which contribute to Dalit studies and subaltern studies as sites of intellectual inquiry and public engagement.

Dalits in Durban, 2001

Twenty years ago, an impressive number of Dalit activists and intellectuals made their presence felt on the international stage set by the non-governmental organization forum (i.e., the NGO Forum) that accompanied the United Nations' 2001 World Conference against Racism, Racial Discrimination, Xenophobia, and Related Intolerance (WCAR) in Durban, South Africa (Harrison 2001, 2005). Dalit delegates—their rallies, exhibits, workshops, and plenary presentations—underscored the parallels that casteism shares with racism. Some even went so far as to claim that casteism *is* racism, invoking race as more than an analogy because of its close family resemblance with caste in a context of human rights advocacy in which anti-racism provided the tactical point of departure for addressing the injuries, traumas, and dehumanizations that birth-ascribed, descent-based inequalities inflict on human beings. United Nations' (UN) world conferences (which are affairs among states) and the companion NGO forums (which feature the voices, goals, and tactics of civil society organizations and social movements) seek to advance the agenda that the UN has promulgated in its charter, declarations (including the Universal Declaration of Human Rights), covenants and conventions. The convention on combating racism is the International Convention on the Elimination of All Forms of Racial Discrimination (ICERD). This is a treaty among nation-states that the General Assembly adopted and presented for ratification in December 1965. It went into effect in January 1969. The momentum for ICERD was built up after the 1963 adoption of the Declaration on the Elimination of All Forms of Racial Discrimination. The major catalysts, those with the most global visibility, for this declaration were the 1960 Sharpeville Massacre in South Africa and the escalation of the civil rights movement in the United States (US). ICERD sought to translate the declaration's vision and ideals into government and civil society policies and practices that the Committee on the Elimination of Racism (CERD) was established to monitor, with the intention of ensuring broad international compliance with the treaty's principles and stipulations. That good intention, however, has yet to be met.

The 2001 NGO Forum's Declaration and Programme of Action, which went further than the more conservative conference's document (which reflects India's refusal to recognize the legitimacy of Dalit grievances and embrace of ICERD), and periodic reports from special rapporteurs and working groups have aimed to clarify the direction for moving forward against racist, xenophobic, and caste oppressions. Those documents reiterate the terms that ICERD spells out in its Article 1, where it states the following:

> In this Convention, the term 'racial discrimination' shall mean any distinction, exclusion, restriction or preference based on race, colour, descent, or national or ethnic origin which has the purpose or effect of nullifying or impairing the recognition, enjoyment or exercise, on an equal footing, of human rights and fundamental freedoms in the political, economic, social, cultural or any other field of public life (emphasis mine, United Nations Human Rights Office of the High Commissioner, ICERD, https://www.ohchr.org/en/professionalinterest/pages/cerd.aspx).

The Durban NGO Forum's Declaration concurs with this definition by pointing out that the 'hidden apartheid' of caste is manifested in discrimination based on work and descent (Articles 84–90 of the WCAR NGO Forum *Declaration and Programme of Action*; September 3, 2001, https://www.hurights.or.jp/wcar/E/ngofinaldc.htm; also see NGO Forum Secretariat, 2002, pages 14–15). CERD, world conferences, and the subsequent review conferences (for example, Durban II, III, and IV in 2009, 2011, and 2021, respectively) have recognized that critiques of caste, specifically untouchability, as a form of structural violence, and the envisioning of new strategies for combating its systemic violations of human rights and human dignity are integral to transnational discussions and exchanges on racism and related intolerance. Such an inclusive approach does not ignore or silence the cultural, national, or historical specificities that condition the ideology, structure, and experience of caste in India. We cannot understand caste without appreciating the multiplicity of ways that Dalits negotiate and resist the power and terror of caste.

Caste in the Wake of Durban

Before participating in the NGO Forum and the conference, both of which I attended as an anti-racist scholar-activist, I had only been exposed to the basics about untouchability and the Dalit predicament. As a sociocultural anthropologist and interdisciplinary social scientist, I had read some of the literature on the varieties of social stratification in human societies, including those based on birth-ascribed distinctions such as caste and race. Since one of my areas of academic specialization was comparative and interlocking social inequalities, I had been exposed to and even taught (post)graduate students on the multiple systems of stratification and hierarchy as they have existed over historical time, geographical space, and sociocultural difference. The wider body of research on the underlying logics, the moral norms, and the sociopolitical dynamics of achieved and ascribed statuses provides a rich theoretical and evidentiary context for situating our understandings and our *mis*understandings of how our home societies operate vis-à-vis societies that are far away, unfamiliar, and, through an ethnocentric lens, strange to us.

This is the intellectual framework in which my students and I have sampled from the extensive scholarship on caste in India and in other parts of the world—from Nigeria to Japan—where caste or caste-like systems also exist. We have gained important insights from the analyses of a number of scholars (Channa 2005, Channa and Mencher 2013, Singh 2014) whose writings illuminate the cultural and political significance as well as the structural underpinnings of the Indian caste system's religious beliefs, symbolic meanings, and ritualized behaviours.

Sociologist Hira Singh (2014) has shown that India's caste system is much more than a social structure driven by cosmology and religion, as Louis Dumont (1980) appears to claim in his normative interpretation of caste hierarchy. In Singh's view, the historically contingent relationship between ideology and the political economy of land and the social division of labour is a necessary focus in order to understand the dynamics and the material stakes of struggles over the inequities and injustices that caste inflicts, often entangled with factors related to class. Scholars such as Eva-Maria Hardtmann (2011) illuminate the multi-scalar practices and connections, from grassroots to global arenas, which shape the contours of collective Dalit agency, including the social action and political mobilization related to building new social movements. These movements have made it possible to translate grounded and embodied understandings of caste discrimination into an international discourse deployed to demand humane modalities of change consistent with the moral and legal standards of what are purported to be universal human rights.

We witnessed some of the outcomes of these internationalizing processes in Durban in 2001, where Dalit NGOs clearly situated caste oppression along the continuum of the 'racism and related intolerance' that the forum addressed. The inclusive focus on racism, xenophobia, and related intolerance is clearly inscribed in the NGO Forum's *Declaration and Programme of Action* (2001). The work and descent-based discriminations the document describes apply to caste as well as race. In that official document, which represents (or represented twenty years ago when it was drafted) a collaborative blueprint for moving social justice and human rights work forward, race and caste are treated relationally as two distinct yet interrelated modes of social inequality and oppression organized around descent-based differences. This approach provides a common ground for building intercultural and transnational relationships of affinity and solidarity for advancing the human rights and dignity of all.

Caste Before Durban: A US Perspective

Long before the awareness that Durban promoted, there were committed visionaries, social reformers, and advocates of radical social transformation who understood the importance of establishing connections and building coalitions across the geopolitical territories of nation-states and continents. Their hope was that they could organize and coordinate concerted action both at home and abroad to disrupt the logics of local and global (sometimes called 'glocal') forces that operate to sustain, and too often, intensify divisions along the lines of gender, religion, class, race, and caste. Dr Babasaheb Ambedkar has been the leading source of inspiration for Dalit activists, intellectuals, and artists. He was also known and respected among African–American internationalists such as W.E.B. Du Bois, who was an anti-colonialist, Pan-Africanist, and one of the leading scholar-activists in the struggle for the civil and human rights of African Americans and of African people globally.

In July 1946, Du Bois exchanged letters with Ambedkar, who had expressed his interest in receiving a copy of the National Association for the Advancement of Colored People (NAACP) human rights petition that Du Bois was preparing to present to the UN on behalf of Black Americans (Ambedkar 1945). Within two years, Du Bois would send 'An Appeal to the World' to the UN, asking that human rights violations against African Americans be redressed. In his letter to Du Bois, Ambedkar wrote that he was considering a similar petition on behalf of untouchables. In their letters, both men noted the parallels in their respective struggles. Du Bois wrote: 'I have often heard of your name and work and of course have every sympathy with the untouchables of India. I shall be glad to be of any service I can render if possible in the future' (Du Bois 1946). The spirit of Du Bois' sentiment of solidarity was also felt by Dr Martin Luther King, Jr., who acknowledged the similarity between the oppressions of Dalits and African Americans when recounting his 1959 trip to India (King 1965).

Beyond these two renowned figures, there have also been others in the US who have noted similarities, as well as differences between the unjust social distinctions that caste and race represent. Anthropologist Gerald Berreman (1972) wrote that: '[race, caste, & gender as oppressive social assignments are] . . . all invidious distinctions imposed unalterably at birth upon whole categories of people to justify the unequal social distribution of power, livelihood, security, privilege, esteem, freedom—in short, life chances' (Berreman 1972: 410).

Decades before Berreman published his classic article in the British journal *Race*, later renamed *Race and Class*, Allison Davis and his co-authors Burleigh and Mary Gardner, who saw their research on African American and Euro-American 'castes' in Jim Crow Mississippi as a study in comparative sociology, used the concept of caste as a heuristic device for analyzing the relations between the dominant and subordinate segments of a rigidly racially segregated, bipolar city in the southern region of the US (David, Gardner, Gardner 1941). In that context, racial 'castes' were endogamous formations of power-mediated social (rather than biological) origins.

The boundary between castes was punitively policed to prevent any shifts in membership and access to privileges and property. In that situation, so-called 'half-caste' children born from illicit, extramarital unions of biracial parents, usually white men and black women, could only belong to the lower, downtrodden caste. Upward mobility could only occur along lines of class, a status that could be achieved despite fixed and permanent caste assignments. At a period when ideas of race were automatically associated with intrinsic biological differences, Davis and the Gardners, who comprised a biracial research team, wished to punctuate the sociocultural basis of race's construction to shift the paradigm away from a discourse anchored in biological determinism. The caste analogy or interpretive metaphor appealed to them for this reason.

Analytically, caste went out of style after the social science debates of the 1930s and early 1940s. Perhaps liberal, integrationist idealism shaped the expectation that race relations, especially outside of the southern region, would eventually become more fluid and diminish in social significance. The hope was in the wake of civil rights legislation along with economic restructuring that would purportedly provide greater opportunities for all to achieve the American dream, race and its caste-like attributes would wither away. Despite the expansion of the African American middle and upper-middle classes, the salience of race has not declined. Race seems to exhibit a considerable degree of permanence (Bell 1992). Perhaps because of this, there are thinkers, most notably Isabel Wilkerson (2020), who have revived the idiom of caste in thinking about the enduring burden of descent in relegating ethno-racialized people into zones of nonbeing, nobodies, and social death (Hartman 2007, Patterson 1982).

Relevant to this view is the unrelenting persistence of anti-Blackness, increasingly recognized as a problem of structural, existential, and ontological implications, sustained by what Afro-pessimists theorize as the 'afterlife of slavery' with its intrinsically related social death (Hartman 2007, Patterson 1982). The Movement for Black Lives, to which the #BlackLivesMatter network belongs, has played a leading, albeit controversial, role in mobilizing against the anti-Blackness manifest in disproportionate extrajudicial killings of African Americans and other racially subjected people (for example, especially Latinx and Native Americans) by police officers and vigilante civilians. The state-sanctioned devaluation of Black life, police impunity, and mass incarceration constitute a problem of crisis proportions that ignited the massive civic unrest we witnessed in the US and in many other places during the summer of 2020, after George Floyd, Breonna Taylor, and several other Black individuals lost their lives from unjust police violence. The antiracist uprising, the COVID-19 pandemic, the devastating effects of the lockdown on the economy with its intrinsic disparities and dispossessions, climate-change-related catastrophes, and the crisis of legitimacy in political leadership during the 2020 presidential campaign merged in a convergence of crises that in many respects is unprecedented in its severity and scale. Of course, this convergence is not at all limited to the US. Its scope, manifestations, and deleterious effects are global—with implications for the precarity, social suffering, collective action, and embodied creativity of Dalits in India and in the Indian diaspora.

The Limits of an Oprah [Winfrey] Book Club Selection on Caste

This is the sociopolitical milieu in which the Pulitzer Prize-winning journalist Isabel Wilkerson's book, *Caste: The Origins of Our Discontents* (2020) was released last year. She organizes her compelling narrative about racism around her interpretation of the concept and several pillars of caste. Her book has received a great deal of media and scholarly attention, and it has revived the debate over caste's relationship with race. This is a matter that the postcolonial and subaltern studies historian Gyanendra Pandey (2013) addressed several years ago when he juxtaposed African American and Dalit autobiographies and memoirs in examining processes of otherization and minoritization in these two markedly different countries. That academic treatise received much less of a response from critics and readers.

Many of the reviews of Wilkerson's book criticize her misuse and unconvincing application of a culturally specific concept and principle of social organization of which she has only a cursory understanding. Dalit journalist Yashika Dutt, author of *Coming Out as a Dalit* (2019), commends Wilkerson's interpretation of the caste logics undergirding the hierarchically graded cross-racial dynamics in American society. Nonetheless, Dutt acknowledges Wilkerson's failure to address the present-day social and political life of India's Dalits—both at home and in diaspora. Despite arguing at least implicitly for the comparability of Dalits and Black Americans, Wilkerson 'ignores the horrors of India's caste structure' today while using caste as a lens for reinterpreting racism in the US and Nazi Germany (Dutt 2020). Wilkerson's widely read book gives caste the public hearing it deserves, but by 'overlooking the ongoing horrors and implications of the Indian caste system on Dalit lives [her book] ultimately serves the dominant caste's straw man argument that casteism is a fading reality in the Indian subcontinent' (Dutt 2020). Dutt goes on to write that reading the 400-page book made her feel 'like being left out of [her] own history.' Paradoxically, she, a Dalit writer, felt like an outcast.

The Value of Dalit Voices, Storytelling, and Counter-Storytelling

In the brief and incomplete intellectual background I have sketched here, race and caste have, at times, been approached as analogies, interpretive metaphors, cases for comparison, and oppressions whose mutual relationality can potentially lead to transnational solidarity against forms of structural violence that should be abolished in favour of 'world-making otherwise'. For any of these approaches to be more than superficial, it is imperative that we understand more about the Dalit experience, especially from Dalits' own points of view. We should seek out and embrace work that helps us acquire this depth of understanding. Moving beyond the debates on race and caste, which have become a preoccupation in the US, it is more than worthwhile to expand the awareness of an international audience on the intricacies of Dalit experiences and struggles. Towards that end, the field of Dalit Studies is an important trend of study in India and transnationally. Within this context, the study of Dalit literature is, without a doubt, a worthwhile endeavor (Gaikwad 2013, Jamdhade 2014).

Baliram N. Gaikwad's contributions to understanding the literary and cultural significance of Dalit authors are seminal (Gaikwad 2013). Building upon and enhancing his scholarly record is his translation of *Fakira*, the award-winning novel of the distinguished Dalit writer, an activist and a theatrical actor of repute, Tukaram Bhaurao Sathe, better known as Anna Bhau Sathe (1920–69). Sathe is the most important writer and activist, recognized as the founder of Dalit Literature. Largely self-taught with very little formal schooling, he produced an extensive corpus of novels, short stories, plays, a travelogue recounting his trip to the Soviet Union, and lavnis, the vernacular or folk songs that rural and urban working people have long enjoyed. Several of his novels and short stories have been translated into many languages and adapted for the movie screen.

Despite his remarkable impact on India's literary and popular culture, Anna Bhau Sathe lived and died in paucity. Apparently, he did not aspire to live a life of affluence and comfort. He was a devoted man of the people and wanted his songs and stories to be informed by his lived experience and embodied knowledge of socio-economic and political marginality rather than by having to imagine or fantasize what poverty was like from an existential distance and from childhood memory. He developed his commitment to writing Dalit life stories and counter-stories—i.e., stories told against the grain of the dominant regime of truth—in his childhood. He and his family were part of a Mang or Matang community in the state of Maharashtra that the authorities, both British colonial rulers and their Hindu compradors or agents, defined both Mang and Mahars as criminal and, therefore, deserving of the colonial regime's punitive policing and repression.

The Matang's livelihood was based on physical labour, serving the landlords in the villages and through entertainment, the street performances of folk music, storytelling, and martial arts. As a young child, he sang songs of devotional poetry that was critical of caste hierarchy and social inequalities, hence, social criticism of caste was an integral part of his every day, vernacular life. After he came of age, Sathe shifted from singing traditional folk songs to performing for the purpose of raising consciousness over social and economic inequalities and the necessity for revolutionary change. He became a leader in the notable Sanyukta Maharashtra Movement (Integrated Maharashtra Movement) due to which Mumbai became part of Maharashtra.

Anna Bhau eventually shifted from Marxism to Dalit activism under the influence of Dr B.R. Ambedkar, becoming a staunch Ambedkarite and spoke, wrote, and sang of working-class people and toiling Dalits having the responsibility of playing a central role in maintaining the earth's balance and in combating global structures of power and political economy, identified as capitalism (Gaikwad 2013, Attri 2019). This perspective departed from the Buddhist influence that most Dalit activists espoused in their opposition to Hindu dominance and nationalism. (Ambedkar founded the Dalit Buddhist Movement, also called Neo-Buddhism and Navayana in the 1950s. It exerts a strong influence on Dalit activism.) Throughout most of his life as an activist, a radical and perhaps a revolutionary reformer, Sathe mobilized his creativity and criticism to resist and refuse the intersecting oppression and exploitation of caste and class. The strengths of his contributions and interventions are reflected in *Fakira*, a compelling text that evokes the vibrant resilience, resistance, heroism, and dignity of Dalits as protagonists who make history rather than merely being victims of it. Sociopolitically promulgated stereotypes of untouchability emphasize the latter.

Final Reflection

I am truly heartened by what I have learnt about this novel, its author, and Dalit literature more generally. I have already begun planning to integrate *Fakira* in a course I hope to develop on social inequality in cross-cultural perspectives. I would like to organize it around themes from the writings—fiction, theoretical essays, autobiographies, ethnographies, and even blog posts—of authors mainly from the Global South and minoritized zones of knowledge in the Global North. I am eager to have my students read intertextually across genres, disciplines, cultures, national borders, and hemispheric geographies as windows on the life-worlds of various peoples engaged in negotiating, resisting, and, at times, refusing the structural violence and ontological terror of systemic subjugations of various sorts. They navigate diverse landscapes of social inequality while finding critically creative ways to affirm, assert, express, and perform their full humanity.

—Faye V. Harrison

References Cited

Ambedkar, B.R., 1946, Letter from B.R. Ambedkar to WEB Du Bois. Ca July 1946. W.E.B Du Bois Papers, University of Massachusetts, Amherst. Available at: https://credo.library.umass.edu/view/full/mums312-b109-i132. Accessed on 25 May 2021.

Attri, Pardeep, 2019, *Politics: Remembering Annabhau Sathe, The Dalit Writer Who Dealt a Blow to Class and Caste Slavery*, *HuffPost India,* https://www.huffpost.com/archive/in/entry/annabhau-sathe-dalit-writer-marathi_in_5d415c3ce4b0d24cde082f0d. Accessed 1 June 2021.

Bell, Derrick, 1992, *Faces at the Bottom of the Well: The Permanence of Racism*. New York: Basic Books.

Berreman, G., 1972, *Race, Caste, and Other Invidious Distinctions in Social Stratification*, Race, XIII (4): 385-414.

Channa, Subhadra Mitra, 2005, *Metaphors of Race and Caste-Based Discriminations against Dalits and Dalit Women in India*. In *Resisting Racism and Xenophobia: Global Perspectives on Race, Gender, and Human Rights*, Faye V. Harrison, ed. pp. 49-66, Walnut Creek, California: AltaMira Press.

Channa, Subhadra Mitra and Joan P. Mencher, eds., 2013, *Life as a Dalit: Views from the Bottom on Caste in India*, New Delhi: Sage Publications India Pvt Ltd.

Davis, Allison, Burleigh B. Gardner, Mary R. Gardner, 1941, *Deep South: A Social Anthropological Study of Caste and Class*, Chicago: University of Chicago Press.

Du Bois, W.E.B, 1946, Letter from W.E.B Du Bois to B.R. Ambedkar, 31 July 1946, W.E.B Du Bois Papers, University of Massachusetts, Amherst. Available at: https://credo.library.umass.edu/view/full/mums312-b109-i133. Accessed on 25 May 2021.

Dumont, Louis, 1980, *Homo Hierarchicus: The Caste System and Its Implications*, Translated into English by Mark Sansbury, Chicago: University of Chicago Press.

Dutt, Yashika, 2019, *Coming Out as a Dalit: A Memoir*, New Delhi: Aleph Book Company.

Dutt, Yashika, 2020, Review: *Feeling Like an Outcast*. FP (Foreign Policy), Available at: https://foreignpolicy.com/2020/09/17/caste-book-india-dalit-outcast-wilkerson-review/. Accessed 26 May 2021.

Gaikwad, Baliram N. 2013, Manifestation of Caste and Class in Anna Bhau Sathe's *Fakira* and Baburao Bagul's *Jenvha Mi Jaat Chorli Hoti. The Criterion: An International Journal in English*, Issue 12 (or Vol 4[1]), February, https://www.the-criterion.com/. Accessed on 1 June 2021.

Hardtmann, Eva-Maria, 2011 *The Dalit Movement in India: Local Practices, Global Connections,* New Delhi: Oxford University Press.

Harrison, Faye V., 2001, 'Imagining a Global Community United Against Racism', *Anthropology News*, Public Affairs column, December 2001.

Harrison, Faye V., 2005, 'Introduction: Global Perspectives on Human Rights and Interlocking Inequalities of Race, Gender, and Related Dimensions of Power', In *Resisting Racism and Xenophobia: Global Perspectives on Race, Gender, and Human Rights*, F.V. Harrison, ed., pp. 1–31, Walnut Creek, California: AltaMira Press.

Hartman, Saidiya, 2007, *Lose Your Mother: A Journey Along the Atlantic Slave Route*, New York: Farrar, Straus and Giroux.

Jamdhade, Dipak Shivaji, 2014, 'The Subaltern Writings in India: An Overview of Dalit Literature', *The Criterion: An International Journal in English*, Vol. 5, Issue III, June 2015.

King Jr., Martin Luther, 1965, 4 July sermon at Ebenezer Baptist Church, The Martin Luther King, Jr. Research and Education Stanford Institute, Stanford University. https://kinginstitute.stanford.edu/chapter-13-pilgrimage-nonviolence. Accessed on 28 July 2021.

NGO Forum Secretariat, 2002, NGO Forum, South Africa: 2001 World Conference against Racism Declaration and Programme of Action, As adopted at Kingsmead Cricket Stadium, 3 September, 2001, Durban, South Africa: South African Non-Government Coalition.

Pandey, Gyanendra, 2013, *A History of Prejudice: Race, Caste, and Difference in India and the United States*, Cambridge: Cambridge University Press.

Patterson, Orlando, 1982, *Slavery and Social Death: A Comparative Study*, Cambridge, Massachusetts: Harvard University Press.

Singh, Hira., 2014, *Recasting Caste: From the Sacred to the Profane*, New Delhi: Sage Publications India Pvt. Ltd.

Introduction

FAKIRA—A Literary Miracle

Thinking about Anna Bhau Sathe, I must begin by mentioning an enigmatic French writer. Jean Genet, author of *The Balcony* and *The Maids*, known primarily as an outstanding playwright, was the son of a prostitute who offered him up for adoption when he was only a seven-month-old child. Though adopted by an affectionate family, Genet got into the life of petty crime and became a vagabond. He was jailed several times and expelled from several countries. But later he decided to give his life a new turn and met Jean Cocteau who helped him get his first novel published. After ten convictions for all the crimes and 'indecency' he had committed, he was to be punished with a life sentence. But Cocteau and Jean-Paul Sartre intervened, and the President of France decided to set aside the sentence. Thus was found a great French writer, celebrated throughout the world for his plays, dramatic productions and non-fiction about the Middle-East. I think of Genet every time I think of Anna Bhau, who was no less in literary talent than Genet. However, Genet had his Cocteau and Sartre to support him. Anna Bhau was, unlike Genet, an entirely self-made man.

Another great literary figure that comes to my mind when I think of Anna Bhau Sathe is the Marathi poet Narayan Surve (1926–2010), born just six years after Anna Bhau (1920–1969). It is difficult to say if he was born an orphan or if he was abandoned, but all that he remembered was growing up as a child sleeping on the Bombay footpaths. He too had barely any literacy and had to teach himself. His first collection of poems was published in 1962 and the next one, *Majhe Vidyapith* (My University), 1966, brought him into limelight. Surve's literary genius, his work with workers' unions and his Marxist political leanings make him comparable to Anna Bhau Sathe as a literary genius. Sathe and Surve in Marathi compared with Genet of France show that the struggle of the downtrodden Marathi writers, though of the same epic tenor as of comparable French or German writers, has dimensions that make it even more heroic. In the case of Anna Bhau Sathe, it was even more so, for he was a trendsetter, innovator and experimenter without a match in the history of Marathi literature.

Not having the benefit of any decent schooling, having to slog off his precious childhood years as a stray labourer, having to leave behind his village in the Sangli district of south Maharashtra and to work in Bombay in order to stay alive, Anna had no leisure to think of poetry and music. Yet, like a bolt from the blue, he found the efflorescence of deeply moving poetry and heart-changing theatre coming out of him. He made use of his talent to motivate people and get them to think of the poor and the wretched of the earth. During the movement for a 'united state of Maharashtra', Anna Bhau's song '*My Beloved Is So Far*' moved millions involved in the movement and acquired an iconic stature that hardly any other single poem in Marathi had ever gained before. The literary forms he used range from songs, poems, ballads, the Tamasha theatre to prose, fiction, and public orations. It is quite astonishing that he excelled in each of these genres.

Anna Bhau's life was short. He died before attaining the fiftieth year; and this short life was filled with many political movements and a harsh struggle for survival. Yet, Anna Bhau managed to be a prolific writer, producing thirty-five novels, just to mention one among the many genres he handled. Of these, *Fakira* was recognized immediately on its publication as the work of a genius. In the times when Marathi fiction writing had made sentimentality, melodrama, and romance as its core, *Fakira* brought in a completely new sensibility. Its impact on the Marathi literary sensibility was so deep that within a few years of its publication, it motivated a large number of young writers to write about socially realistic themes and about Dalit communities. Anna Bhau's work inaugurated a brilliant literary movement, which later came to be known as Dalit Literature. He was for it what William Wordsworth was for British Romanticism.

In 2021, the plot of the novel may not strike one as unique; but at the time it was published, it was a completely unprecedented one in a style that was entirely fresh. It tells the story of a young man and his crusade for the rights of people of his community in the British regime. The story deals with the religious practice or ritual called 'Jogin'. It is a sad reflection on the Indian literary scene that the work remained untranslated for such a long time. I am glad that Dr Baliram N. Gaikwad decided to bring it out in English to mark the birth centenary year of the writer. In 2020, all over Maharashtra, there were a number of (online) seminars and lectures on Anna Bhau Sathe's contribution to social movements and literature. There already exist statues of Anna Bhau in several small towns and cities in Maharashtra. Yet, the popular adulation that he received during the five decades since his death does not take away the fact that his literary output remains unknown outside Maharashtra. In that direction, Dr Gaikwad's English translation being published through a renowned publishing house such as Penguin is most welcome. Like thousands of his admirers in Maharashtra, I have a sense of delight that an iconic work of a writer whom I most admire is being brought to the notice of readers in and outside India.

G.N. Devy, Literary Critic and Cultural Activist
17 June 2021

Translator's Note

Fakira, recipient of the Government of Maharashtra's 'Best Novel Award', is the seminal work of the veteran author, playwright, novelist, folklorist, poet, freedom fighter, and actor of repute, Anna Bhau Sathe. I read *Fakira* as a recommended text for my MPhil. course at Dr Babasaheb Ambedkar Marathwada University, Aurangabad. But it was after reading numerous critical works on *Fakira* and African American literature while I was pursuing my Fulbright Post-Doctoral studies at the University of Florida, that I gained a deeper understanding of the text. My supervisor, Dr Faye V. Harrison, introduced me to an exhaustive list of African American authors and ensured my direct interaction with the African–American community through authors and activists. My friend, Dr Tricia Nunn also involved me in community interactions and local visits to churches and historical plantations. This collective exposure gave me the socio-literary insights and an understanding of the mutual inspirations derived by African–American literature and Dalit Literature. The comprehensive comparative study of this subject also equipped me with a profound understanding of the similarity of the collective experiences as in social atrocities, and their long battles to obtain justice, freedom from caste, racial discrimination, and a dignified social status. Both these literatures are not meant for entertainment but for social awakening. My intense response and reaction to these similarities inspired me to undertake the challenging project of translating *Fakira*.

I consider it a privilege to translate *Fakira* from Marathi to English. *Fakira*, now in its forty-sixth edition, has been the first and foremost Dalit novel in Marathi. The versatility of the novel can be fathomed from the fact that *Fakira* was soon made into a film in 1963 in which Anna Bhau Sathe himself played the lead role of *Fakira*. Six of his other novels were also made into films. Anna Bhau Sathe, the Dalit author who had not received any formal education, produced literature of such high standard that for the last three decades, his works have been prescribed as textbooks in many Indian universities and also have gained substantial attention in the research arena.

Besides being Marxist, in the early phase of his life, Anna Bhau Sathe was a follower of the philosophy of Dr B.R. Ambedkar. The significance of the novel *Fakira* is underscored by the fact that it is dedicated to the mighty pen and gigantic social contribution of Dr B.R. Ambedkar. Anna Bhau Sathe was also an avid reader and admirer of Dr Martin Luther King Jr. It has been learnt recently through an interview of retired military officer Dr Hadolikar that when Dr King was assassinated in 1968 in Tennessee, Anna Bhau Sathe conducted two condolence meetings in Worli, Mumbai, and impressed upon the gathering that Dr Martin Luther King's life and movement should be a fountain of inspiration to the Dalits in India. Anna Bhau Sathe's works seems to be the confluence of the ideals of Dr King and Dr B.R. Ambedkar.

Caste and class struggle, eradication of caste, identity politics, and love for a unified and glorious Maharashtra are some of the broad areas his dexterous pen covered. The thematic concerns, socio-political portrayals, a message to fight against injustice through education, cultural awakening and a ceaseless quest for the common man's welfare are his dominant themes. Deliberate use of a dialect of Marathi turns out to be the required strategy to bring authenticity to the work. During the process of translation, utmost care has been taken to retain the subtleties, the cultural connotations, and tone of the original Marathi text.

It is beyond a doubt that Anna Bhau Sathe's *Fakira* has been the most celebrated novel which received Government of Maharashtra's 'Best Novel Award' in the year 1961. It has been translated into Hindi and Punjabi languages. Anna Bhau Sathe reinvented the tradition of oral history which stands parallel to the written history. Of course, subjective base of the oral history cannot be as rational as objective truth portrayed in the written history. However, some phenomenon and everyday experiences of the common folk receive consent in the conceptualization of the public reason, spiritual, temporal, other worldliness, or *Lok Dev*. Public reason, *lokmanas,* unlike enlightenment, provides space to the accommodation of customs like revelation and belief. Anna Bhau Sathe traced out myriad shards of cultural practices like beliefs, customs, and perceptions, which he transformed into creative myths and constructed the theme of his novel. Sharad Patil, an acclaimed Indologist and scholar, remarked that Anna Bhau Sathe draws our attention to the spiritual divine marriages, which he attempted to revive in his novel in the form of jogani.

The common myth was that of winning the right to hold jogani fair in the village. It was a collective traditional belief that such jogani fair will bring in sufficient rains, bumper agricultural production and the prevention of epidemic spread. Symbolically, jogani (a piece of dry coconut covered with yellow cloth) epitomizes self-motivation and brings prosperity in the village. Here, jogani also symbolizes a divine marriage and good luck. Actually in this marriage, a person of gurav caste acts as joga, while a beautiful person of sutar caste acts as jogani, and they were called respectively called bride and groom. Any village that is able to snatch the jogani from the hands of the groom will win the game and a fair would be organised in their village.

This novel begins with romanticizing the story of a bloody contestation between two villages, namely Shigaon and Vategaon, for bringing jogani forcibly to their own village.

A tough fight between Ranoji and the villagers of Shigaon results in a heroic win for Ranoji. Bapu Khot of Shigaon violates the customary rules and crosses the boundary of Shigaon in chasing him to get back the jogani and Ranoji Mang is unlawfully beheaded by the chasers. Learning from his mother, the inspiring stories of heroic deeds of his father Ranoji, Fakira in a herculean fight against the Khot of Shigaon brings back the jogani, the lost pride to Vategaon. By this exemplary act, both Ranoji and Fakira were not called by their caste Mangs but instead they become the *Lok Dev*—a jagrut (live) place of worship, faith, and belief. Fakira becomes a hero and an icon not only for fulfilling the dream of his father, Ranoji, but also for devoting his life to the interest of the village and more so for bringing about welfare of the downtrodden neighbourhood in the region.

Despite the critical comments about the over romanticism in the novel losing the touch of psycho-emotional facets, undoubtedly Anna Bhau Sathe's through *Fakira* rewrites the history of vulnerable masses, Mangs, Mahars, nomadic tribes and criminal tribes.

He also demonstrates how these communities revolted against all odds in their daily lives and how they revolted against the coercive rule of feudalism and imperialism.

Anna Bhau, knowingly, paid less attention to the artistic values in his writings. What he gave paramount importance to, is the lived experiences of the common folk in everyday sociology, and he also expressed how the protagonist and his followers played a significant role as an agency of emancipation for the vulnerable masses. For instance, this novel addresses the issues of poverty and hunger of Mangs and Mahars in the village, emphasizing the imperatives of survival strategies. During famine, when repeated requests to the British government for food supply failed and peasants were dying of hunger,

Fakira, with his men, loots the kothar (British grain stores) and distributes it among the hunger-stricken Mangs and Mahars. The colonial administration begins to harass Fakira's family when Shigaon police reports this incidence to administration. Secondly, when the lives of all downtrodden Mangs and Mahars turned out to be on the verge of an end, to overcome this terrible situation, Fakira goes on to loot the British treasury and distributes it among the sufferers. The British government, with all its might, was after Fakira but failed to catch him. However, when the British forcefully imprisons the villagers, Fakira surrenders himself in order to save the lives of his villagers.

A special characteristic of the novel *Fakira* also needs to be understood here. 'Parushi', the sign language of the Mang caste, is embedded in the oral dialogue of the characters in the novel. Anna Bhau Sathe preserved this highly attractive language which is imprinted on the minds and souls of the readers. Readers get engaged with the narrative style and linguistic artefact here. The author has taken sufficient care that the clever use of Parushi language in the novel does not overshadow other facets of the novel but lucidly integrates in it. I would also like to underscore here that through *Fakira*, many words in the Parushi language have been added to the dictionary of Marathi literature. Anna Bhau Sathe has simultaneously documented the Mang Parushi language through this novel. While the merits of any novel are determined on the premises like content, technique, and style, Anna Bhau's *Fakira* not only fulfils all the prerequisites but also engages the readers in applying the hermeneutics for understanding the underlying meanings of the oral traditions and decoding the myths, cultural practices, folk rituals, and law and justice.

The protagonist Fakira, revolts against the orthodox system prevalent in the rural areas especially, and the British Raj, to save his villagers from utter starvation, caste discrimination, and humiliation. A protagonist and his community are subsequently arrested and tortured by the British officers and Fakira eventually surrenders, to save the lives of his villagers. A British officer Mr John releases 200 villagers only after Fakira's surrender, and ultimately, Fakira is hanged. His sacrifice for the villagers reflects the philosophy of humanism too.

Fakira becomes the symbol of protest against the intentional social cruelty imposed on the Dalits for thousands of years. Prolonged oppression of the Dalits: the Mangs and Mahars, the pathetic lives of landless labourers, agricultural workers, and the merciless exploitation of these men is integral to the novel. It also poses a strong resistance to the social stigma, based on the notion of purity, impurity, and untouchability. For researchers and readers, the Hindu religious traditions, rituals, customs, rites, festivals among these people, are the unexplored anthropological sites in the novel.

Evidently, Dalit Literature is the truest reflection of Dalit lives and Anna Bhau Sathe, the first distinguished Dalit writer who started projecting Dalit lives with inherent philosophy, stated in the introduction of *Fakira*:

> *It's my belief and personal experience that if any creativity which is not in accordance with the*

> *universal truth and truer reflections of life then it is useless. If the truth is without the base of life, creative potential is ineffectual much like the mirror in the darkness. Then,. however hard one tries he cannot see the reflection in the mirror and defeats imagination. Like the wingless birds, creativity cannot soar high. I am too heavy and incompetent to take flights of imagination of that kind. As creativity needs to be supplemented by truth and factual; imagination also demands the wings of life and if self-experience is not influenced by compassion then we would never reach the unfathomable truth of life.(Anna Bhau Sathe)*

Anna Bhau Sathe, both in *Fakira* and in his other writings, wrote with extreme compassion towards all the strugglers and the minorities in the world.

He writes:

> *While writing I am always compassionate because for whom I write are my own people, living human beings. Their concern is my chief concern. Even this Fakira is mine. As an author, I am not equipped to and don't intend to 'make real what is not in existence'. I wrote and write what I see and experience personally. I have been and will be writing based on what I personally see and experience in real life.*

Anna Bhau Sathe was the first Dalit to foreground the Dalit experience with an authenticity, honesty, and accuracy because it was his lived experience. That gives his work an internal integrity. His characters are real because he writes about them with compassion and affection since they are his people, they belong to him, and he to them.

Considering the changing times and the growing awareness of Dalit Human Rights, especially since the 2001 UN World Conference against Racism, Racial Discrimination, Xenophobia, and Related Intolerance, it has become necessary to translate some major texts of Dalit literature for global cognizance and attention. This English translation of *Fakira* is an effort in that direction.

I hope the endeavour of rendering *Fakira* into English, a global language, and sharing the enormous value of the novel will internationalize the Dalit issues and literature as well. It would be most appropriate to dedicate this translation project to the Indian Dalits, African Americans, Native Americans, Aboriginals of Australia, and Ainus of Japan and all those who are fighting their battles for pride, dignity, and recognition around the world.

Mumbai
22 March 2020

One

The sun had set, but it had left a streak of pink light along the western sky. In the gleaming steel greyness below it, there was a faint glow where the sun had been. And the blanket of darkness was spreading over the whole world, right from the narrow fertile valley, from the Warna to the Krishna. Just as the sun had illuminated every inch of this gigantic world, the night was now blackening it out. Light after darkness and darkness after light, the rhythm of nature was playing out its course.

Vategaon's very presence had disappeared. The 1200 dwellings had been swallowed by the murky waves of night. The barren lands around the village, even the mighty seven-gorged mountain of the Sahyadri, were engulfed by the darkness. Only the light at daybreak could restore the presence of the village. The cart track which came from Tambakhadi entered the village, and as it headed towards the chavadi, it went past Vishnupanta Kulkarni's magnificent wada, then circumambulated Shankarrao Patil's wada and straightened up before reaching the Mahar Mang settlement. From there, beyond the enormous tamarind tree near the Mang Wada, you have to take a turn to get to the homes of the Mangs. This cart track wound its way eastwards, meandering through fields and farms before it entered Shigaon. The four-mile distance between Vategaon and Shigaon had been converted into a six-mile journey because of the curves and bends the path had taken. That path had now been wiped out by the darkness.

Gradually, the monsoon winds rose and before long began to run amok. Dark clouds crowded the sky. And like a fish cutting through the water, lightning shimmered in the clouds. And in these brief bright flashes the sky looked like it was about to collapse. The clouds assumed frightful, ugly shapes and began to somersault, as the wind tossed them about like cotton balls.

Quiet descended on the village. All the lanes seemed deserted. One by one the dimly glowing lamps started shutting their eyes. Dogs became mute. Silence reigned. The timid atmosphere stood dejected and forlorn. The village made not a whisper.

Shankarrao Patil was sitting on the wooden swing, all alone. He wished someone would come and sit with him, talk to him. He had waited for so long, but no one had turned up and he was peeved. He had drawn his knees up to his chest and rocked the swing gently, as he stared intently at the path ahead. His ears were pricked up to catch the whisper of a passerby. But in vain. No one had come to talk to the Patil. People had closed their doors and laid down on to sleep a long while ago. And that's what had annoyed Patil further. Work hard all your life and in the end, die—that's what he didn't approve of at all. He believed that man should be happy, work hard and enjoy life. Tomorrow was the last day of the month of Ashadh. Tomorrow was also the jogani fair at Shigaon. He felt a surge of envy for Bajiba Khot of Shigaon.

The entire jogani jatra had been organised by that Bajiba Khot. As a young man, he had battled valiantly against the whole of Kalgaon, captured the jogani vati, half a dry coconut that symbolized the jogani—a local deity—and brought it to his village. Since that day Kalgaon had given up holding the jogani jatra and it now took place at Shigaon. Had the people of Kalgaon caught Bajiba that day, they would have beheaded him and hung his head by the boundary gate of the village. But Bajiba was a big, strong man. And that's why Shigaon thrived and prospered. People there celebrate fairs and jatras three times in a year.

And here, in our village? Nothing at all. When the day ends, not a word is heard, not a human seen. No sports, no tamasha, no nothing! One jatra in twelve months and that too as if people have gathered for a funeral. Such a big village, to what purpose, Patil thought.

Patil was overpowered by this whirlwind of thoughts but he tried to shrug them off. Just then, he heard the sound of a horse's hooves approaching. Patil strained his ears to catch the sound. Suddenly the horse neighed loudly, shattering the surrounding silence. The sound reached Patil's horse who responded with its own neighing. Peering into the darkness in the direction of the sound, Patil called out, "Who goes there?"

"Me, Ranoji Mang," said the man alighting from his horse.

"Come, come, have some paan before you go." Patil urged him with a sense of urgency in his voice. "You are late today?"

"Yes, late night," Ranoji replied, looking up at the sky. "Aba, the rain, it's coming," he grumbled.

"You come and sit. The wind is howling; it won't rain," Patil assured him. Ranoji reined in his horse, dismounted and went and sat on a stone near the swing.

"Not slept yet? Why are you awake?" Ranoji asked.

"What to do, sleep not coming."

"Why, what happened?"

"Nothing. Feeling dejected. No challenge or spirit in our village." Patil expressed his innermost thoughts. "There is no life left in the village. Soon as the sun goes down it becomes dead-like."

"Then what should it do? It goes to sleep from exhaustion."

"Don't others get tired? Don't they have responsibilities?" Patil asked. "Don't those people of Shigaon feel fatigue? Three jatras in a year they conduct, along with living their routine lives."

"Their village has the jogani vati, so they hold it. What can we do?"

"Jatras don't happen on their own. You have to make them happen. Tomorrow if we decide to conduct the jatra, will anyone stop us? Hold us back?"

"Then why don't we organize it?"

"How is it possible?" Patil retorted. "After sunset not a stray dog stirs in this place. Then who thinks of a jatra? In the British neighbourhood beyond, people are enjoying their lives. In that Shigaon, the joga and jogani will be taken in procession. The jogani vati will be proudly displayed tomorrow. Unless our village produces a brave hero like Bajiba Khot, how can we host the joganis? He was solely responsible for it."

"Bajiba? How?"

"He charged into the Kalgaon jatra, created a disturbance and in the ensuing confusion grabbed the jogani vati and rushed back to his village. Do we have such a daring man in our village?"

"Why not? Big people like you or Panta, you two can challenge a tiger!"

"It is easy to take on a tiger, but fighting against a whole village is not easy. One needs a courageous heart as large as a mountain and I don't have it. As for our Vishnupanta—so good at nudging and pushing the law, he will not give up his service even if he loses his life."

"I'm going to the jatra tomorrow. What about you?" Ranoji asked.

"I never go to any jatras," replied Patil despondently. "I don't like to be welcomed and felicitated in other people's villages. When our own homes are in darkness, celebrating in the bright lights outside doesn't appeal to me at all." So saying, Patil handed a prepared paan to Ranoji.

Both of them chewed on the betel leaf paan. Ranoji was about to get up when Patil said abruptly, "This pandhari, our village, desperately needs a person like Bajiba Khot if it is to prosper and gain glory. Bajiba did Shigaon a great favour by his courage. We also need one such warrior to take birth here."

Hearing this, Ranoji became extremely serious. His mind was in a turmoil. Twisting the leather whip in his hands, he stared into the darkness. The flat barren plain between Vategaon and Shigaon, the winding track, the muddy path and the clumps of thorny nivadung bushes along the way—these images floated before his eyes.

"Go now," Patil said, "Daulati must be waiting for you."

Ranoji stood up and started walking, his head full of thoughts. His horse followed him. When he turned the corner, he heard Kondiba Mahar singing his bhajans. Kondiba could not be seen in the deep darkness, only his gruff voice and the sound of the accompanying tarya was heard. Ranoji broke out of his reverie. He looked in the direction ahead at Mang wada and leapt onto his horse.

Mang wada, just a shout away from the village, lay motionless. The nivadung cactus, tall as five men, encircled the fifty houses lying within its arms. Two of these arms met at the huge tamarind tree, leaving gap for a narrow path leading to Mang wada.

Those hutments among the cactus had somehow managed to remain standing. Their sugarcane-leaf thatches looked alarmed today. The dark sky was threatening to collapse on them. Suddenly an owl hooted. A nightjar chittered. The deadly cobra slithered to hunt the doves, and its arch-enemy, the mongoose, tried to attack the snakes. Sounds of the scuffle between cobras and mongooses were heard. They made the panic-stricken children crawl into their mother's arms, with knees drawn into their bellies. Death wriggled about by their heads and feet.

The village had no idea of how many people lived in the Mang wada. Nor did anyone really care what they lived on.

But they all knew that Mang wada existed among the nivadung cactus. The law too had acknowledged that the Mangs were the official sepoys and the yoke of protecting the village was on their necks, they being the servants of the village. The Mangs were responsible for whatever happened in the village and the fields. Even if one bundle of hay went missing, the Mangs were held responsible. Every Dashera they performed the puja to honour the sword. Two things enjoyed a unique coexistence in this colony—poverty and pride, pride of the sword!

When the Mangs were awarded a small patch of land, there were only three families living there. Now there were fifty. The land was just not enough. Branded as legitimate sepoys, they did not have the means for farming. So now they were helpless and exploited.

When rain started pouring down from the sky, tears would start streaming from Mang eyes. With employment opportunities drying up, the fire of hunger would begin to burn. Children would cry for food, old men would succumb to starvation, young people would drink water and gird themselves to face the situation. Theirs was a life of oppression. For this proud community, begging was humiliating. With hungry stomachs they would think and think and exhaust themselves. And only one way out appeared before them.

The men would congregate with their weapons and in the pouring rain, in the dead of the night they would raid far off villages and fields. Risking their lives, they would rummage for whatever they got and return home to appease their insatiable appetite. This had become a practice, a custom. Not for a day but year in and year out.

Between the harvest and the monsoon season, they were forced to become thieves. Habit had made it a profession for some. What good could abject poverty yield other than this evil?

Yet from within the embrace of the prickly nivadung had sprung the strongest men, the toughest, the hardiest, the bravest. All of them weighed equally against the other. Like an ember fanned into a flame or a sandalwood tree sprouting in an arid land, this tiny Mang settlement had taken shape. Daulati Mang, Appa Mang, Bhairu Mang and many such elders were active there. Be it in the Mang colony or the main village, they would roar like tigers. No one would dare to cross them! Just like the elders, the youngsters such as Daulati's son Ranoji, or Bali, Pandu, Dagadu, Ninya, Savalya, Gonda and many others would strut around like shimmering swords.

Daulati, now in his fifties, had some silver glints in his impressive moustache, but his muscular physique still had the strength of steel in it. His son Ranoji was a mature young man and looked after the house and his government duties. Daulati's wife Rahibai, his daughter-in-law Radha, grandsons Fakira and Sahadeva, fondly called Sadhu, and son Ranoji had filled his life with a sense of satisfaction and joy. Daulati was spending his remaining days without any cares.

But today Daulati was worried. His son Ranoji was unusually late returning home. Rahibai was restless. Fakira and Sadhu too were waiting for their father and kept asking their grandfather why their father had not come home yet. Rahibai tried to distract the children by telling them stories of gods and goddesses. Radhabai was stirring the bubbling pot of broken rice. Daulati's ears were impatient for the clip-clop of a horse's hooves. The ten-year-old Fakira said plaintively, "Baba, why doesn't Gabarya come?"

"Gabarya will be here any moment now . . . with your father," Daulati comforted Fakira.

Once a group of Pendhar tribals had made a halt on the outskirts of the village and one of the Pendhars had gifted a young colt to Daulati. Daulati had taken great pains to turn it into a magnificent steed. He had christened him Gabarya. The entire village had grown fond of Gabarya. Instead of asking when their father would come home, Fakira and Sahadeva invariably asked when Gabarya would come. They were quite sure that Gabarya was in charge of their father. As soon as he turned by the tamarind tree, Gabarya would neigh loudly and the children would jump up and down with excitement. Gabarya's whinnying and snorting became a signal of their father's return. Knowing that it was Gabarya who carried their father away in the morning and brought him safely back at night, the children would wait not for Ranoji but the sound of Gabarya's trotting hooves to enter the lanes of the village.

The half-hearted responses to their grandmother Rahibai's stories indicated that their ears were actually tuned to catch Gabarya's neighing. And sure enough Gabarya's neighing at the tamarind tree proclaimed, "We have reached!" The boys jumped up with delight. Gabarya had come! Gabarya stopped by the door and snorted. Daulati tethered the horse and carried his saddle and bridle into the house. Ranoji sheathed his sword and gathered the children to his waist. Rahibai released a sigh of relief. Radha stole a shy glance at him and looked away. A heap of corn cobs rolled towards the kitchen fire. "Very late today?"

"Late, yes, Patil stopped me on the way."

"During rain and lightning you should hurry home," said Rahibai. Radha merely glared at him. Fakira and Sadhu took the freshly roasted corncobs and perched on their father's lap, listening intently.

Radha served the food.

As they were eating, Daulati asked, "What did Patil say?"

"Not much! The matter of the Shigaon jogani came up.'"

"Did you run into Panta?" he asked, referring to Vishnupanta Kulkarni. They did not take the names of the elders from the village.

"No. But Aba, what is the issue about the jogani?"

"Issue? No issue at all. It's just a popular custom among the twelve balutedars, the public servants of the village.

"Two baities, young effeminate men, enact the role of the jogani and joga, the bride and her bridegroom. A wedding procession is taken out. The jogani holds in her hands a vati, half a dry coconut wrapped in a yellow cloth. If someone dares to snatch it from her and take it away, the village loses its right to hold the jogani jatra. The village where the coconut vati is taken then gets the privilege of holding the fair. This is an age-old custom. However, if the one who tries to steal is caught, it is also the accepted custom for him to be beheaded."

"What! Breaking off someone's head for a piece of coconut?" asked Fakira indignantly.

"It is not just a coconut vati, it is a symbol. It carries the prestige of the village," Daulati explained.

Young Fakira turned to his father. "Why don't you grab that vati, then?" Everyone laughed and Radha laughed the loudest. Then she whispered, "Very clever boy you are! You want to eat that coconut vati or what!"

"Of course! What's the big deal," Fakira replied confidently.

"But the snatcher may lose his head, child!" Daulati said. With a furrowed brow, young Fakira declared, "Let them break heads, you go and steal it for us." Once again the house was filled with laughter at Fakira's words. Rahibai was delighted to see her grandson talking the language of a brave, valiant man, the language of their community, even though innocently. She retorted, "Going outside to pee when it is dark terrifies him and he says let the heads get broken but get the jogani vati!"

This remark crushed Fakira into silence. Why had the old woman brought up his pissing in public like this? Then Radha said to him, "So go then, and get that jogani!"

Biting into the corn that his father had brought, Fakira replied, "Wait and see, when I become as big as Aba, I will definitely get it for you."

Ranoji held Fakira close. In good spirits they all lay down to sleep. Fakira and Sahadeva were fast asleep, curled up against their father, one on each side. But Ranoji lay awake. With his mighty hands resting on his boys, he was thinking about the morrow. His unbridled mind troubled him. It was running wild at one moment, rushing into the crowded fair ground and getting into a fight at the next, leaping on to Gabarya and galloping away, and then suddenly becoming still and wondering about the next day:

If I win back the jogani vati, it would be a great honour for my village. "What Bajiba had done, a Mang has dared to do," they will say. Our village will host the jatra. People from neighbouring villages will take part in the fair. Everyone will say, "It is Ranoji who made it possible." Shankarrao Patil will say "shabas" in appreciation! If I live, I will get pats on my back and if I . . . then . . . I will earn a name! "He gave his life for the village," they will proclaim! Death . . . death is inevitable, it will come when it has to; but if it comes while claiming the jogani for my village, it will be a tribute and a matter of pride for my people. The gaping wounds on my body will be engraved on the hearts of my fellow villagers. The thundering of Gabarya's hooves will be etched in their memories.

But what will happen to Aai, Aba, Fakira, little Sadhu and Radha? How will they survive? Who will support them in their old age? It will be ten years before my boys grow up. How will these five lives manage till then? What will happen to them?

What's going to happen to them? Nothing. They will live. People did exist even when I wasn't around. They will continue to live. And Patil will be reassured that the warrior who made this village proud was born here. Vishnupanta Kulkarni will be pleased.

With closed eyes, Ranoji lay there thinking. Darkness had dissipated and dawn had taken over. Birds began to chirp and flutter in the thorny nivadung clusters. Myriad colours streaked the eastern horizon. The sun slowly emerged from behind the rain-bearing clouds. Seeing it, the koel sang her sweet ku-huuu song. The breeze caressed the nivadung thickets and they were refreshed.

A smile played on nature's face. The entire river valley between the Krishna and the Warna was bathed in light. The Sahyadri Mountain to the west of the village stood proud, baring its chest. Stirrings of life were seen all around. Fearlessness filled the air. With dogged determination to bring the jogani of Shigaon to Vategaon, Ranoji got up.

Morning turned to afternoon. Ranoji set off for Shigaon. Carrying Fakira and Sahadeva, he walked a while and paused under the tamarind tree. Daulati brought the sword and the horse, Gabarya. Putting the children down, Ranoji took the sword into his hands. The glistening six-inch-wide steel blade had a heavy grip. Attached with it was a foot-long dagger. With this magnificent sword in his hand, Ranoji leapt on to his horse.

Daulati spoke, "Don't quarrel with anyone, and don't get into a fight. Come back before dark." Ranoji nodded and turned towards the east. Gabarya began to trot. Fakira and Sahadeva shouted after him, "Aba, bring us pedha!" Suddenly Ranoji's stomach churned. He dug into the horse's flanks. Gabarya was startled and began to gallop, his neck arched like a bow and his forelock swaying like a dancing peacock's crest.

As the sun made its slow descent in the west, Ranoji was marching towards the east. Both were now in an unprecedented hurry to return. Ranoji's eyes were surfing the fields where the hard tilled earth lay in furrows. Some farmers were sowing in the black soil of their land with a strong belief that the same black soil will turn into a lush green expanse. They laboured so hard with an infinite trust that their efforts would yield a harvest next year. Seeing them Ranoji muttered to himself, "What you sow, you will reap!"

The Shigaon jogani procession had started with full fanfare. Every lane and alley in the village was crammed with people. Men, women and children thronged the place. Having gorged on puran poli, the men belched, satiated and ran around attending to things. Firm in their faith that once the jogani was conducted successfully all the ills of the village—misfortune, grief, poverty—would be routed, the villagers rushed to pray to the jogani and ask for a long life.

Once the joga and jogani turned back, the Tamasha performance would begin. The following day, a kusti, a wrestling contest was organized for which people from the neighbouring villages had already assembled in large numbers. The wrestlers strutted around with their yellow langots to be worn during the bout later, thrown over their shoulders. There were people everywhere. The bride and her groom, the jogani and joga would often pause, and people would bow down low to them in great devotion.

The strong men of the village had formed a human chain around the joga–jogani. They were protected by a group of young men carrying naked swords in their hands. Their stern gaze surveyed the scene. Thus the religious procession of joga–jogani moved ahead in the protective shadow of the swords. The procession was led by multiple musical instruments played in perfect harmony. Holding the coconut vati wrapped in yellow cloth, the jogani was inching forward. The nhavi, the barber, was fanning the jogani with a soop, a winnowing pan as he walked alongside her. The chamar, the cobbler of the village, pushed the crowd away with a thorny wooden staff. Believing that a touch of that staff was a bad omen, people tried to stay far from it.

Bajiba Khot's son, Bapu, with a drawn sword in hand, rode his wilful horse and circled around jogani some distance away. Like a hawk, he swooped and dived among the people, exhibiting his prowess and speed to warn them not to dare to even look at the Jogani with evil intent.

On the other side, Gajya Mali was trying to rein in his restless horse. Like him, many vigilant horses hovered around, keeping a strict watch on the jogani.

Hiding his sword under his arm, Ranoji moved stealthily thorugh the crowd. He had tucked the packet of pedhas into his waistband and was deeply engrossed in his plan of action. He had tied his horse Gabarya near a stream that flowed through Shigaon. At what point to attack the group, how to grab the jogani vati, how to reach Gabarya from there in the shortest time and how to dodge the guards, all these manoeuvers had been thought out by Ranoji's master-mind as he walked with the procession, alongside the jogani. As the decided spot was approaching, Ranoji became oblivious of his surroundings. His body and mind became numb. He had forgotten Daulati, Rahibai, Radha, Fakira and Sahadeva.

It was as if he had transcended into a new world of his own. His mind and thoughts were governed by something lofty and sublime. The toughest and strongest link in the human chain around the jogani was Ramya Lohar, the ironsmith. His bloodshot gaze skimmed over everyone, allowing no one to come anywhere near the jogani. Ranoji's eyes were fixed firmly on the ironsmith. He had decided that he would attack the powerful ironsmith as soon as they reached the inner courtyard of Kaikadi. Whom to kill, where and how had been punctiliously planned as he continued walking with the jogani procession.

The jogani had reached the marketplace when Ranoji met Bhairu Ramoshi. "Ranuda, when did you come?"

"Long while back. You just come away from here."

Ranoji almost dragged him out.

"Ranuda, what's the matter?"

"Go to our village immediately."

"And do what?"

"Tell Patil and Panta . . ."

"Tell them what?"

"Tell them that I am on my way with the jogani. Ask them to meet me . . ."

"Meaning?"

"Meaning nothing, Bhairu, just run. People with weapons must come there quickly. Very soon, I will be starting from here."

"But how will you fight alone?"

"Wait and see just how I fight."

"Then I will stay here. You proceed with the jogani vati and I will hold them back, stop them from chasing you. In front of Pirsu . . ."

"No Bhairu, this is not the time . . . You just go, run!"

Ramoshi was speechless! He went to a secluded spot, tucked his dhoti up and sped away. He ran fast! How to reach the village before Ranoji snatches the jogani vati and starts from Shigaon was the only thought in Bhairu Ramoshi's mind. Every moment was to him like an age.

Through a narrow lane, the jogani reached the courtyard of Kaikadi, a slightly elevated plain, with a path for bullock carts leading from it. Beside it was the stream where the watchful Gabarya was waiting for Ranoji.

As the crowd reached the open space, the strict vigilance slackened. Everyone was looking for a place to relieve themselves–some went behind the shrubs, others chose an open field. A few opened up the chanchis with betel leaves and nuts, some dipped fingers in chuna and rubbed the tobacco in their palms with it . . . while many a bidi was lit on many a lip.

At that instant, Ranoji leapt up and with one blow struck Ramya Lohar, and snatched the yellow-cloth-wrapped coconut vati. Immediately, he saw a mighty sword about to attack him but he knocked it down. Came another sword soon after, but that too he struck down. And before the eye could blink, Ranoji sprinted towards the narrow bullock cart path. Swift and straight as an arrow he ran and a hue and cry arose. "The jogani is gone! The jogani vati is lost."

The guards of the jogani rapidly moved forward when Ranoji spun around and yelled, "Dare to take one step forward and I will have your head!" Chaos and confusion prevailed. People ran helter-skelter. Sounds of "jogani is lost, jogani is gone" rent the air.

Attacking those who attacked, avoiding a few, taking on some, handing others serious blows, deflecting some attackers, evading some sharp assaults, Ranoji ran towards Gabarya. Ranoji was even more impassioned. The frenzied cries of "jogani's lost!" caused a stampede. All the horsemen of Shigaon village panicked. Nobody knew who was running away with the jogani. Bapu Khot's horse was stuck in a cramped lane. People running from the opposite direction were hindering him, blocking his path. In utter exasperation, Khot drew his sword and waved it about, scattering the crowd, making way for himself. Bapu Khot's random action had injured many people. That led to greater chaos but Khot was least bothered. He entered the Kaikadi courtyard and said, "Who snatched the jogani vati?" But the men on run did not reply. Gajya Sutar came. Some more horses appeared. They saw Ranoji emerging from the stream astride Gabarya. Six horses of Shigaon hit the ground hard as they took off. "Catch him! Kill him! Don't let him escape!" Their cries added to the frenzy of the crowd.

Instead of covering the six-mile distance to Vategaon's boundary along the bullock cart path, it was better to take the short cut alongside the mountain, thought Ranoji and turned Gabarya in that direction. On reaching the maidan, he looked back at those chasing him. Suddenly he leaned forward, threw down Gabarya's reins and bridle, rolled up the dry coconut vati wrapped in a yellow cloth into his waistband and held his mighty sword aloft. Putting his mouth close to Gabarya's ear, he cried out loudly, "Gabarya, take me home to our village bounds. Take me there fast. Don't leave me here. Run, run!"

Gabarya ran. His legs acquired lightning speed. His hooves pounded the hard ground. Cutting through the powerfully blowing wind, Gabarya galloped. And the word "speed" lost its meaning. Gabarya was trying to reach the boundary of his Vategaon. Displaying the raw courage nurtured amongst the cactus, Ranoji, the sharp broad blade glinting in his hand, was rushing towards victory.

Khot was close behind Ranoji and was spurring his horse for more speed. His horse's hooves dropped on a ground rhythmically like drumsticks beating on a tasha drum. Gajya Mali's horse was also charging with same pace as that of other horses, ear to ear.

The thundering sounds fell on Ranoji's ears and Gabarya became a whirling top.

Shigaon's boundary was crossed.

Vategaon's boundary limit began. Bapu Khot, crazed with revenge, continued the chase. Seeing him, Ranoji thought that at no cost should he be allowed to grab the jogani vati and take it back. So he took it out from his waist cloth and bit it, then chewed and gobbled it up.

Gabarya was galloping at the speed of light, snorting and blowing as he ran. He had never run that fast in his life.

"Ranoji is on his way with the jogani!" This news had already been delivered by Bhairu, and before anyone could say "What? What?", the cry was echoing all over Vategaon. There was great excitement among the people. In no time at all, the entire village was thronging the bullock cart track. Weapons, implements and tools clogged the path. When the news reached the Mang colony, Daulati was astonished. Rahibai was shocked. Radha ran up to the door and wailed. Climbing on the tamarind tree, Fakira looked out for his fiery father. Sahadeva began to cry. The Mangs gathered their battleaxes. The Mahars quickly prepared themselves. Shankarrao Patil mounted his horse without a saddle. Vishnupanta's horse also started cantering like the other steeds. Soon the entire village was moving to Ranoji's aid.

But Ranoji had not taken the cart track. He had reached the village border from the mountain side. Khot had not given up the chase. He had not turned back. In fact, he was even more incensed. The horses were running till their hearts were almost blasted. They sometimes came close, sometimes they fell back. Gajya Sutar was almost upon Ranoji, when Khot shouted, "Gajya throw your spear, boy!"

Gajya righted himself in the saddle, gathered all his strength and hurled his spear. The heavy blade pierced Ranoji's back. His already numb body was beyond pain. It twitched and shuddered slightly. Ranoji was bathed in blood. With the spear still in his back, Ranoji looked out for Gajya. When Gajya Mali came closer, Ranoji raised his sword and brought it down on Gajya's head in one quick stroke. It cut through the turban and stopped at the tip of Gajya's nose. Gajya crashed to the ground, under the horses' feet. Seeing Gajya fall, Khot let out a bellow of rage and started screaming insanely. Hearing this, the mob moving along the bullock cart path was taken aback. The scream had come from another direction, across the fields. But it was not easy to traverse that piece of land. It did not have even a muddy trail.

As Gajya fell, Bapu Khot steered his horse close to Ranoji and gathering all his strength, threw his spear. It pierced Gabarya's flank. The exhausted Gabarya's forelegs folded under him. His lungs were bursting from all that galloping and he started vomiting blood. Even before Ranoji could balance himself from Gabarya's precipitous fall, innumerable blades struck him again and again. And then that valiant Mang, gripping the hilt of his sword, collapsed onto his most loyal, devoted Gabarya.

Khot started searching for the jogani vati. When he couldn't find it, he turned back with the severed head of Ranoji. Just then, the people of Vategoan reached the spot. What they saw stunned them. What Khot had done shocked and then inflamed the people of Vategaon. He had actually trespassed a mile into Vategaon territory. The Shigaonkars had broken the strict code, the tradition.

Daulati threw himself on his son's body, began beating his chest and wailing loudly. Rahibai and Radha rolled on the ground, weeping uncontrollably. The children were moaning piteously. The entire village came together. The young and the old. They raised a lament. The women of the village tried to console Rahibai and Radha.

Vishnupanta arrived. He saw Ranoji's headless body. His face darkened. All the villagers looked at him expectantly. What would he say? In a choked voice, Vishnupanta declared, "Khot has committed a felony by intruding one mile inside our boundary. He took away our head. This body will not be cremated till the severed head is brought back. I will not sip a drop of water until then. Either I will get that head or give up mine." Saying these words, Panta dug his spurs into the horse's sides.

His black and white stallion darted towards Shigaon. Shankarrao Patil eased the sword from Ranoji's grip and roared, "I will annihilate Shigaon! If I fail, I'll set fire to Vategaon and will immolate myself! Let's go!"

Once more, the ocean of men headed towards Shigaon. Bhairu Ramoshi was running wildly with the axe in his hand. Maruti Chauhan was bounding with belt-swords. Tayanu Mahar was struggling hard to run ahead of all with his razor-sharp metal spear. Axes gleamed. Naked sword blades glistened. Benumbed by grief, Daulati was running along with the throng. Daulaji Dhekna, Nana Dongra, Pandu Nangara, Bali Mang, Appa Mang, Savala Mang—every man, young and old, was charging along the mountain side.

"We will get back Ranoji's head or sacrifice our own," they chanted.

Only Bhairu Ramoshi thought differently. "For one Mang head, I will get fifty of theirs," he told himself.

Ranoji had given up his head, his life for the village. Now the entire village was ready to give up theirs for him.

Two

Hatred raged like a fire in the hearts of the Vategaonkars. Young and old rushed about with revenge on their minds, shouting and screaming. Their cries of "Burn Shigaon down, turn it to ashes!" rent the air. For Bapya Khot had broken the rules and committed an unforgivable crime by trespassing into their territory.

Now the Vategaonkars were prepared to kill or be killed. Their hands were restless as they gripped their slingshots, charged and ready to use.

On the other side, Shigaon was fearful and tense. The havoc created during the jatra was more or less under control. Children who'd got lost in the fair had returned to their homes, so there was relief but the fear persisted. Since Ramajya Lohar, the blacksmith had been felled by a single stroke of Ranoji's sword, the lohar lane was in mourning. Learning that Gajya's body was lying in Vategaon territory, the carpenters' homes were plunged in gloom. Visitors from neighbouring villages were running helter-skelter, their pagotis tucked under their arms instead of sitting on their heads, crying, "Run,

run, fellows, along with the grain the insects too will get ground." The maidan was strewn with broken footwear and ghongadis, their coarse woollen blankets. Many stout sticks and axes lay unclaimed and abandoned. Amidst all this, Bapu Khot had brought Ranoji's head, hung it on the village gate and gone home, bathed in blood. Proud and pleased with his son's valour, Bajiba Khot went around reassuring the villagers. "Don't be afraid, my Bapu has brought back the head of the one who stole the jogani vati. We have not lost our jogani. Come, let us start the fair once more. Come, all is peaceful now."

No one dared to venture out. But Bajiba did not notice it. When Bapu had returned with Ranoji's head, Bajiba had asked him, "Who was he?"

"Ranya Mang, from Vategaon."

"Where did you find him?"

"On the maidan."

"How many of our people were lost?"

"Four here and two on the plain."

"Six? He was quite formidable then!"

"I cut off his head and hung it on the village gate."

"Shabas!" saying this, Bajiba rushed out. Triumphantly, he shouted, "We have not lost our jogani. All is not lost. Come out of your houses!"

Just then, Raghu Manya trotted up. When he came near Bajiba, he reined in his horse and stopped. "Vategaon villagers are on the maala, ready for battle. The maidan is overflowing with them."

"How many?"

"Can't tell."

"Order our people to come out and pick up their weapons," Bajiba shouted. "Don't allow them to enter the village. Hold them off, outside the boundary."

At that moment, Bapu came cantering in. He had brought Bajiba's horse along, saddled and ready. Immediately Bajiba leapt on to the saddle and rode through the marketplace.

"Come out, don't let the Vategaon villagers enter our village, otherwise our village will be reduced to ashes!" he exhorted the villagers.

They realized the seriousness of the situation. With old Bajiba on the field, their morale got a boost. They came out in large numbers. The lanes of Shigaon were filled with men, valiant and aggressive. Some manned check-posts. Others raised stone piles at a number of places and readied their slingshots. The womenfolk prepared to defend their houses as the sun slunk behind the hills.

Slowly darkness engulfed the surroundings. Hollows and ditches, rivulets and streams, all appeared to be levelled. The crowd from Vategaon halted. They camped on the maidan. Vishnupanta advised them, "Be patient. Lie low till sunrise. It will be wrong to enter another's village in the night time. We will start our operations at daybreak. In the meantime, we can assess the mood of the Shigaon villagers. Do not speak the language of aggression!"

Heeding his words, the crowd quietened down. They decided to remain calm till sunrise. Gradually, their anger dissipated. Hot heads cooled down. The rage that had erupted on seeing the inert and lifeless bodies of Ranoji and Gabarya vanished and sanity returned. However, anger against the injustice and the thirst for a fight remained. "We will either take back Ranoji's head or give away ours," many were heard saying. "Only if we take fifty heads will we be worthy sons of the Ramoshi caste," declared Bhairu. Nobody in the village of Vategaon had ever bothered to give the Mang community a thought. No one had ever asked, who are those that live amongst the nivadung cactus? Births, deaths, whose son is this, whose grandson is that? No one cared. But when a person from that community gave his life for the village, for the village jatra, all of a sudden the centuries-old chasm disappeared. Every single person vowed to avenge him, mourn him, as if he was a family member.

A new worry besieged those who had stayed behind. The whole village had gone to Shigaon to get Ranoji's head. What would happen there? If there was a fight, who would die? Who would survive? The eyes of the women and children were fixed in the direction of Shigaon.

Shigaon had lost six men, many were injured.

The British regiment was watchful, but did not act.

As the Queen's proclamation had promised that they would not interfere in any religious matters, they were bound by that promise. By declaring the jogani jatra as a religious matter, they could remain aloof. Besides if these people were dying, fighting each other, it was no mean advantage to them.

The night was dark, storm clouds rumbled in the sky, hanging low in monstrous ghost-like shapes. The villagers of Shigaon and Vategaon were camped on either side of the stream. They were waiting for the sun to rise. Their weapons were taking a rest. Every now and then, the stars would shine briefly and in that intermittent starlight, the weapons would show their fangs.

An eerie silence prevailed. Heavy lids drooped over sleepy eyes, tense bodies relaxed. Some stretched their legs, some lay down. A calm and peaceful atmosphere reigned.

Suddenly a loud cry rang out, "Listen, oh you Vategaonkars!"

Everyone was startled. They recognized it as Bajiba's voice. Vishnupanta responded equally loudly, "What do you have to say?"

The men scrambled up, awake and alert. Their arms at the ready.

"We say, you go back peacefully."

"And why should we do that? You trespassed into our territory and killed our man."

"Where is the proof?" said Bajiba, advancing towards them. There was a collective outcry.

"Don't you dare come forward!" snarled Bhairu.

"I won't. But who says we crossed your boundary?" Bajiba queried.

"Why, do you need a lamp to see in the daylight?" retorted Shankarrao Patil.

Bajiba replied, "Very well, we will make inquiries in the morning. If you are proven right, we will return the head. Is that acceptable?"

"Acceptable, acceptable, acceptable," everyone cried out in chorus.

The sun rose. Five men from each side were appointed as the panchas, and they began the inquiry. Bajiba, Vishnupanta and Shankarrao went back to Vategaon.

They saw the spot where the corpses lay. After checking out the landmarks they knew that Ranoji was deep into the village limits. But Bapu had advanced into Vategaon territory and beheaded him. He had committed an offence by breaking a tradition, they decided. Vategaon had won.

Bajiba went back to Shigaon and returned Ranoji's head. The Vategaon villagers rejoiced as they took the head back and cremated his body. His horse was buried at a spot nearby. It was a big victory for Vategaon. The whole village was overwhelmed by a mixture of grief and happiness. The fair would take place exactly twelve months from that day and it would continue taking place till the sun and the moon shone in the sky. Because of the sacrifice of one man, an old tradition would be revived and a new law enacted. Everyone sang Ranoji's praises as they grieved for him. They danced and they wept for Ranoji. But in the Mang wada the morale was as flat as the ground. Darkness had settled in the eyes of Daulati, Rahibai, Radha, Fakira and Sadhu. The sky had collapsed on their heads. Their kinsmen were mourning because their leader had fallen. But Daulati's ship had sprung a leak. Either he would flounder for the rest of his life or he would drown.

The villagers came to the Mang settlement and offered words of comfort to Daulati and the community. They gave them sound advice. "We will together take care of Ranoji's two boys. He has made such a big sacrifice for our village. We will try to repay it. The village will stand by the Mang community."

On the third day, Vishnupanta himself came to Mang wada. This Kulkarni, with his flowing dhoti, the brocade turban on his head and shindeshahi footwear, made a handsome figure. He had a grave face, bright eyes, sharp nose, bushy eyebrows, impressive black moustache. Vishnupanta, whom even the British saluted, had never set foot in the Mang settlement. So when they saw his regal presence at Daulati's home, all the Mangs crowded around Daulati's door. Daulati quickly spread out a mat for him to sit on.

"Dhani, why you have taken the trouble?"

"This is no trouble, Daulunana, when compared to giving up your son's head!" Vishnupanta's words moved Daulati and he started sobbing like a child. Vishnupanta also became emotional.

"Nana, don't cry. Believe your Ranoji is still alive."

"He used to sit on this mat."

"I will sit on it," Vishnupanta said and sat down. Everyone was surprised. Then Panta, as he was popularly known, added emphatically, "Both his sons must live."

These comforting words and Panta's moist eyes gave Daulati some hope. His tears of grief turned into tears of happiness.

Shankarrao Patil also visited them and gave Daulati the same assurance. But then his heart broke every time he saw Radha's blank forehead, without the kunku, as a widow's was meant to be. She lived only for the sake of her two boys, Fakira and Sadhu. The villagers were puzzled by Rahibai. How, at such an old age, could she survive the death of her only son? They wondered. But only one thought kept her going. And that was revenge.

Fakira, however, was deeply affected. "Lose your head but grab the vati," he had told his father just before he left. In his young mind, he was convinced that his father had heeded his words. Now he would never see his father again, never get any pedhas from him, nor sit on his lap . . . And Gabarya will never neigh again! Fakira wept, hugging Gabarya's saddle and reins. Sadhu's repeated questions about his father made Radha cry . . .

When Bajiba returned home after handing over Ranoji's head, Bapu Khot was livid. He yelled at his father, "What were you thinking when you gave back that head? You have called upon adversity, invited misfortune, you have insulted me, insulted the whole village."

"You acted wrongly," snapped Bajiba, "Like a fool, you entered their territory and brought back Ranoji's head. Are you not ashamed to talk like this now?"

"Who says I acted wrongly?"

"I say so. That spot says so. Gajya who died there says so. You fool! You couldn't even bring back the dead body of your companion. You are not fit to live. If you were so valiant, why did you allow him to pass through our territory? Tell me!"

"It's not true. I caught him inside our boundary."

"Don't say more. Had you been alone, he would have cut off your head and taken it away, but . . ."

"But I cut his head off and you gave it back."

"That was the right thing to do. What if those people had entered our village and cut my head off when I brought the jogani? But that didn't happen because there was and is a tradition. They abided by it. You didn't. That's why I returned it and it was a good thing."

"No great good it was . . . There will be cow dung . . ."

"Bapya!" shouted Bajiba and slapped Bapu hard across his mouth. Bajiba's body was shaking with rage. Without thinking of what he was saying, he yelled, "If you have so much vengeance in you and if you are of my bloodline, you will bring the jogani back in my lifetime. Get out of here!"

The Shigaon villagers were burning with indignation. They couldn't bear the thought of a lonely and morose joga being taken in procession in their village while the jogani jatra would be celebrated in Vategaon. They felt that their village had lost its glory, now that they could no longer hold the jogani jatra. A tradition had been broken.

The news that Shigaon's jogani had been taken away by Vategaon spread to the neigbouring villages. Now onwards, the joganis will be held in Vategaon. What is left in Shigaon now? Only a lonely joga! What is there to see in him? A real man, that Ranoji . . . Single-handedly, he fought the Shigaonkars and snatched away the jogani.

The jogani affair was much talked about in the surrounding areas.

Those who had seen Ranoji's valour began singing ballads in his praise in their own villages. The Vategaon Mangs became famous in the valley.

The rains, restrained so far, spread out their limbs. The skies broke into heavy showers. Flashing bolts of lightning and deafening claps of thunder shook the countryside. Seeds germinated in the soil and small sprouts raised their tiny heads above it. Slowly, the black soil donned a green mantle. A new creation emerged, a new fragrance spread, a new warmth engulfed the world. Men's hopes and dreams came into the realm of reality.

The sun freed itself from the clutches of the rains and appeared new and refreshed.

The rains went away and the skies became clear. Birds started performing their acrobatics in the blue skies. The damp earth started sighing. It was time for the harvest, and preparations for the harvest activities gathered momentum in the fields.

In the meantime Daulati went to Pandharpur on a pilgrimage. Since Fakira was still mourning for Gabarya, Daulati brought back a pure white pony. Fakira fed him with handfuls of straw. The boys named this pony also Gabarya. But this Gabarya did not whinny as yet.

When the harvesting began, Daulati went around looking for work—reaping, harvesting or threshing. When the farmers saw him, they remembered Ranoji and placed heaps of corn cobs before him. Daulati's house was full due to the generosity of the villagers. Rahibai wandered among the thorny scrub with her two goats. Her efforts were towards obtaining milk for Fakira and Sadhu. The boys helped their grandmother. Radha accompanied the other womenfolk for modani, to break the ripe cobs off the stems. She kept herself busy throughout the day since it helped her forget the pain in her heart. The onerous prospect of spending the rest of her life with a kunku-less forehead lay heavy on her mind.

That day, Radha had set out for the fields as usual. The other women had gone ahead. There was nobody around. The boys had gone with Rahi to the maidan, and Daulati was working in the fields. Radha was hurrying to Choughula's field with a basket on her head. Now she had to take care of not only the two boys, but also herself. She was still young, strong and supple.

As she was striding ahead, she saw a bullock-cart coming from the opposite direction. She wondered for a moment who it might belong to. The cart climbed the bank of the stream and started along the track towards the village. The bullocks were trotting along merrily. Quickly, Radha moved away to the edge of the track. When the cart came nearer, she was surprised to see it belonged to Patil.

When he saw her, Patil abruptly pulled in the reins and stopped the cart. "Where to, Radha?"

"Going for modani."

"Whose field?"

"Choughula's."

"Go back home," he told her, turned the bullocks around and got the cart moving.

Without thinking, Radha began to follow the cart. Shankarrao did not glance back even once till they reached the tamarind tree. The cart halted. Radha also paused, staring at the ground below her feet. "Is Daulati at home?" Patil asked.

Just then Daulati, who had come back to take the pony out to graze, saw Patil and Radha and came forward. "I've just come back from Sonataki for the pony . . ."

"That's all right, Daulati," said Patil looking grim. "But this is not good. If Ranoji hears that Radha is toiling like a labourer, he will come down from up there and take my head. Do not send her to work again. You need grains? Here, take . . ." So saying, Patil started unloading sacks of grain from the cart.

One . . . two . . . three . . . Is he going to empty the whole cart here, wondered Daulati. "Enough, gaokar, enough!" he exclaimed.

"It's enough? Then listen to me. Radha will not go to the fields. Her husband endured a mountain of hardships, at my behest, as the Patil of this village. He did it so that the jatra could be held in our village, and I could strut around proudly during the fair. He did it to bring honour to our village, and left Radha kunku-less, made orphans of two young boys. If this is how we repay his favour, we all will go straight to hell. You will reap what you sow."

"Patil, why do you say such things?"

"What I say is right. You can't compare offering a few sacks of grains with giving up one's head. Grains grow in fields, not heads. This is a matter of the prestige of one who fought Khot and sacrificed his life. It is worth the whole world. My loyalty is not enough to equal it."

"That's why I am living," said a tearful Daulati, as he tried to control his trembling lips. "I would have died. It is your words and Panta's words of comfort that have kept me alive . . . No, I will not send Radha anywhere from now on."

"Do that." So saying Patil went away looking straight ahead. Radha went inside the house. The sobs held back for so long burst forth. Daulati got two men to carry the sacks of grain inside. He untethered the pony and was about to set out when Fakira came in with a bale of fresh grass. When he saw Daulati about to lead the pony out, he shouted rudely, "Ay old fellow, where are you taking it?"

"To graze in the pasture . . . Why?"

"Don't. It is better off in the house."

"Arra, but why? It needs to graze or no?"

"Na . . . Aba took Gabarya to Shigaon and killed him. Now you will take it to the fields and kill it . . . what you will do who can say." Daulati smiled to himself and with a loving look replied, "You're right. You take care of your Gabarya. I will go to the fields." Saying this, he went off.

Radha called Fakira inside. "Why did you fight with your Ajja?"

"He was taking Gabarya to the pasture."

"So what? What's wrong with that?"

"Aga Aai, I was just teasing him."

"You mustn't tease old people!" she said with a smile and quickly picked him up. The ten-year-old, well-built Fakira sat in his mother's lap and felt he had reached the skies. But then he remembered his father.

"Aai!"

"What?"

"Khot killed Aba?"

"Yes."

"When our Gabarya grows up, I will kill that Khot."

"He will be an old man by then."

Just then, Sadhu came in.

Sadhu was plump and had chubby cheeks. He spoke very little.

The sun was overhead. Shadows hovered underfoot. The green fields acquired a sheen under the sunrays. The golden valley was breathtaking.

Radha got busy with her work.

Fakira and Sadhu ate their bhakri and went out. They decided to play under the tamarind tree.

"Let's play kurghodi," Fakira said, "Yes, ride the horse . . ." Sadhu nodded. Fakira went behind the tree trunk and returned with both fists closed. One contained goat droppings, the other a tamarind seed. He held his hands out in front of Sadhu and said, "Lendi or chinchuka?"

"Chinchuka," saying this, Sadhu pointed to Fakira's left fist. Fakira quickly opened the other one and yelled delightedly, "See, lendi! The seed is here, in the right hand!" Sadhu had lost. He had to be the horse. He bent down and Fakira mounted his back. The game began.

"Leap horse, horse leaps over the dome, and how many eggs in the saheb's home? Tell me . . ." Fakira held up three fingers, still riding Sadhu's back. Sadhu, struggling under Fakira's weight, gasped, "Five, five."

Fakira jumped off Sadhu's back and showed Sadhu the three fingers. Sadhu was disappointed. He bent down again to let Fakira climb onto his back. Fakira repeated the rhyme and again Sadhu did not guess the correct number.

Their game continued for a while. Sadhu could not guess the number of eggs correctly, so Fakira continued to be the rider and Sadhu the horse. Soon Sadhu was wet with perspiration, his back was hurting. He thought of abandoning the game and running away, but Fakira wouldn't let him. Sadhu was on the verge of tears. Just then, Radha came out of the house and saw Fakira sitting on Sadhu's back and Sadhu staggering under the weight. Fakira asked him again to guess the number of eggs. "Leap horse, horse leap, horse leaps over the dome, how many eggs in my home?" cried out Fakira with four fingers stretched out. "Seven, seven," Sadhu stuttered.

Seeing this, Radha got angry. She came forward and scolded Fakira. "He can't even count the number of fingers, how can he guess the number of eggs, haan? You want to kill him or what, riding on his back like this all day? See, he is soaked in sweat."

"And what if it was my turn to be the horse?"

"So what? You are clever, he is not . . ."

"And what if he rides on my back?"

"Will you be able to guess correctly?"

"Of course I will."

"Then show me!" Radha challenged him. Fakira was equally determined. "See, I am bending down," he said.

"Come, Sadhu, climb up. Let's see if he guesses right." Sadhu sat on Fakira's back. Then he repeated the rhyme and held up his fingers. Fakira was looking at the ground in front of him. He could see the shadow of Sadhu's fingers. Immediately he cried out, "Two, two."

Radha was surprised. She pulled Sadhu close to her and said, "No re baba, don't play this game . . . too smart he is for you!"

"Now give me my turn."

"It's enough!"

"No, I must get my ride."

"Look at him, he is almost in tears."

"My turn!" Fakira insisted. His eyes filled up with tears of rage.

What he was really angry about was that his mother was trying to protect Sadhu by being unfair to him. Stamping his feet, he shouted, "Aai, I want my turn!"

Radha quickly turned around. Fakira was crying. Setting Sadhu down, she quickly hoisted Fakira onto her back. "Here, take your turn," she said and carried the boy back to the house.

The sun was now at its own doorstep. Its rays had cast a brilliant glow on the seven-valley hill below. A huge brown cloud was spreading itself just above the horizon, and the sun looked as if it was sitting on a brown carpet. The dense forest on the hillside stiffened itself to become one with the darkness.

People who had been working in the fields all day were returning home. The cattle were lowing on their way back. Grunting bullocks were lumbering along the stream. The villagers' efforts were finding their rewards.

Radha started preparing the wood fire to cook the meal. Sadhu was breaking twigs to kindle the fire. Fakira was sulking in a corner. Just then, Rahibai returned with the goats. Radha was telling Sadhu, "You are like your grandfather and this Fakira, he is like his father. Your grandfather used to say, though we had a sword in hand we begged so that the community could survive. Your father would laugh at that. Actually it angered him, but he covered it up with laughter."

"Don't abuse my Aba," growled Fakira in a shrill voice. Radha laughed but before she could say anything, Rahibai said, "Fakira, she is not finding fault with him! How hot-headed you are!"

"Why is she taking my father's name?"

"So what? You shouldn't be grumbling all the time." Then turning to Radha, she said, "Look, Bai, stop teasing him. There's no cure for one's nature."

Radha smiled and drew Fakira into her arms. "I was just joking," she said. He slowly released himself from her arms and went to the door. Radha went back to her cooking. A few minutes later, Daulati came. He rinsed his mouth, stretched his legs and asked, "Where is Fakira?"

"He just went outside," Rahi replied. Daulati started calling out to him but Fakira didn't come. Then Daulati got worried. "Aga, the child is not to be seen," he muttered anxiously as he peered outside.

Hearing this, Radha's heart gave a jolt. Going to the door she looked around and started calling his name, "Fakira, Fakiraaaaa . . ."

Her calls travelled a long distance and then went silent. There was no answer. Now her stomach was knotted. She quickly glanced westwards. Only a quarter of the sun was left above the horizon. Soon it would be dark. Where will I look for Fakira then, she thought and almost went crazy with worry. A sob rose in her throat.

Daulati and Rahi started running around amidst the nivadung cactus. People from their lane gathered outside their home. They started chasing shadows. Fakira's friends Bali, Mura, Isha, Kisha began to look for him. Radha stood like a statue in the doorway. Sadhu started to cry. Slowly, the shadows were wiped away by the falling darkness. All hearts were thudding fearfully.

"Hai, look for him, look before it gets completely dark," cried out Bhairu Mang. "Go look into the well in front."

Hearing the word "well," Radha let out a wail. The thought was unbearable! Just then Bali exclaimed, "There he is."

"Where? Where is he?"

"There, see, see up on the tamarind tree, he's sitting there!"

There was a clamour below. "Come, come, all . . . hey!" they shouted looking upwards.

Fakira was sitting there swinging his legs nonchalantly and watching the chaos unfolding below. Radha looked up still crying. Daulati said in a cajoling voice, "You rascal, you almost killed us . . !"

Fakira didn't bother to glance at him. Then Rahi said, "Come down, it's getting dark."

Everyone tried to coax him, "Fakira, come down, it will be night very soon."

But Fakira continued to sit, still as a log, with not a "hoon" or a "choon" out of him. He didn't move. Then Bhairu said, "Boys, climb up and bring him down."

Hearing this, Fakira dared them, "Try climbing the tree and see . . . I will jump."

Everyone panicked with this threat. Their mouths went dry. Then Radha pulled down the sari pallu and spread it out in front of her. "Here, I am begging you, come down."

Daulati went down on his knees. "Don't jump Fakira, my babya, come, climb down."

Rahibai was trembling with fear. Fakira calmly climbed down the tree and immediately Radha pounced on him. Holding him close to her chest she began to sob. Everyone felt as if they'd been saved from the gallows and heaved a sigh of relief.

"Don't nobody say anything to him," Bhairu advised.

But Daulati blurted out, "Fakira, why did you? Don't make us die like this . . ."

"Aai calls me names," Fakira hissed.

"She is mad. If anyone calls you names, I will break their heads. But you don't let it turn your head."

No one said anything more. And ever after that everyone was careful about how they addressed Fakira. As for Radha, it was a lesson she would not ever forget.

Three

The winter came and went. The sharp Chaitra sun was scorching. The heat flowed like molten steel and painted the sky with a shimmering blue veil. The trees were decked in the new leaves of spring, exuding freshness, proving that even ugliness pales in the bloom of youth. The wild scrub and thorny bushes displayed new growth. With the recently added palm-shaped leaves, the nivadung cactus stood even taller. Their large red fruit were eye-catching and the needles on their leaves were ready to sting.

There was hectic activity in the Mang settlement. Every house had set up rope twisters by its door and the work of twining the ropes had begun in earnest. The elders were releasing the loose strands while sitting in the shade of their doorways. Some children went back and forth carrying the twining wheels, their heads covered with pieces of cloth to protect them from the sun. The heated wheels were making a squeaking sound. Wisps of loose fibres and dust were flying everywhere. Those youngsters who were habitual shirkers were running in and out of the cactus like mongooses, trying to hide and give their parents the slip. Fakira and Sadhu had started a game of viti-dandu under the tamarind tree, since Radha had forbidden them from playing kurghodi. Daulati had gone to the village office, Rahibai had taken the goats to graze and Radha had dozed off where she sat.

Slowly, the shirkers Isha, Kisha, Bhiva, Bali and Mura joined in the viti-dandu game. A little while later, Savala Mang's son Ghamya arrived on the scene. He had brought some fresh news, he said. Ghamya seated himself in the centre. And the curious boys gathered around him.

Ghamya was quite tall, had a long face, a fair complexion and a rather long nose. His thin neck was long too as was the shendi, the tuft at the back of his head. But it always stood stiff and erect. Like his father, he was vain and shrewd. The boastful Savala had named his beloved son Ghamandi, meaning vain. Important news and information from the surrounding areas would reach Savalya first, and then Ghamandi would plant it in the houses and in the alleys. Today also he had brought an interesting news item. Pleased to have the boys around him waiting eagerly, Ghamandi began, "An army unit, a laskar has camped on the Rajewadi plain near the government bungalow. Want to come and see it?"

"Ay, what's a laskar like?" Isha asked and Ghamya replied, "It has white soldiers; it is very mighty."

"But what are those white people like?" asked Mura and Ghamya was puzzled.

"Come on, tell us how the white people look," Fakira urged him.

"That I don't know," blurted Ghamya, and immediately Bali declared, "Let's go and find out then."

"But Rajewadi is pretty far away," said Fakira looking east towards the mountains.

"Arra, it's just three miles. Come on, let's go," said Ghamya excitedly. And all the boys set off for Rajewadi. Fakira told Sadhu, "You don't come. Your feet will burn. Stay here. I'll take a look and describe everything to you."

"Come soon," said Sadhu solemnly.

"I will, but don't tell Aai," warned Fakira. The boys trotted off along the cart track. The seven of them then crossed the stream near the village and broke into a run. They were in a hurry because they wanted to see the laskar and come back before their parents missed them.

The sun was making its presence felt. The path along the maidan was covered with soft sand which felt like live coals under their feet. Gusts of hot wind blowing above the thorny bushes created a haze of fine dust and the boys cut through it, drenched in sweat. Soon they reached the Rajewadi village limits and stood there looking around. Their eager eyes were taking in everything.

The vast maidan and everything on it was searing hot. There was just one solitary babhli tree on one side of the path, but that did not offer much shade. The boys headed towards it with their tired legs and suddenly stopped. Chandu Attar from neighbouring Vategaon village was cantering towards them on his dark grey horse. He had wound a huge silver-coloured patka on his head. With his wide forehead, bushy eyebrows, grey tightly twirled moustache, thick grey beard, short neck, powerful chest under the English jacket, he easily attracted people's attention. He was pressing his feet into the horse's sides to make it go faster, impatient to reach Vategaon at the earliest.

Seeing Attar, the boys moved to one side to make way. But as soon as he neared them, Chandu Attar stopped. The boys looked at him fearfully. Attar glared at each one of them.

Fakira was standing right in front. He was wearing a circular pairan and loin cloth below it. His face was glistening with perspiration. The hair on his head was tousled and sweat dripped onto his neck. Looking at his brown complexion, grey eyes, straight nose, broad forehead and intelligent face, Chandu Attar shifted his gaze to Bali. Bali was short in stature. He had a handsome face. He too was dressed like Fakira, in a pairan and langot. Mura stood nearby, his hands clamped tight in his armpits. The old turban on his head and the shirt on his thin body were tattered. He looked nervous. Behind him was the scrawny Kisha, looking frightened. He only wore a loincloth whose loose rear end flapped like a tail, making him look like the young one of a monkey. Bhairu Mang's son Isha had taken off his pairan and thrown it on his shoulder. He was thinking of making a run for it. Savalya Mang's Ghamya was shuffling his feet and grimacing because his feet were burning in the hot sand. Appa Mang's son Bhiva was silently cursing Chandu Attar.

Having taken a careful look at all the boys, Chandu Attar raised his bushy eyebrows and lifting his head high asked, "Ay you abismuthe ki fauj (you army of little imps), where are you running to? Planning a dacoity or what? Speak up, say something . . . have you lost your tongues?" He then addressed Ghamya, "You are Savalya Mang's boy, aren't you? Then definitely a robbery is being planned."

Nobody dared to say anything. With lowered eyes they looked at Attar's beard. Attar then turned to Fakira.

"And you, you are Ranoji's, na re?"

"Hunh," said Fakira. Immediately Attar's tone softened. "Even stones are turning into popcorn in this hot sun, and where are you fellows rushing off to in the heat?"

"We are going to look at the laskar army," said Fakira. "What is there to look at in the army?" asked Attar tauntingly. "Why not go to Vithoba's field and watch the monkeys there instead?"

"Our feet are burning," Fakira raised his voice.

"So what should I do?" snapped Attar.

"Allow us to go," said Fakira.

"Then go!" Attar said and dug his heels into the horse's flanks. Once again, the horse set off at a trot.

The boys started running like birds released from a cage. They reached the road leading to Rajewadi. And under the cool shade of the banyan trees which lined both sides of the road, they stopped to catch their breath. Some of them simply lay down.

A little further down, the government bungalow stood to the right of the road. There were a number of pure white tents pitched around it. Several white soldiers were lolling about in the mango groves. A pile of large halters and bridles was lying on one side. Security personnel carrying guns stood guard at intervals. From their place under the tree the boys observed the guards in their strange attire—pleated knee-length skirts, long-sleeved tunics, and their red faces, flat noses, chubby cheeks and peculiar voices. It was a novel sight for them. Their tiredness vanished and they began to laugh.

Suddenly they saw Bapu Khot from Shigaon riding towards the camp at great speed. Seeing him, the army horses started neighing and snorting. Some reared up, shaking their manes, pawing the ground. The guards turned slightly to look at him. Khot entered the camp and was in there for a very long time. He had come to invite the senior-most officer for dinner.

Ghamya recognised Bapu Khot and said, "Look at him; he is Bapu Khot from Shigaon. He is the one who killed Ranunana."

Hearing these words, Fakira frowned and his eyes became hard. He muttered, "He killed my Aba . . ." There was anger and pain in his voice. "And he killed our Gabarya too."

Sitting on a large root of the banyan tree, Ghamya said, "A son of the devil he is, the scoundrel."

"And it looks like he is a friend of the white saheb," remarked Bali.

"So maybe . . . this laskar is also of Khot's caste?" Ghamya wondered. And immediately Kisha said, "No doubt about it, they probably have the same nature."

"Then we don't want anything to do with the laskar. Let's go back," Fakira burst out angrily.

Just then they saw Khot come out, talking to the senior white officer and moving in their direction.

The boys got frightened. The foolish Ghamya, thinking of something, picked up a stone . . .

When the people of the Mang settlement realized that seven boys had gone missing, there was panic. Everyone rushed around in search of them. Their parents ran about calling for their children, weeping and wailing. Hearing the commotion, Radha came out of the house. When she saw that Sadhu was alone, she asked, "Where's Fakira, ra?" Sadhu stuck out his lower lip in answer. A deep fear gripped Radha's stomach. She started calling out Fakira's name. Then Daulati arrived. "Where have the boys gone? Where are they?" The clamour increased. The parents of the missing boys gathered in front of Daulati's door. Savalya Mang also came with his axe.

This Savalya Mang was of medium height, slender but sturdily built. He was obstinate, short-tempered and like a vengeful snake when disturbed. Hence the people called him daukhel Savalya. He was as cunning and given to stealing as he was courageous and daring. The police officers looked upon him as an enemy and he felt the same about them. He was friends with all the unsavoury characters in the surrounding area and was a respected figure in criminal circles. He used to say that a theft should be committed only to fulfil the hunger in the belly and should be just enough for that purpose. He didn't like show offs, pomp and grandeur, though he himself was quite vain and boastful. That is why he had named his beloved son Ghamandi—the boastful one. Whatever he did in his house, Ghamandi would broadcast it to the whole of the Mang settlement. And now Ghamandi was missing. Believing that Ghamandi had done so at Fakira's behest, Savalya Mang was very angry. With raised eyebrows and wide eyes he said to Daulati, "Nana, our sons have got spoilt; your boy is leading them astray."

These words infuriated Daulati. Nobody had dared to speak to him with a raised voice so far, but today Savalya had. Daulati replied, "I know very well what a good boy your beloved son is. Put a bridle on his feet and tether him. He is already a ringworm, where's the question of spoiling him?"

Savalya's temper rose when he heard Daulati. He rushed forward in frenzy and shouted, "Don't say that. My son is like a god. What wrong has he done?"

"So if he is like a god, how can my boy make him wicked?" Daulati asked.

"How did . . . Where have they disappeared?"

"Why do you say that Fakira has led them?"

"You pamper him too much . . ."

"Our child, we will pamper!"

"Don't argue with me!" Savalya was indignant.

Just then Kondi Mahar, who had heard the uproar, turned up there from the Maharki. He had heard the exchange of words and said quietly, "Stop! Don't blame each other. I saw some boys a while ago, running along the maidan. Ghamya was bounding ahead of them all."

"Did you hear that?" snapped Daulati. Everybody rushed towards the maidan. Savalya was ashamed because he had snarled at Daulati unnecessarily. He marched ahead silently, but in his mind he was seething at Ghamya.

Radha's tear-filled eyes were searching for Fakira. She wished fervently that he would appear on the maidan so she could grab him and hold him close to her bosom. It was a loving mother's maternal instinct that made her melt like butter. Her gaze ran far ahead of her and returned disappointed when it couldn't find Fakira. She was desperate. Suddenly, she bent down and tried to see if she could find Fakira's footprints in the hot sand. She suddenly cried out, "Attu! This is my Fakira's footprint. He has definitely gone this way."

"Radha, have patience, Fakira won't go anywhere," Rahi attempted to reassure her.

The search party had crossed the first stream when they saw Chandu Attar coming towards them.

"Where are you going? What are you all so agitated about?" he asked them.

"Since afternoon our boys have not been seen," said Daulati.

"Where will they go? They have gone to see the army camp," Chandu said, playing with the reins in hand. "I saw them some time ago. They must be on their way back now."

"That will be good," Daulati said with a sigh of relief. Chandu interrupted him. "Where else can they go, Daulunana? Isn't he your grandson? He is a good boy, just like his father. And this lady in tears must be his mother? Ay, what are you crying for? Has he gone to attack the army camp? Nana, take care of your boy. He will become a tiger, yes, a tiger. A tiger gives birth to a tiger not a jackal. And you Savalya, that jewel with a shendi, he is yours, isn't he? As cunning as you are, you . . ." Everyone burst out laughing. Chandu Attar proceeded on his journey. Savalya was furious.

They crossed a small hillock and reached the plains of Rajewadi. Then they slowed down. Seven boys were running towards them at a tremendous speed. Seeing them, anxiety fled their faces. They were happy. Everybody sat down. Tobacco pouches were unrolled.

But Radha didn't stop. She kept running. Like the wind. Fakira came towards her guiltily. She grabbed him and held him in a tight embrace. She kissed him and wiped his sweat with her pallu. She wiped the dust off his feet. Her lips trembled.

"Where did you go, ra?"

"To see the army," said Fakira without looking at her.

As Ghamya came near, Savalya picked up two stones as large as coconuts and pushing the pagota to the back of his head and screamed, "Come here, you rascal. I will kill you to death . . ."

"Arra arra, what are you doing? Stop!"

"Leave me, Bhairudaji. This rascal is full of evil."

"Arra, what is the use of thrashing him?" Appa shouted and Savalya, driven to tears said, "Today, because of him I insulted Daulunana . . . I will bury the scoundrel alive, let me go."

"Shut up," snarled Daulati glaring at him. "A child and an ox, both are the same."

Savalya calmed down. The boys came closer. They were confident that Radhakaku would save them from a beating. They all headed back to Vategaon. Ghamya, however, was dragging his heavy feet along.

It had become dark by the time they reached home. Immediately, Radha went to the kitchen and started cooking. Sadhu and Fakira took the first hot quarters of bhakri and went and sat by the door munching on it. Rahibai helped her daughter-in-law. Daulati, who was officially a sepoy at the village office, had gone to the chavadi after finding the boys. He had not yet returned from the chavadi.

Sadhu who was pulling on his dripping nostrils as he ate the spicy chutney and bhakri, whispered to Fakira, "Did you see the laskar?"

"Yes, I did, idiot."

"What is it like?"

"All white men, guns, swords, horses."

"What do they wear?"

"Loose pants and hats like shoes on their heads."

"You didn't take me. You left me behind."

"Sadhu, my feet burned. I got blisters on my soles."

"You always say that. It is thorns during the nights and blisters during the day. Then when will I . . ."

"No longer. No longer will I say that."

"Those sahebs, are they like people?'

"Of course they are, but they behave like monkeys."

"Meaning? They jump around on trees?"

"No ra, they don't jump, but they talk very funny."

"They scream?"

Both of them laughed. Fakira said, "Gitchmid, gitchmid, ra, all gitchmid . . . Then that Khot from Shigaon came there and . . ."

"The one who killed Aba?" interrupted Sadhu.

"Arre ho . . . yes, the same one." Fakira had stretched out the word "yes."

Rahibai and Radha were listening to them talking from inside the house. When they heard the mention of Khot's name, they came to the door to hear better. Fakira continued, "While talking to that saheb, he walked towards us. Ghamya got angry and picked up a stone. He said, 'This is the one who killed our Ranunana.' But I held his hand. Otherwise . . ."

"Why did you stop him?" said Sadhu angrily. "You should have let him hit the rascal."

"But then the whole army would have come after us," said Fakira fearfully.

"Oh, yes. I had almost forgotten." Sadhu realized his mistake.

"All the sahebs are that Khota's friends," said Fakira.

"Then they are all bad men. We don't want them," said Sadhu disapprovingly. "I won't come now to look at them."

"I too won't go," Fakira replied.

"Mother cried a lot," Sadhu muttered.

"You told her?"

"No."

"Shabas! You should never tell."

"Why not?"

"Because then mother will call me names and say I am bad. That's why."

"Then why did she cry?"

"Because I am her son."

Radha couldn't hold herself back. She came out. She took both of them on her lap. With tears dripping on their heads, she ran her hand over the soles of Fakira's blistered feet. In a choked voice she said, "My child, I will never call you a bad boy, never."

Without warning the sky changed colour. Rain-laden clouds gathered menacingly overhead. Before they knew it, the month of Ashadh was upon them.

Again Ranoji's name was on every lip. Vategaon's joganis were round the corner. Preparations had begun. Every house got ready for the festival. It was declared that the procession of the Vategaon joganis would take place on Amavasaya, the day of the new moon. Hoardings announcing it were displayed in all villages. A reputed Tamasha troupe was invited to perform. A huge sum was declared as prize money for the wrestling competition.

Shankarrao Patil knew that Bapu Khot would not sit still on the day of the jogani and so he was alert. He gathered the youngsters of the village and prepared them. We will give our lives but we will not let the joganis go, they vowed. In the Mang settlement, the Mangs started sharpening their swords. Bhairu Naik sharpened his axe on the grinding stone.

And then the day of the new moon dawned, bringing joy to the village with it. Polis sizzled on tavas in every home. Children pranced around in shiny new clothes. A joyful haze hung over the village. It bustled with guests and visitors. Early in the morning, the village barber put on a sari and dressed as the jhadapin went from door to door seeking alms. From each house, he received half a dry coconut and a one paisa coin. Nobody refused him that day in the hope that the following year would be good. The day was a very special one in the history of the village. A new practice was being established. The jatra was being celebrated anew. Young and old alike were intoxicated with excitement. But one doubt lurked in all their minds. Would Bapu Khot create a ruckus and try to grab the jogani from them?

There was some mourning in Daulati's house that morning. Exactly one year ago, death had come to Ranoji. Thinking that it was not right for them to weep and wail when it was a joyful occasion for the whole village, Daulati, Rahibai and Radha comforted each other and joined in the happy atmosphere. The government of the princely state had donated the cost of one and a quarter maunds for the naivedya, an offering to honour the memory of Ranoji. So Radha wiped her tears and rolled out polis early in the morning. Then Daulati, Fakira and Sadhu carried the offering in a brass plate to the field. Fakira was carrying a bale of fresh grass to offer to the brave Gabarya. Fakira had not forgotten his loyalty.

Daulati paid no attention to the tears falling from his eyes and made the offering. Swallowing the sob rising in his throat, he said, "Boys, bow down to respect and honour your father."

Fakira and Sadhu touched their foreheads to the ground at the exact spot where their father had been slain. They didn't actually say "Let us inherit your strength, your fame, your courage" but the soil from that maidan inadvertently stuck to their foreheads as if the earth was giving them its blessings. Daulati saw it but he could not bring himself to wipe it off their foreheads. Then the grandfather and his two grandsons returned home. Radha took one look at their foreheads and burst into tears. She recognized that soil. Daulati said, "This is the soil from that very place."

"Yes, yes, I recognized it."

"It was not deliberately applied. It just stuck to their foreheads. How can that earth on which he had danced with his sword, the packet of pedhas tied to his waist, forget these two?" Daulati didn't say anything more. Rahi was serious. Her tears had dried up a long time ago.

Radha took both the boys inside the house and asked them, "Did you touch your father's feet?"

"Yes, we did. Ask Aba . . ."

"So what did you ask from him?"

"Nothing!" said Fakira. Looking at his forehead, Radha said "But your father has given you everything without you asking him. That soil will never forget you. You too should never forget it. The Khot has committed a crime on that soil. Don't forget it till you die. Become big. Big like your father. I will not die till you are grown up."

Radha was blabbering away incoherently. All the words that she had held back found their way out that day. She wiped her face with the end of her sari. Then Fakira and Sadhu went and sat near Daulati and Rahi. Fakira turned Daulati's face towards himself and whispered, "Baba?"

"Yes?"

"Aai says she is not going to die. You?"

"Even I won't die."

"And what about big Aai?"

"We will not let her die either."

Afternoon came. Food from the one and a quarter maunds sanctioned for the occasion was served in the Mang colony. Soon a message from Vishnupanta arrived. "It is time for the procession of the jogani. Come quickly."

To the clashing of cymbals and beating of drums, the Mangs started in procession towards the village with their swords held high. Guests from other villages also joined them. The lane was crowded with swords, axes, spears and shields. Fifty young men were on guard, fully prepared and ready to give their lives if it came to that. About a hundred-two hundred strong crowd of young and old accompanied the sword bearers. The throbbing beat of the halagis created an air of excitement. The village appeared to have filled up. Daulati Mang, officially designated sepoy of the government walked proudly at the back of the procession. Shankarrao Patil in a silk turban was astride his magnificent steed. He had curled his thick moustache and his bushy eyebrows were raised. With the unsheathed sword in his hand and grim expression, his broad face looked fierce that day.

Vishnupanta had appeared on his smartly saddled grey horse. There was an air of resoluteness about him. He had personally made all the preparations for the jogani procession. He had appointed horsemen to guard all the approaches to the village and was riding around making sure everything was properly controlled. Many people commented that the spirit of Ranoji the Mang seemed to have entered the brahmin Panta's body and completely possessed it!

The sun neared the western horizon and the jogani procession began. All the instruments started playing together in harmony rising to a crescendo. In one voice, the entire village cried out "Hara Hara Mahadeo!" The jogani set off on its way. Young Dinu Gurav was playing the part of the bridegroom joga and an equally good-looking Ranga Sutar was in the role of jogani. To play joga and jogani, the male–female in the service of God on that day, was an honour. They were walking under a canopy of swords. All the lanes, bylanes, dilapidated walls and hutments swelled with humanity. The jogani and the joga advanced through the crowd. The believers piously joined their palms in prayer. As the joganis approached, Ranoji's name fluttered on their lips.

The mother-in-law and daughter-in-law, Rahi and Radha were standing on a small rock. Fakira and Sadhu were beside them holding their mother's hands. The jogani was to pass in front of them. Radha had chosen this spot and had been waiting there for a long time so she could get a close view of the jogani. A storm of thoughts had arisen in her mind. About twelve months ago, a life had been lost forever. But the loss had brought long-lasting happiness to the village. Because his blood was spilt, this huge jatra is taking place. That blood is closely related to me. So all this is happening because of me. The decorations, the festoons, the drums, the swords, the people rushing about, my soul has permeated it all.

Radha was lost in her thoughts until the cacophony of approaching musical instruments startled her out of her reverie.

Savalya Mang was leading the joganis with his axe held aloft. He was wearing a double, twin-pleated dhoti and had wound a tapar around his head. Bhairu Ramoshi was beside him. Today, his already huge body was puffed up with pride, making him appear like a rakshasa, a demon. Panta had warned them not to let anyone who tried to attack the jogani from the front, turn around. "Make sure it doesn't happen," he'd said. Sakhuji Mahar kept the crowds back with the sickle in his hand. Vishnupanta and Shankarrao Patil were in front and behind the jogani.

The jogani reached Radha and then continued to move forward. Suddenly Panta cried out, "Stop the jogani right there."

Everyone abruptly halted. Panta dismounted, went up to them and said, "The ownership of this Jogani lies here. Allow her to worship first." He went to Rahi and Radha and said to them "Yes Kaku, touch the jogani's feet first. It's all due to you."

Rahi and Radha were confused. They didn't know what to say, what to do. So Panta came forward and led Fakira and Sadhu to the jogani so that they could have a good look. Both of them joined their hands and bowed their heads.

"Proceed!" commanded Patil. Once more, all the instruments started playing, and the jogani procession moved on. The jogani went right across and through the whole village and then as the sun went down, returned to the starting point. The procession had ended. The festivities were over. People bid farewell to the jogani. A burden was lifted off Vishnupanta's and Patil's heads. The villagers let out a huge sigh. Bapu Khot had not appeared, but even if he had been there, he hadn't been able to do anything. Their first jogani had gone off without any hitch or impediment. But who knows what will happen the next time! With this thought, the villagers returned to their homes.

Radha was elated because Panta had halted the jogani procession for her sake. It made her forget her sorrow. His words had given Rahibai much reassurance. She felt that though her son was dead, his sacrifice was being appreciated. Sweet words uplift one's soul and raise one's spirits.

And after a whole year, Daulati twirled his moustache that day.

Four

In the middle of Ashadh, the rains became really heavy. The Mangs starved. In Daulati's case, the villagers were generous, but the other Mangs were stricken. They had no patrons, no masters. Savalya Mang couldn't bear to see their pitiful plight. He set out in the downpour. Bhairu Ramoshi and he wreaked havoc in the neighbouring villages. They were especially severe with Shigaon. Khot was so troubled by this harassment that he became desperate and went to Satara where he met the district collector and lodged a complaint against Savalya Mang.

The collector had heard of the infamous Savalya. He promptly rushed a sepoy to Vategaon with a letter addressed to Vishnupanta Kulkarni. The letter said:

"Send Savala Daji Mang from your village to Satara. We have something to discuss with him."

Hearing this, Savalya was alarmed. "I will not go to Satara. There will be treachery there," he told Vishnupanta. "The letter says, to discuss, not to arrest. So go," Panta told Savalya. "If anything untoward happens, I will come there myself," he assured Savalya.

When Savalya reached the collector's office and saw Khot there, he guessed that the letter had been written because of a complaint from Khot.

The collector had a good look at Savalya. Seeing his bearing and manner, and his gleaming axe, he was convinced that the man must be a dacoit. He soon realized that Savalya was quite garrulous too. The collector asked the first question.

"The other day, a murder took place in Bhatwadi in the British territory next to your village. We need information on that."

Savalya smiled. "If your officers who consume two chickens a day can't get information, how can a grass-eater like myself have it? Besides, the murder wasn't committed after informing me," he said.

"You talk too much," admonished the collector, "Answer only what I am asking you."

"I cannot measure my words, sarkar!"

"You mean you can speak and behave without restraint, do you? You Mangs have committed that murder!"

"Who says so?" Savalya snapped back. "Mangs never kill anyone. Corn cobs can be cut and stomachs filled. Not heads. Cutting off heads is what ruffians like Khot do, not us," he added, nodding at Khot. Khot turned pale and looked nervous but said nothing. The collector got angry.

"Don't take the names of others to hide your own wrongdoing. I can arrest you."

"Arrest me, then!" said Savalya defiantly. "You can blame me for a crime, sarkar, but you are hitting the ground thinking it's the snake. If what you say is true, I will shave off my moustache . . . Mangs do not commit murders. Killing people won't fill our bellies . . . In fact, we wish for people to live long lives, cultivate their fields and reap rich harvests so we can get a small share of the yield."

"Which means you loot standing crops?"

"That is right."

"You burnt down the Shigaon crops?"

The collector started firing his salvos at Savala. "Khot beheaded a Mang while he was taking away the jogani. In retaliation, you have been ransacking the Shigaon fields! Is that not true?"

"Now you speak the truth," said Savalya with a false smile. "It is clear that you summoned me here because Khot complained . . . If we wanted take revenge for Ranoji's death, sarkar . . . Khot's head was not kept under lock and key . . . We could have cut it off anytime, anywhere, and . . ."

"And what?"

"And even now, if Khot tries to take back the jogani from us, we'll knock his head off on the spot. I am no son of a Mang if I don't . . . I will die but before that I will leave this message for my children and my future generations . . ."

"You are boastful."

"That I am, sarkar!"

"I have work to attend to. We will talk again tomorrow," said the collector and left. Giving Khot an oblique look, Savalya went to a local dharamshala to stay for the day.

That same night, a special dispatch came with the news that Khot's entire sugarcane crop was reduced to ashes. On hearing this the next morning, the collector saheb was convinced that Savalya had nothing to do with the looting and plundering in south Satara, that someone else was responsible for it. So he ordered Savalya to go back home. Twirling his moustache arrogantly, Savalya returned to his village.

Everyone was certain that Savalya would be arrested. They were pleasantly surprised to see him back home. Savalya went straight to the chavadi to meet Vishnupanta. It was getting to be dusk and the sun was down low on the horizon. Panta was about to finish his work and go home when he saw Savalya. Savalya bent low in a mujara and the two of them started walking towards Panta's wada. On the way, Savalya told Panta what had transpired between him, the collector and Khot in Satara.

"Then what was the reason to summon you to Satara?" asked Panta.

"No reason, nothing," Savalya retorted. "Khot made allegations and poisoned their minds."

"How do you know that?"

"The collector said that we are taking revenge because Khot cut Ranoji's head."

"Was Ranoji's name mentioned?"

"The collector didn't take the name but said that since a Mang was killed, you are doing all this looting—plundering."

"Very well. Go now, and be careful. Don't get caught in other people's territory," Panta advised him and entered his wada. Savalya headed home. On the way he met Bhairu Ramoshi. When he saw Savalya, Bhairu said, "Savalya, when you were not there, I felt as if my arm was broken, ra."

"I don't think my arms will be free for long now, Bhairu."

"Why, ra? What is the problem?"

"The Government has woken up. Big people like Khot are whining away to the sarkar. I feel something bad will happen . . ."

"What did Panta tell you?"

"Stay within the boundaries and don't get caught across the borders."

"If Panta says so, then something is definitely wrong."

As they were walking and talking, they reached the Mang settlement and Bhairu whispered in Savalya's ears, "I was the one who set fire to Khot's sugarcane."

Hearing this, Savalya laughed. "Good thing you did. Because of that, my neck was saved!" Saying this, he hurried to his house.

Barely a fortnight had elapsed when the British police arrived with an order from the government of the princely state. Panta, Patil and the whole village was bewildered. Another calamity had descended on the Mang settlement. Panta read out the order in a loud voice from the village office.

"In view of the Mang community of your village entering into British territory and creating havoc there, this order has been issued so as to maintain peace and order in the area. As per this order, Savalya Daji Mang is to be detained in Belgaon. This order is to be immediately implemented and the accused handed over to the Government servant carrying this letter. If the accused wants to bring his family members with him, the Government has no objection to it."

Vishnupanta finished reading and looked at the faces of the respected elders sitting in the chavadi, then flung the paper to Shankarrao Patil.

"But what is the Mang's crime?" asked Patil sharply. Pointing at the paper lying in front of him, Panta retorted, "Ask that notice."

"I don't understand this government policy."

"It certainly cannot be understood. A man is not a stone that you can pick him up and put him somewhere against his wishes. It is gross injustice. That is the injustice present in this order. Today it is Savalya, tomorrow it may be Daulati, then Bhairu."

"But what about the consequences of this?"

"It is quite clear that the government is not bothered about the consequences. That there will be repercussions, there is no doubt. The administration of the village will slow down, trade transactions will come to a standstill. There will be a Mang uprising and then they . . ." Panta swallowed the rest of his sentence.

The sepoy went to the Mang settlement and brought Savalya to the office. When he heard the order, tears came to Savalya's eyes. In a broken voice he said, "What must I do? What is the opinion of the grey heads here?"

"Right now, you better go. I can't say anything at this moment," Panta told him.

"I'll go and get ready to leave and then come back," Savalya cried.

"Yes, go."

Savalya rose and started towards his house. The constable followed him. Shankarrao Patil got annoyed. He shouted to the constable, "Ay, where are you going? He will come back. Don't get agitated. Don't be impatient."

"And look here," Panta warned the sepoy, "Behave properly with him on the way to Belgaon, don't be rough or rude . . . He is like a tamed tiger. He can easily tear you apart. Keep that in mind."

The policeman sat down, intimidated. Savalya returned fully prepared. He had worn a fancy turban on his head, slung a bundle under his arm and carried a thick heavy stick in his hand. He strode as if he was going to a jatra. In no time, the news spread through the whole village. People gathered to walk with him till the village border and bid him goodbye. Mang women and children began to shed tears. Ghamya let out a bellow of grief. It was as if the supporting pillar of the Mangs had been dislodged.

People came up to the maidan. Savalya touched Panta's feet and said with a heavy heart, "My people are orphaned, gavkar. Watch over them. I am going away. If anything bad happens here, I won't be there. You will."

"Go! Don't worry," promised Panta.

Savalya cried out to all the Mangs gathered there, "You turn back now. I am off. Don't be afraid . . . If anything goes wrong, I will rush back from the white man's land. Go, be resolute, be brave."

He touched Daulati's feet, embraced Bhairu and held Ghamya close. He reassured his wife and headed out on the road to Belgaon. Today, I am leaving this place, this earth where I was born. Now, I will live as an outsider in another village. I will not see my family, my village. Though I am a native I will be a foreigner; though I have a home I will be homeless. Who will I find there who is dear to me? These thoughts wrenched his heart and the Savalya, who was tough as a rock, broke down and sobbed like a child.

The same law which had expelled Savalya from his village now swept across the province. It exiled thousands of Mangs; it dispossessed hundreds of Mang children. Caste became more important than the right to land. "A Mang can never be worthy" became a catchphrase. The word "worthy" was dissociated from the entire Mang community, and because of that many Mangs were cut off from their villages, their lands and their families. It was an attempt to deprive the Mangs of their dignity. The sole intent of the law was to bring the valiant spirit of the Mang people to its knees, to suppress it and to make them slaves, helpless and dependent on the charity of others.

As a result, the homeless Mangs became wanderers and accepted whatever work they could get in the neighbouring villages. Many took their families with them when they left their homes. They became like gypsies. This law pulled its noose so tight that it became difficult for them to survive as Mangs. "No pardon for a Mang," became the dictum for the police. So the Mangs began to hide their identities. Many of them became snake charmers. The British managed to hold the entire tribal community of the Mangs of Maharashtra on the sharp edge of the sword.

In Belgaon, Savalya picked up the traditional work of a wadar, breaking stones. He sorely missed his village and became restless and uneasy. The jogani will be taken out. Bapu Khot will snatch it away. We will lose our prestige; Ranoji's sacrifice will go in vain . . . thoughts such as these tortured him. Unable to bear it, one day he grabbed the supervisor's feet and pleaded, "I will work here as a wadar. I will make sure not to trouble anyone."

"What exactly do you mean?" asked the officer.

"Allow me to visit my village every year, on the new moon night of the month of Ashadh."

"That will depend entirely on your behaviour," said the officer.

So Savalya behaved very well. He became the perfect stone breaking wadar. The officer-in-charge gave him permission to visit his village for just one day. On the new moon day of Ashadh, Savalya reached his village in time for the jogani. With his long flowing beard and glinting axe, he had pride of place and walked right beside the jogani. That night he met everyone. After greeting Panta, Shankarrao, Daulati, and his own family, he returned to Belgaon.

Thereafter, Savalya worked hard so he could visit the village every year. He was afraid that in his absence, the jogani would be snatched away. The efficient way he broke the rocks earned him the nickname Wadar. Savalya did look like one, anyway.

For four consecutive years after he was forced to leave the village, Savalya was given permission to return home. But in the fifth year, the supervisor was transferred and a new man took his place. Savalya failed to convince the new officer and for the next five years, he was not allowed to visit his village. He was heartbroken and despondent during those five years. Whenever Ghamandi or his wife visited, they brought news of home. Savalya had to be satisfied with that.

Finally in the ninth year, when he did come home for the jogani, everything had changed. The old cactus arms had shrivelled up and new ones had sprouted in their place. New people resided in the old houses. Daulati, who was determined not to die, was clinging on to life somehow. There was a different kind of contentment about him now. He had nurtured and raised the two little twigs into big strong trees and was ready to take his last breath with Savalya by his side. His fierce moustache shone like silver. The grey eyebrows merged with the sandal paste dot on his forehead. His still-strong bones and prominent veins stood out from under his taut skin.

Rahibai, who had kept herself alive with dogged determination to see that her grandchildren's reputation would be just like her son's, was now unafraid. She had developed tremors in her neck, the hair on her head had all turned grey and her face was full of wrinkles. Even today, she wore a big round kunku on her forehead and took care of the goats.

Radha felt that all her hardships had borne fruit. The struggle of the past eleven years had proved worthwhile. It was very difficult to live without a kunku, as a widow, but Radha had managed to do it. Today, she had not one but two sturdy young sons in her home. Daulati and Rahi had two Ranojis in front of them. Fakira and Sadhu were carrying the responsibility of the household on their strong young shoulders. New winds of happiness were blowing through that old house of theirs.

Fakira had now come of age. Following in the footsteps of his father, he behaved in a manner befitting his father's reputation. He was loved by everyone in the village. People felt happy when they saw his sparkling eyes, fresh radiant face and a body tough like steel. His mother had brought him up well. His speech, when he did speak, was measured. He lived in his own world, by his own rules. He had an aversion for frivolity. He felt that he should behave like Panta. He was no longer stubborn. And he worshipped Ranoji's sword kept in the devhara, the altar for the gods in his home. He was very attached to the old Gabarya's saddle. He now placed it on the new Gabarya's back and flew across the maidan like a free falcon.

Sadhu had taken up a government job.

Vishnupanta too had aged. His luxuriant moustache showed streaks of grey and his broad, handsome face had become more solemn. That added to his original resolute demeanour.

Old age had begun to catch up with Shankarrao Patil too. But the arrogance had not diminished. Some people are born arrogant and they die arrogant. Shankarrao Patil was one of them. People like Bhairu and Appa had become old but they had not lost their fiery temperament. On the contrary, with age, their irritability had only increased. The children Isha, Kishya, Bali, Murari, Ghamya, Bhiva had grown up and had begun to behave like tigers.

Seeing all this, Savalya felt very happy.

Ashadi amavasaya, the new moon day was here once more. The village was gripped by fervour and excitement. People had come from all over to see the joganis.

Five

"If you have so much antagonism in you and claim to be of my blood, then you will bring back that jogani before I die." Bapu Khot had not forgotten these sharp words from his father Bajiba. They had been burned into his heart. For the last ten years, he had been trying to bring the jogani back but had been unsuccessful. The Vategaonkars were fully aware of his intentions. Bapu Khot, the one who had broken the custom and intruded into their village and killed one of their men would not rest until he had recovered his jogani; they knew and so lived in constant preparedness.

Bapu Khot had spared no pains to get the jogani back but Shankarrao, Panta, Savala, Bhairu Ramoshi and Tayanya Mahar had risked their lives and neutralized Bapu's efforts. With six men having been killed and the jogani not recovered, the Shigaonkars had lost their nerve. No one spoke about offering their heads in the fight to regain the jogani. So what could Bapu Khot alone do? Making his father's words come true with the backing of government officials and support from friends of other villages was beyond Bapu Khot's capacity. He first needed help from his own village. And that is exactly what was not happening. Though many people did feel bad looking at the lone joga taken out in procession every year in their village and would have liked to sacrifice their lives for the sake of prestige, the thought, "What can I alone do?" had prevented them from acting.

Bajiba had aged. He didn't have the spirit any longer to leap onto a running horse. Sadly he stared at the mournful joga but never uttered a word about the jogani. The others didn't have it within them to do so either. Nobody could openly speak about retrieving the jogani. Because when they uttered the word jogani, the images of Bhairu Ramoshi and Savala Mang with their glistening axes danced before their eyes. So these thoughts remained trapped in their minds. They thought that if they said anything about the jogani and it was conveyed to Bhairu—that demon of death would come and finish them off. Of course, that fear had somewhat lost its edge now, especially as Bapu Khot's influence over the youth of the village was growing. He had leased out his lands among them and made them indebted to him. And they were openly talking about launching an attack to bring the jogani back. This emboldened many of the older villagers.

During this time, something unexpected happened. Bapu Khot gave his daughter in marriage to Raosaheb, a member of Shankarrao Patil's extended family. After giving the proposal serious thought and keeping in mind the possibilities in the future, he paid a dowry of Rs 14,000 to finalize the match. He knew that though

Raosaheb was not holding the post at that time, it would come to him after Shankarrao. Raosaheb commanded much respect in the village because of that. Bapu Khot was sure that he would do exactly what his father-in-law expected him to. He knew he could achieve a lot through Raosaheb, his son-in-law. This gave him confidence to think seriously once more about the jogani.

Several young boys had gathered in the open veranda of Bapu's house. Many old men sat leaning against the pillars. Bajiba, seated on a chair was listening quietly. Bapu Khot was saying, "I am not afraid of death . . . my heart is not in my stomach; it is on my back. But what can I do on my own? Though I have power, it is not enough. I need backing, support. I could have gone alone and got killed, fighting. But now the time has come for all of us to say 'We must have our jogani back.'"

"So what should we do? Just tell us," said Gajya Mali's son Galu Mali with his nostrils flared. Bapu recalled Gajya's valour. He said, "Galu, the minute he was told, 'Throw it, ra,' your father threw his spear that landed on the Mang and finished him in one blow. I need that kind of courage, that kind of determination . . ."

"I am prepared," said Galu, swelling with pride at these words of praise for his father. Ganu Kumbhar who was sitting with his back to a pillar said, "Yes, I saw Gajya's wound. The sword that had hit his head had reached his nose."

Bapu was shaken. He quickly made Kumbhar shut up and said, "Whatever happened has gone with him. Talk about the present now. I am getting fifty men from outside. They will assemble here on the veranda. Another fifty or more we can round up from the village and . . ."

"And let us cause a disturbance," said Dnyanu Sutar full spiritedly.

"Yes, there must be a dangal, a riot," said Khot. "No point holding out any longer. Either the head gets broken or the tail gets cut . . . Whatever has to happen will happen . . ."

"Should we get into an open fight?" someone asked in a doubtful tone.

"No. My son-in-law is in that village. My men from outside are camping there. Some of them will block the swords of the Mangs while the others will go with Raosaheb to the jogani. They will carry out the important task. We will remain at a distance, watching discreetly. Once the rioting starts, we must go in, cut the legs of those following the jogani and rush back to our village."

"All right. But what do we do about Bhairya Ramoshi?" another doubt was raised and Bapu Khot shot back sharply, "Yes, eight of our men will be near and around Bhairya Ramoshi and Savalya. Their two bodies will be the first to fall in the fighting."

"Done! It's done then!" The unanimous cry echoed through the veranda, as if Bhairu Ramoshi and Savalya Mang were already reduced to corpses. A weight seemed to have lifted off their chests!

The strategic meeting ended. Everyone got busy with their tasks, taking different routes to Vategaon. Bapu made preparations as if he was getting ready for a war. The people of Shigaon hid their weapons in the folds of their ghongadis. Some kept their horses ready on the outskirts of Shigaon. Some had already reached Vategaon. Others spread themselves out, in anticipation of a call. Some started looking for Bhairya. Others went in search of Savalya. They all merged with the crowds.

The sky was as clean as freshly washed rice. The sun had begun its swing to the west. Its rays had become slightly less sharp and a refreshing wind was blowing across the plain. The neem trees in the village were rustling and bending low in the breeze. The furrowed black soil waited impatiently for the seeds to be sown. The tamarind tree near Daulati's house swayed cheerfully.

The time for the jogani procession to start was near. Wearing freshly washed clothes, Daulati, Rahi, Radha were bustling about. The village was buzzing with people. The twelve professional balutedars, who were part of the servant-cum-caste system prevalent there, were busy getting their tasks done. Shankarrao had decked up his horse with ornaments. He had placed the saddle on a silken cloth and was sitting astride it with the sword fixed to the jin, the sheep's wool underpad. The horse kept rearing up every now and then impatiently, and the visitors to the fair gathered around to see this prancing steed.

As per tradition, the Mang swords led the procession to the accompaniment of the musical bands. Mura, Bali, Kisna, Ghamandi, Ishwara, Bhiva, Sadhu, Piraji from Chinchani, Nilaji from Sajur, Bali from Ghonchi were among the powerful Mangs. In full preparedness, they held their swords aloft. Many were carrying sharp pointed spears and shiny axes. The halagi drums started throbbing. In one voice the entire gathering cried out, "Here comes the sword of the Mang!"

Fakira loaded old Gabarya's saddle onto the young Gabarya's back, and taking the sword from the devhara in his hands, he was about to set off when he received a summons.

"Come immediately."

Fakira took the straight cart path and flew like the wind towards Panta's wada. On the way, Galu Mali was sitting in wait. He looked at Fakira with wide eyes and asked a visitor to the fair, "Who that is?"

"He? Fakira," came the reply.

When Fakira reached Panta wada, he saw Bhairu and Savala sitting there looking worried. Immediately, Fakira suspected that something had happened. These men of steel wouldn't look so disturbed otherwise. He dismounted and went inside. When Panta came to know that Fakira had arrived, he came out. He was also looking worried. He said in a serious voice, "Fakira, there will be an ambush today. Shigaonkars have sneaked into our village."

"Who says?"

"Savala and Bhairu."

Fakira frowned.

"Why didn't you tell earlier? Outside the village only we could have dealt with them."

"How to do that without informing Panta?" Savala replied.

"Yes," nodded Bhairu. "Would be unnecessary trouble otherwise . . ."

"Let it be now," said Panta in a conciliatory manner. "Before or after, what does it matter? We got the information, that is important. We are now alerted. Had we been caught off guard, there would have been trouble. Now keep a strict watch. Savala, Bhairu, you both are experienced people, teach the boys how to fight." Panta suddenly paused. He looked at Fakira carefully from the hair on his head to the toenail on his foot, then asked, "This is Ranoji's sword?"

"Yes," Fakira muttered nodding.

Panta said, "Fakira," then paused once more. Turning to the sepoy he said, "Natha, tell Shankarrao that I have called him immediately. Go, hurry."

Natha ran off and Panta said, his voice raised, "Fakira, Bapu Khot had entered our territory and had cut off Ranoji's head. If such an attempt is made, and there is no doubt he will do it again, do not allow him to leave our boundary. The prestige of that sword is very high and it now rests in your hands . . ." Fakira didn't utter a word. For no reason, his eyes welled up. The valour in his heart was reflected in them.

Savala retorted, "If the Khot escapes from our border, then I am off to heaven."

"Do your best. Don't delay. I will go now and start the jogani procession."

As Fakira, Savala and Bhairu headed out of the wada, Shankarrao came in. Panta said to him "Patil, what is happening in the village?"

"Good thing you called me," said Patil. "I feel something is going to happen this year. Unknown faces are seen in every lane of the village. Strange new people are thronging Raosaheb's wada."

"It means the Khot has buried a granary under us and is going to set fire to it now. Let it burn! Ten years have gone by waiting . . . Our days are getting shorter . . ." Patil was angry. "Let it end once and for all, today only, if . . ."

"It is going to, today itself," Panta interjected. "Keep an eye on Khot and when trouble erupts, guard Fakira's back. I will get the jogani out. You carry on." Saying this, Panta paused. Patil said nothing. Both had the same feeling in their minds at that time. Suddenly Patil embraced Panta. Panta's hands encircled Patil. Patil said, "If I live, we will meet again."

All the instruments began to play together. The bugle sounded. The jogani set out. There was a huge din. The sky echoed with the sound. Dhangar cymbals clashed and the tiles on the roofs started dancing. *Dhamb dhamb dhamba* . . . The tasha and the Mang halagi drowned out human voices.

Under the protection of the swords, axes and spears, the jogani moved along. Daulati, Rahi and Radha waited at a spot on Mahar ground. They had stood there every year.

Jogani had gone ahead somewhat when Fakira called Sadhu beside him and whispered, "You stay behind me. If anyone attacks me from the back, knock him off. Call Mura here." Saying this, he turned and looked back. Shankarrao was riding nearby with the reins held tight. He signalled with his eyes, "I am here." Mura came. He addressed Fakira as Daji now.

"What, Daji?"

"Be careful. There is going to be trouble. Treachery." Fakira bent down from his saddle and said, "Protect the necks of your companions. If anyone tries to attack the jogani, cut him down instantly. Tell Chinchanikar, Sajurkar and Ghonchikar, do not retreat. Go!"

Mura went. He told Bali. As soon as Bali heard it, he turned back sharply and ran up to Fakira. Standing on his toes, he asked, "Daji, how many men from Shigaon are there?"

"However many—100, 200, 1000 . . . no matter. Whoever dares to advance, cut him to bits. Go! Tell the Ramoshis."

One person spoke to another, then he told third, and another and soon the message reached everyone. There were some furtive movements. The Ramoshis gave the ghongadis on their shoulders to their accomplices and stood up straight. The children who had gathered around the jogani vanished. Fakira was leading Gabarya where there was a little bit of space, and where Fakira went, Sadhu followed. Shankarrao riding his horse with care followed them. Ahead of them were Bhairu and Savala as also Panta on his mount.

The situation was turning tense. The moment when the skirmish was expected drew near, Fakira's eyes were open, unblinking. The jogani reached the Mahar territory. Daulati bowed low in a namaskar, then touched his moustache. Rahibai could see Ranoji in front of her eyes. Radhabai silently gave her blessings to Fakira and Sadhu and prayed for their well-being. jogani moved ahead. The new arrivals began to crowd around. Naked weapons licked their lips.

The jogani reached the sandy area in front of the Mahar settlement and suddenly, along the cart track from under the tamarind tree near the Mang settlement,

Bapu Khot emerged, his horse at a gallop. Everyone's attention was drawn to him. They stared bewildered. For a moment, the guard around the jogani slackened. The jogani was surrounded. Immediately, the Ramoshis spun around, and the Mangs jumped to their rear. Swords started clashing, people started falling. Savala, Bali, Nilu, Bhiva, Ishwara were bloodied. Bhairu started swinging his axe blindly.

But Fakira didn't move. Like a hawk, he had his eyes fixed on Khot. The fighting reached its peak. Suddenly someone cried out, "The jogani . . . the vati is gone!"

One man separated from the crowd and ran towards Bapu Khot. Fakira slowly nudged Gabarya into a trot. As he moved, Sadhu followed him. Shankarrao stood by watching. He was wondering what Fakira's next move would be.

The man who had run away from the crowd handed over the vati of the jogani to Bapu Khot. Khot turned his horse around. And Fakira's Gabarya charged.

By that time, the disturbance near the jogani had been brought under control by the Ramoshis and the Mangs, and they turned around to see what would happen next. Fakira had closed in on Bapu Khot. On the open fields of rich black soil, the two magnificent horses were watched by a thousand pairs of eyes. All breaths were stuck in their chests because the jogani had been snatched away. As he galloped, Fakira turned Gabarya to the left of Bapu Khot's horse, making it difficult for Khot to attack with the sword in his right hand. In spite of that the provoked Khot raised his sword. Fakira, who had his eyes fixed on it, knocked it out of Khot's hand along with the fist holding it. He rushed at Khot. It was horse upon horse. The two horses collided, and Khot who had lost his hand was dazed for a moment. He jumped off the horse. For just a moment, Gabarya was unsettled. Then he recovered, turned around and came at the fallen Khot and was about to trample him. But Fakira held him back. Khot quickly got up and with a pitiable face, started pleading for mercy.

"Don't kill me . . . Here, take the jogani."

Fakira stopped. He couldn't bring himself to do it. It's not easy to kill a man. He took the jogani vati and warned Khot, "All right. Let the sword lie there. Take the horse and run for your life. Don't look back even once. Never forget that here, death by the name of Fakira is roaming around on Gabarya's back."

Bapu Khot jumped onto his horse and headed towards Shigaon. Soon, the fighting and the disturbance were quelled and everyone ran towards Fakira. Panta rushed forward through the crowd and asked, "Fakira, what happened?"

Fakira showed them the sword with Khot's fist attached to it and also the jogani vati. Everyone cheered and threw their ghongadis up in the air. Pant smiled quietly and asked, "Why didn't you cut off his head?"

"But that there is his head," said Fakira, pointing to the sword. At that, Panta patted Fakira's back.

"You have upheld your father's name and honour!" he said.

"By removing this thorn you have relieved me," said Shankarrao Patil, embracing him. Fakira roared, "Who handed over the jogani to Khot?"

"Dula Mang from Satara," said Mura.

"Where is he?"

"In the chavadi," said Panta. "Come on, let the jogani proceed."

After sending the sword with Khot's fist still gripping it to the village office, Patil continued with the jogani procession. All those who had dispersed gathered together once more. Daulati, Rahibai, Radha all hugged Fakira. Radha pulled the end of her sari to wipe the perspiration on Fakira's forehead when she remembered that particular day when the two young boys had gone to make their offering to their father's memory. As they had bowed down and touched their foreheads to the ground, some of the earth had stuck to their foreheads. Radha had reached out but then drawn back her hand, lest she wipe off the sacred earth. She had wiped her tears instead!

People attended to their wounds and joined the jogani. After the ritual ended and the ceremony was completed, Patil and Panta went to the village office. There they saw Dulari Mang tied up and Savala and Bhairu standing guard over him. He was interrogated in the night. Threatened with being beheaded, he came out with the whole truth.

Dulari was a government servant in Satara. By regularly tipping off the police about the criminals and miscreants in the area, he had risen to a fairly high position. An officer in Satara had introduced him to Khot. Later on, they had become friends and today he had come there to help his friend. He had stayed in Vategaon for two days in Raosaheb's wada as a Patil and hatched the plot from there. Raosaheb was fully aware of it.

Panta and Shankarrao were stunned by this story. When he heard that Raosaheb had joined hands with Khot, Shankarrao felt that he had a coiled snake under his pillow. At the same time, he was pleased that he had been alerted to the danger.

Taking into consideration the fact that Dulari was a government servant, Panta warned him, "Though you are a government employee, you meddled in matters that do not concern you. Also since you are a government servant, we pardon you on this one occasion. Go away, right now."

"But the Ramoshis and the Mangs will not let me escape alive," Dulari howled.

"All right. We will send someone to accompany you." Saying this, Panta turned to Bhairu. "Bhairu, you accompany him till Satara," he ordered.

When he learnt that it was Bhairu who would escort him, Dulari started crying even louder. "This man will take me to heaven, not Satara," he wailed.

The jogani incident had caused a sensation. Thousands of visitors who had come for the jatra returned singing praises of young Fakira. Like bees carrying honey from flowers, they carried Fakira's fame from village to village. Everyone started saying, "Fakira is the bravest warrior . . . He defeated Khot. He cut off his wrist holding the sword and broke the sting in the scorpion's tail. Khot has been completely disabled."

The whole village was mighty pleased with Fakira's conduct on that day. Fakira's exploits on Gabarya had begun. Savala and Bhairu were more pleased than Daulati, Rahibai and Radha. They forgot their own injuries. The reputation of a highly accomplished person reaches far and wide. Many are impressed for a moment on hearing about it but no one pays attention to the sacrifices and hardships that go with the reputation.

The next morning, Savala got ready to go back to Belgaon. Before he departed, he went to see Fakira first. He embraced the young man. His eyes were full of tears but he was laughing aloud. On hearing him laugh, Fakira was perplexed. Daulati, Rahi and Radha were also astonished.

"Why you are laughing, ga?" asked Fakira. "An old memory . . . I remembered the incident when you all had gone to look at the laskar and I had a fight with Daulati-aba," Savala replied.

Saying this, he again became serious. He raised his eyebrows, flared his nostrils and said, "Yesterday, you acquired a reputation; it was what I had wished for. An insect in the dung does not remain in the dung."

"When you will come back?"

"How can I say?" said Savala helplessly. "It would have been better if I had committed a murder. At least I would have been sentenced to a fixed term in Kala Pani and would have finished serving it by now. But this terrible law won't leave me alone."

"Nothing can be done?"

"Who will take the trouble?" said Savala dejectedly. "We are voiceless people. Marked as criminals. Who will pay heed to our pleas?"

"Why didn't you talk to Panta?"

"And say what? Can he not see?"

"I will talk to him."

"Talk. Do something." Savala sounded deeply hurt. "Eight–nine years I spent. A very hard time it was. Though a native, I am now an alien, a homeless wanderer." He stopped, his voice thick.

Fakira said, "And now?"

"Now I don't feel like leaving the village!'

Hearing this, Fakira was saddened. He felt a wrench in his heart. He said in a firm voice, "You go now. I will do something. I will not sit quiet and will not allow Panta to keep silent either."

"Yes, yes," said Savala smiling. "Don't let me die in a far-off land. Let my bones fall in this settlement. Let my dead body be carried to the graveyard in our village. I should not die a dog's death—that's all I want."

The comment hit Fakira at his sensitive core. He said harshly, "Don't go then. Stay here. Let whatever happens, happen."

"No, no," said Savala. "The village told me to go, so I must. I cannot act against their wishes."

"So go then."

Savala departed but his words, "Don't let me die a dog's death in that faraway land," ignited a fire in Fakira's heart. He was distraught, thinking about what he could do for Savala. For a long time, he stood leaning against the tamarind tree.

The sun slowly came up. Its early rays settled on the branches of the tamarind tree and started to spread over the leaves. A golden light splashed on the green cactus. The village cattle came to the stream. People got ready for work. Vishnupanta set out towards his fields. Hearing the horse's hooves, Fakira became alert. The horse stopped under the tamarind tree. Mang wada was astonished to see Panta stopping there, all for this young man. Leaning forward, Panta looked piercingly at Fakira and asked, "What is the matter, Fakira?"

"Nothing, Aba," Fakira smiled.

"What nothing? Your face says something is wrong."

"Aba, Savalunana has gone."

"Where? To Belgaon?"

"Yes, to Belgaon."

"So? What do you want to say?"

"Why did he have to go?"

Panta was in a bit of a dilemma. After thinking for a moment he said, "He has been exiled by the sarkar . . . as a criminal."

"What was his crime?"

"Actually, nothing. The government has no proof of any kind."

"Then someone will have to question the sarkar about it."

"I know. They must be questioned. I will do it myself. You go home."

Panta's horse sped away. Fakira turned to his house. Daulati was standing in the doorway. Radha came out. The Mangs had gathered around. Daulati said, "What did you ask Panta?"

"About Savalunana."

"What did he say?"

"He is going to question the sarkar."

Hearing this, the Mangs were overjoyed. Now our days will be happy! If Panta goes to Satara and fights there, then this law will lose its teeth and we Mangs will not be abused any longer. We will bear pain but will eat happily. Our bones will fall here, in this village, in this soil, in this land—no matter if it's a small piece—where we were born, and that's how it should be. With this thoughts, the Mangs returned to their homes.

Fifteen days later Panta left for Satara.

Six

When Vishnupanta went to Satara, Bhairu Ramoshi had gone with him. It was in his capacity as a government sepoy that he had accompanied Panta since there was the danger of robbers attacking people as they climbed the Satara ghat. They met Dulari Mang just outside the collector's office. He did not recognize Panta immediately, but as soon as he saw Bhairu, he hastened towards him.

"What village you are from?" he asked, almost blocking their path.

Panta replied, "From a place far away . . ."

"The place has some name or not?"

Hearing this, Bhairu got angry. He had recognized Dulari and was about to say something when Panta replied, "We are from Vategaon. Why? And who are you?"

"You don't recognize me?"

"No, we don't," Bhairu retorted. "Why? Are you a king or something?"

"That you will find out soon enough. But my name is Dulari Waghmare."

"You may be anybody . . . now get out of our way," Panta said, his voice raised. "I haven't come here to find out who you are. I am here to meet the collector."

"The other day, this fellow had beaten me, made me fall at the feet of a stone in the maidan," said Dulari angrily. That's when Panta realized he was the man who had accompanied Khot to the chavadi. He had been arrested and kept in the chavadi and later on, he was sent back, escorted by Bhairu. Bhairu had beaten him on the way and that's why he was so angry now.

"So why had you come to our village?" asked Panta sharply. "Make way for us or I will set the horse on you." Saying this, Panta spurred his horse. A commotion started. The officials came out and Dulari became meek. The collector recognized Panta and led him into his office. Bhairu went and sat under a tree.

The government officers were aware that Vishnupanta was a stern and upright man. Mindful of how one should speak to him, the collector started the conversation.

"So, tell us, what brings you here?"

"I come every year to Sajjangad for darshan. That's why I have come. Also, this time I have to lodge a complaint with you."

"Tell us then, what is the complaint?" asked the collector. "I am pleased to meet you. Do tell me what you have to say."

"A Mang from my village has been held in Belgaon for the last eight–ten years."

"All right. So what about that?" said the collector staring at Panta.

"That man is a gazetted sepoy. He has land of his own, but he is in Belgaon . . ."

"It is like this," interjected the collector, "such people are rascals. The government will not give them any consideration."

"Such people? What exactly does that mean?"

"'Such people' means thieves," said the collector quietly. "They commit petty crimes and harass the common people, who then lose faith in the government. Other unruly elements get emboldened. That's why such people, rather such communities are troublesome. There is no pardon for them."

"Please don't say that," said Panta in a reconciliatory tone. "Grinding the insects along with the grain is not the right way of creating confidence in the administration, I believe. The government must apply balm where it actually hurts. Only then justice is served."

"I agree with you," said the collector. "We are taking care to prevent meting out injustice . . ."

"Certainly not!" Panta exclaimed. "Had it been so, Savala Mang would not have been confined in Belgaon for ten years. Nobody hears a dumb man."

"Since he had created unrest in that area, considering him, no, proving him to be a petty thief, he was expelled from his village, in accordance with the Criminal Tribes Act."

"What is the proof that he had created unrest in that area?" In a few words, Panta had created a dilemma for the collector. "Is the government of the opinion that after Savala was banished, peace has reigned in that region?" Panta's second question left the collector baffled.

He said, "The Criminal Tribes law has been invoked . . ."

"But is the individual actually a criminal?" quipped Panta immediately.

"Can I say something very frankly?"

"Certainly!"

"Please don't misunderstand," said the collector. "Some upper caste people are using the Mang–Ramoshis to create unrest and anarchy. Those tribals commit murder and loot, and these respectable people fill their houses with gold and then go about defending the criminals."

"Have you finished?" asked Panta very calmly. "There hasn't been a single dacoity in my area, so there is no question of gold or wealth entering my home. Besides, I am not here to defend or plead for a criminal; rather I have come to inform you about the just and fair side of a gazetted sepoy, Savala. This is not a justification, rather, like I said, it is a complaint and a request . . ."

"It seems my words have hurt you," said the collector gently. "Please don't take it in that way."

"I won't," said Panta his voice slightly raised. "I know that the law, which has made it impossible for a person to acknowledge his caste, is capable of finding a supporter of that tribe guilty too. But if I am not considered a supporter, I can't be held guilty either. This is my humble request. Savala's case is serious. Do give it a consideration, otherwise make arrangements to auction his lands."

The collector was silent for a while. After giving it some thought, he said, "Panta, I will make enquiries about Savala . . ." Then he paused. And then, as if he recollected something, began, "And yes, I hear that the other day, a Mang from your village cut off the hand of that Khot from Shigaon. What is the meaning of this?

What is going on? The government is taking a serious view of the matter."

Hearing his words, Panta replied, "Then let me tell you, you must take serious cognizance of the fact that this very Khot had acted against convention, entered our territory and cut off the head of a Mang who had the jogani vati in his possession. This is not a very old story; rather it happened just ten years ago. And now, while trying to snatch away the same vati, it was only his hand that was chopped off, and not his head. He could easily have lost it and since it was a religious matter, you couldn't have done anything about it."

The collector was wide-eyed with amazement. "Your Mangs are such brave warriors?"

Pant, squaring his chest retorted, "They are fighters, not petty thieves. The man who cut Khot's hand is the son of the same person who Khot had beheaded. I say there is no other warrior community that shows so much self-restraint."

"That means this happened when the Khot tried to regain the jogani?"

Panta nodded. "And Dulari Mang was helping Khot that day. We had arrested him but let him go because he was a government employee. It would have been very easy to take his head also, as per the convention."

The collector got very angry hearing this. He immediately summoned Dulari and asked him, "Were you present in the jogani riot at Vategaon?"

"Yes, I was, but I was only watching."

"He is lying," Panta interjected, "He snatched the jogani vati and handed it to Khot."

"What? Is this true?" the collector asked sharply. Dulari started to whimper. With a pathetic expression he whined, "I was ordered by Babarkhan saheb . . ."

"So why did you lie?" growled the collector.

"The Mangs from my village are not like this," declared Panta. "That's why I say that one can't make generalizations about the Mang community from different regions. After all, from a bundle of firewood, a broom may take birth."

The collector had nothing to say to this. Panta left for Sajjangad. As promised, an order from Satara went to Belgaon. A report on Savala's behaviour was received in Satara and an order rescinding Savala's exile was sent to Belgaon.

When Savala returned to his village, he came like the breeze, dancing in delight. He first went to Fakira and touched his feet. He then bowed down to Daulati, Rahibai and Radha. From there, he went to the village and prostrated himself before Panta.

He went around the whole village chanting, "Now I will die in my own land. My family will take care of me." He met Bhairu and embraced him tightly.

"Now, I will not tread on anyone's fallen leaves . . . will not commit any offence . . . I will work hard and be happy with the family . . . hard work turns soil into gold . . . a bad law is like a dog," he kept repeating.

Because of Savala's return, his home acquired a new glow. The Mangs felt reassured. Fakira was also happy to have a large-hearted man back with him.

The Mangs started saying, "On Fakira's suggestion, Panta went to Satara and fought with the government authorities, and Savala got another birth. Fakira brought him back into his own. Otherwise, he would have rotted to death." They understood the value of Fakira's words and even at that young age, they started looking up to him as their able leader.

Mangs came from faraway places just to see him. They became his friends. They found him a unique individual . . . one who instead of stamping a scorpion to death had merely broken off its sting and let it live. Radha too felt the same way. She had always been afraid of him, even when he was a child. She still was. Since the day he had climbed up the tamarind tree in a temper, she had not spoken to him with a raised voice. Even if she was annoyed, she just swallowed her anger and kept quiet. Now she was nervous. Her husband had become famous, and her son too would gain fame. And then what? That Khot will not remain still. His hand was cut off. So what? A centipede does not limp because one of its legs is broken, and Khot is a terrible person. He will not be at peace till he has his revenge. What if he does take it?

The thought was unbearable. But what could she do? How could she tell Fakira about her concerns? Every day, new people were meeting him. That Chinchanikar Piraji, Sajurkar Nilu, several Ramoshis, many Marathas, and that Satya from Kumaj—who had openly rebelled. It was said that there is an order to put him in the mouth of a cannon. He is a friend of Fakira's now. He comes regularly to meet Fakira. Fakira frequently takes his horse and goes somewhere. He comes back at all hours of the night. If Khot takes advantage of this one day?

Radha spent several days tortured by these painful thoughts and then one day she decided to talk to Fakira.

Fakira had gone away for two days and was back early in the morning of the third day. Radha had woken up to the sound of Gabarya's hooves as they reached the tamarind tree. For the last three days, she had sat leaning against the wall. She hadn't eaten anything. Daulati too was waiting for Fakira, his chin resting on his knees. Rahibai was constantly dabbing her eyes. So when Fakira finally returned, they were all relieved. Fakira tied up the horse and entered the house. He found the lamp was burning. Radhabai was sitting with her back against the wall. Daulati looked morose.

Fakira was shocked to see them like this.

"Aai!" he called out. She didn't reply. Tears were running down her cheeks.

"What's the matter, Aai? Where is Sadhu?" he asked worriedly.

"In the chavadi," Daulati replied.

"Aai, why are you crying? Why don't you say something?"

"No one will understand why I cry."

"Why? Go on, tell me," said Fakira as he sat down beside her.

"How can I say it? All my life I have been afraid of . . . even now I am."

"Afraid of me? But you are my mother, my . . ."

"Aai?"

"Yes, yes, my mother."

"Then tell me, where had you gone?"

"To Chinchani—to meet Piraji."

"You had told anyone before you went?"

"No. I hadn't."

"Why? These three lives should burn like an oil lamp?"

"Aai, big Aai, Baba, my mistake."

"She hasn't touched water for three days," said Daulati, pointing at Radha.

"This old woman is waiting for you like a frightened bird. There was food in front of us, but not a morsel would go down . . ."

"Why do you worry so much? Am I a child still?"

"You are grown up now, yes, re baba. But how can I explain it to this heart of mine? An enemy like Khot has been after us for two generations. The wounded snake has only crawled into its hole. We are afraid of him."

"But I am not afraid," said Fakira. "Let him come any time. Even if he as much as raises his hood, I will crush him to death. I am cautious and I am aware of everything. Raosaheb Patil from our village, that Dhondi Chaughala from Kalgaon—they are Khot's burrows. I am keeping a close watch on them."

"But it's not good to say, 'Don't go by the mud path, go along my body,' and inviting trouble," Daulati spoke up.

Fakira laughed. "How can I ever say that? But I will not attack anyone nor will I let anyone attack me."

"And you will continue roaming around during the nights?" Rahibai interjected.

"No, I won't. Henceforth, I will not go anywhere without telling you."

"Do that," muttered Daulati.

"I thought you would not be worried . . ."

"You mean we don't worry about you, is it?" said Radha, "I don't say anything because even when you were as big as my fingernail, you didn't listen . . . I burnt my tongue when . . ."

"I was just a child then," said Fakira. "Now I won't climb the tamarind tree and then threaten to jump from there, Aai. Really, I promise."

"Who can say anything about you, baba," Radha said indulgently and Fakira smiled.

"It is my good fortune that you are my mother. Scold me. You, Baba, big Aai, you all are my world, my haven pandhari," said Fakira and placed his forehead on the ground in front of them. Those three souls were overwhelmed. Daulati leapt up and stroked Fakira's back. A flood built up in Radha's eyes. Rahibai circled a handful of chillies around him to ward off the evil eye. She said, "We have lived only for you two, you and Sadhu."

"Your father was just like you," said Daulati, "He didn't say anything to anyone until he reached for the jogani vati . . ."

"But you don't do that," Radha said. "Tell us whatever you do."

The sun came up. Its first rays crawled into Daulati's hut. Birds started fluttering over the cactus. Gabarya, who had ridden through the night, started whining. The hen which had been forgotten in its coop during the conversation started flapping around. Radha's heart was no longer heavy. As she stood up, she said once more,

"Gather good people around you, avoid bad company, take care of yourself, that's all that we know . . ."

"And that's all I too know," Fakira replied, "My men are steadfast . . . like fine blocks of stone. Set them in the right place and they remain firm there. And Aai, death takes birth before a man and dies taking the person with it. What remains behind?"

"Reputation, goodness," said Radha.

"And that's exactly what I want to achieve," exclaimed Fakira. "You only taught me that your son should not behave badly. I haven't forgotten it . . . I will never forget it. But . . ."

"But what?"

"You must not cry."

Hearing this, Radha laughed.

It was the harvest season. Suffering had given way to happiness. The fields were flush with riches. Birds became plump. Insects thrived. Cattle were frisky. People who had toiled in the fields all day were returning home content. After two full meals, belches of satisfaction were heard. Ravinarayan, the lord of the sky, was standing at his door. His yellow glow spread on the nivadunga cactus and created a bright new shade of green.

The rope twisters were working full-time. Mang children were struggling to turn the wheels and the Mangs were loading new bobbins on to the spindles. We will finish twining this particular rope and then stop, we will twine just one more, another one, and then we will stop . . . this was the refrain as they continued their work. The little wheel turners were ready to cry.

From beyond the cactus, children who had taken the cattle out for grazing were returning home, shouting and yelling. Some who were riding on the backs of buffaloes were lustily singing, "Oh you girl of King Nand—"

Just then, along came a wayfarer. He was sitting on a short horse. Very short. So short that the man's feet were almost touching the ground. He looked like he was riding a donkey. There was a red-coloured patka on his head, and he wore a thick bundi and a zari-bordered dhoti wound tightly around his waist. In his hand, he held an axe with a long slender handle. He was extremely dark-complexioned, had twirled his short moustache into points and flared his nostrils. His bloodshot eyes had anger in them. Seeing him, the boys stopped their clamour. They started communicating with each other in their code language.

"Ai aaril thikayla ra . . ."

"Arra, not aaril, jhimak . . ." the second retorted.

The third screeched, "Aala, vasaru naka . . .'"

The fourth instantly replied, "Pedu dya."

Hearing the children's babble, the stranger stopped.

He asked in a softened tone, "Who do you belong to boys?"

"We? We are of the kuruvadis, farm labourers," one boy piped up a falsehood.

The man was surprised. "Then what, ra, is the language you utter?"

"Poranchi, kid's language."

"What? Choranchi? The language of thieves?" The cunning man tried to tease the boys but they didn't get rattled. Screwing up his nose, one of the boys asked the man,

"You are deaf?"

"Nhai, ba, not at all. I hear very well."

"Then how did you hear chor, 'thief' when we said por, 'kid'?"

Having got the better of the stranger, the boy continued, "In the mind of a thief, moonlight shines . . ." All the boys burst out laughing. The embarrassed wayfarer said, "Ai, don't make fun of me. Tell me, which one is that Fakira's house?"

Once again, the boys became suspicious. They signalled to each other with their eyes. One boy said cheekily, "Which Fakira do you want?"

The man was perplexed. Quietly, Babaji Mang's son Jhingya scampered through the tangle of cactus like a rat and went to Fakira.

After a lot of thought, the traveller asked, "So how many Fakiras are there in this village?"

Instantly the boys replied, "Ahwa, there are four Fakiras here."

Now the wayfarer understood the boy's tone. He realized that these were all children from the Mang community and they were trying to make an ass of him. With that thought, he cleverly asked, "And what are the names of the fathers of these four Fakiras?"

A scrawny, dark-skinned boy stepped forward. "I will tell you," he said. "One is called Shingya, another is Jhingya, the third is called Shirgya and the last one is Mirgya."

The boys burst out laughing. The man was baffled. Just then, Fakira emerged from the arms of the cactus and came out into the open field. Jhingya stood at a distance adjusting his loincloth. All the boys fell silent. Fakira asked,

"Which village from, pavna?"

"Visitor from near Kalgaon . . . Kumaj."

"Who are you visiting?"

"Fakira."

"What do you want from him?"

"I have been sent by Sattu from Kumaj."

Hearing Sattu's name, Fakira was surprised. He said, "I have never seen you with Sattu, pavna," Fakira said.

"I am Gonda Gondhali. I roam around from village to village. Sattu is my friend. He has sent me to meet Fakira . . . "

"Then I am that Fakira. Tell me, what work do you have? Ay you boys, go away now."

The boys went away, steering their cattle. Gondhali dismounted from his horse and said, "Sattu is in deep trouble. Hence he has sent me to you."

"What kind of a trouble?"

"Only if you do something can Sattu's life be saved. If not, there is no hope for him," Gondhali said sorrowfully.

Fakira became serious. "What is the problem? Tell me about it," he said.

"Very well. I will tell you."

The two of them started walking towards Fakira's house. Fakira was very disturbed to learn that a friend of his was in trouble, He wanted to know the details. As they walked, Gondhali asked, "Who are these boys?"

"They are Mangs."

"They told me they were kuruvadis."

"They lied to you."

"How many Fakiras are there?"

"Only one, me."

"They told me there are four."

Fakira laughed.

"On top of that they spoke a strange language," mumbled Gondhali.

"Strange how?" asked Fakira.

"What does 'aaril' mean?"

"Farm labourer, kuruvadi."

"And 'varavala'?"

"That means 'has come'. It is the language of our caste."

"Why do they speak this language?"

"So that the government officials don't understand it."

They had reached Fakira's house.

Gondhali started narrating the incident that had taken place in Kumaj.

"Yesterday, the Patil from Bahadurwadi arrested Sattu. The officer had given the order. He plans to arrest all those who are opposing or protesting against the government."

"How did they catch Sattu?" asked Fakira.

"He was getting a shave at a barber's. Suddenly fifty people surrounded him, caught him and tied him up in Mali. Tomorrow itself they are leaving for Satara. All the upper caste Patils are behind this," said Gondhali.

"So what is Sattu's message for me?"

"The message is, 'Please help me with men and arms. If I survive, I will repay the favour.'" This message touched Fakira's heart. Despondently, he said,

"Why did you take so long?"

"What could I do? All the paths were blocked. Now you hurry, otherwise this Warna valley will lose an exceptionally valiant son."

"How many men does Dada Patil have?"

"Fifty, but all are armed."

"Don't tell me about the weapons, just the number of men."

"Fifty."

"Then let's go," Fakira got up hastily.

"Only the two of us?"

"Why? We will collect the men as we go along."

Fakira called Sadhu and said, "We have to rescue Sattu. Gather our men and prepare to leave."

Darkness had fallen. About twenty-five young men in all, including Mura, Bali, Iswara, Kisna, Bhiva, Ghamya got ready. Fastening Gabarya's saddle, Fakira told Ghamandi, "You go to Chinchani and meet Pira. Tell him to reach Bahadurwadi by afternoon. Go at once. One of you, go and get Hari and Rama."

After making all the preparations, he went to Radha. Bowing at her feet, he said, "Don't be angry. My friend is in the clutches of death. I am going to save him. Baba, big Aai!" Saying this, he clasped their feet. Daulati said in a tremulous voice, "Go, but be careful."

"When will you be back?" asked Radha, controlling her tears.

"By tomorrow evening. Definitely."

"We will not eat anything till then," said Rahi.

"Don't worry about me. Tomorrow evening you will see me here," replied Fakira.

Everything was ready. Gabarya whinnied and set off at a gallop. Radha stifled a sob. She said to Gabarya in her mind, "Baba, please don't throw off my Fakira and come back alone. Both of you return, otherwise . . ."

At that moment, Fakira's horse was trotting towards Bahadurwadi and Fakira could see in his mind's eye, Sattu from Kumaj awaiting death in the Mali. The only word on his lips was Bahadurwadi. He kept thinking of how he could reach Bahadurwadi before sunrise the next day, surround the venue, free Sattu and reach home by evening, as promised to Aai.

Seven

At Kumaj village, the Warna River takes a long leisurely turn and the village nestles in the bow of this circular bend. The fertile soil, black like a cake of kaajal, and the waters of the Warna give Kumaj the reputation of being the richest village in the valley, the Amaravati of Kuber, the deity of wealth. It was a beautiful amalgam of earth, water and hard work, created by nature.

But Sattu had nothing left in the prosperous village of Kumaj. He was worthless like a bare and withered banyan tree. His father had sold his lands to stoke the chillum and smoked it all away. Eventually, it was the same ganja smoke that had despatched him up Kailas-wards. The house from the days of Sattu's grandfather was dilapidated. Except for his old mother, Sattu had no one else in the world to call his own.

By grinding grain into flour in someone's home, toiling in the threshing yard of someone's farm, plastering people's floors with cowdung water and similar household chores, Banabai Bhosale had managed to bring up her son, Sattu. When Sattu was in class seven, she went from house to house to ask the womenfolk for some pickles, papads and other savoury accompaniments for Sattu. And Sattu grew up on these foods. Like a mushroom nourished by a garbage pile, Sattu was nurtured on the heap of indigence. Gradually, Sattu began to catch everyone's eye—because of his appearance, his physique and his good qualities. Most people were impressed by him.

But one day Sattu's eyes opened. He began to see his own abject poverty. He felt extremely sorry for his mother and was extremely ashamed of himself. He dropped out of school in the seventh standard and got a job in the cavalry regiment of the army. With his strong body and sharp mind, he stood apart in the regiment. From marksmanship to wrestling, he was good at everything. His co-workers used to be awed by his fearless horsemanship. The British officers too were impressed. Many of the young English madams licked their lips on seeing him.

Banabai finally saw some happy days in Kumaj. Her once-dilapidated house was repaired. Her feet no longer had to trudge around doing chores. The whole village said that Sattu had repaid his debt to his mother. Many chests swelled with pride because Sattu's achievements had given Kumaja special standing in the army. And a stream of cash started flowing into Banabai's hands.

But then something happened. Sattu got fed up with the meanness of the officers. Their arrogant, wilful manner angered him. He could not bring himself to behave like a slave. It disgusted him. As a result, within a year he gave up his job and returned to Kumaj. People commended him for making a name for himself in the army. But Mathaji Chaugula turned up his nose and said scornfully to Sattu's face, "You've come back from the army, so you think you've become a king or what? A potter's daughter-in-law will only knead clay in the end."

Sattu was shocked and humiliated by Mathaji's words. But he decided to let them out through the other ear and focussed on assimilating into the daily life of Kumaj. He cut grass or worked in fields whenever the opportunity arose. When there was no work, he roamed around with his axe in his hands.

Some days passed in this fashion.

One day, Sattu had gone to the river to take a bath. The harsh Chaitra sun was scorching the earth. Everything had become hot—even the fish in the river had become sluggish. The Warna had draped herself in a silky green shawl of the tender new foliage on her banks. The already ploughed land around was gasping in the heat. The blistering winds were running wild, carrying hot dust with them. The birds, exhausted by the heat, had fallen silent. An eerie quietude prevailed.

Sattu was returning to his house along the mud track when suddenly a woman started screaming somewhere down the path. The banks of the Warna shook with her cries. Sattu ran towards the sound.

Sattu learnt later that a young pregnant Mahar woman had insulted Mathaji Chaugula. She had come there in the middle of the afternoon and broken off a spike from the fence on that arrogant man's land. He had turned up there at that very moment. What he saw infuriated him, and he started hitting the Mahar woman.

When Sattu reached there, he saw Mathaji kicking her viciously as she lay on the ground, screaming loudly. She was rolling around amid the thorns and trying to shield her stomach from the man's feet. Chaugula was beating her with his chappals which he was holding in his hands. He was raining kicks all along her body, from head to toe. He would stop when she lay motionless but when she stirred slightly, he would get wild again and beat her. He seemed to be furious because she wouldn't die. Then, he aimed his foot at her stomach. At that point, Sattu could no longer remain a mere spectator. He grabbed Chaugula's hand and said humbly, "Aba, what are you trying to do?"

"She has broken a spike of my fence, the wretch."

"So that's enough punishment now . . . Let her go Aba . . ."

"No! I will take her life . . . you get back." Chaugula wrenched his hand free and shook his head as he spoke.

Sattu said, "You are going to kill a person for a fence or what?"

"You don't teach me. I will go the gallows if I must."

"Chaugula, she is pregnant. Come on . . ." Saying this, Sattu once more held Chaugula's hand, and Chaugula got very angry. He shoved Sattu away and shouted, "Just go away . . . don't interfere." His anger was rekindled. He started hitting the woman once more. The woman who had so far remained motionless cried out pitiably and implored for help repeatedly. "I have a child in my womb. Don't hit me. I will die. I promise I will never touch your fence again . . . Aaaah . . ."

The Mahar woman's cries roused Sattu's anger. But then Chaugula moved forward and said, "You want to scream, then scream . . ."

Sattu's body turned into a furnace. He shouted, "Chaugulya, you want to listen to me or not?"

"I won't listen." He spun around, his chappals in his hands, his eyebrows raised and his eyes widened. "I am going to finish her."

"And what if I kill you instead?"

"Just try it," said Chaugula and moved towards Sattu aggressively. Sattu roared and raising his axe high in the air, shouted,

"So Chaugulya, you are a dead man now . . ."

And with one stroke, Chaugula fell to the earth. The blows of the axe continued to rain. Chaugula's body lay like the broken thorns of the fence. Sattu did not know when the man actually died. He came to his senses only later. He helped the Mahar woman up and escorted her to the Mahar settlement. That very day, he left Kumaj.

Sattu became an absconder. He had no regrets that he had killed a human being. On the contrary, he felt that he had done something honourable. He gathered fifty men just like himself and started wandering about in the Warna valley.

He had decided he would not spare anyone who was arrogant and wicked like Chaugula, and he started getting rid of them. He crushed many self-centred and egotistical people. His stated aim was to subdue bullies. He went around burning the record books and mortgage deeds of moneylenders and freed their poor Dalit debtors. The banks of the Warna trembled at his name. He persuaded men who had deserted their wives to go back and live with them. Anyone who refused or complained or whined about it was shamed and publicly humiliated. He threatened their doting fathers and humbled many arrogant sons-in-law. He made grown men stand on one leg as punishment! The broken family life of many a young woman was restored, to thrive and flourish. Marriages were happy and girls lived in harmony with their in-laws. Quarrelsome husbands started to fear Sattu and married women looked upon him as a god.

Sattu roamed around the Warna valley like a king, but the government was certainly not asleep. A reward of Rs 5,000 had been announced for anyone who helped to nab him. Notices to that effect had been pasted on the pillars of all the offices of all the villages in the valley. And the notorious crooks in these villages were going out of their way to help the government find him. Khot of Shigaon, Dada Patil from Bahadurwadi and Umaji Chaugula, son of Mathaji Chaugula, followed Sattu like his shadow. They were waiting for an opportunity to ambush him. But Sattu was fearless. He roamed around the mountain slopes and along the grasslands, not sparing anyone who dared to confront him.

Sattu had only his old mother in Kumaj. Whenever he missed her, he went straight to Kumaj to meet her. At such times, it did not matter how many guards were on the lookout or who was chasing him. He simply did not care. He was intensely proud of Kumaj and the mother from whose womb he was born. Besides, he had reduced the heavyweights of that region to nothing and those that remained, they didn't count for anything. Except

Fakira. He considered no man his equal, except that Mang, Fakira. And that's why he kept meeting Fakira. He looked upon Fakira as someone who would give his life for him. It was his firm belief that true valour was sharpened on the whetstone of poverty. That courage does not bloom among the rich, it springs up in poverty. That was his experience.

The festival of Diwali was near and Sattu suddenly remembered his mother. Thinking of her brought back a flood of memories, of the old history. He had started out totally without fear, determined to let no force stop him from meeting his mother—the mother who had swabbed rich people's houses for the sake of her son. He set off for Kumaj with only twelve men accompanying him.

When he reached the outskirts of the village of Nandgaon, the moon was overhead. Venus shone like a lamp in the sky. The world was slowly stirring at the hint of the approaching dawn. Silence was dissipating and sounds were taking shape. Light filtered down from the many-hued carpet of clouds. The eastern horizon was smiling. The breeze was swirling around. The trees had lost their meekness. And birds were getting ready, fluttering their wings. Life was slowly gathering pace.

The small bells around the necks of the bullocks in the cattle sheds tinkled in harmony. Grinding stones had begun rotating rhythmically and the songs of the farmers' wives made sweet music. The clear notes from the throats of these women were cutting through the air like sharp swords. Sattu reached the main market square of Nandgaon and the first cock crowed. Just then, from a house nearby, some lines of a song fell on his ears. He stopped in his tracks. Everyone stopped with him. Sattu listened carefully. The woman sang,

Even if you don't have a maher, a parental home,
you must have a brother behind you
A protector of the poor, like Sattyaba of Kumaja . . .

These words made Satya whirl around. The men stiffened, holding their breaths. Sattu's entire body became his ears. The woman finished grinding the grain and brought her song to an end . . .

My grinding is done, as I offer the last handful,
I pray to my God, give Sattyaba a long life.

The stone took one last furious turn and stopped, and Sattu let out a deep sigh. He was utterly overwhelmed. His lips quivered.

"What is special about Kumaj? My Kumaj is here, my mother is here, and my sister is also here."

Hearing this, the men accompanying him were baffled. Gonda Gondhali said with a solemn face,

"But the sun will rise, won't it?"

"Let it," said Sattu, "Day and night are the same to me. But here is a woman who spreads her sari pallu before God every morning and asks for my long life. I have never set eyes on her. I will not go to Kumaj until I see her."

Like his name, which meant confused, Gondhali was confounded. He said, "So what do you propose to do?"

"Go and get a kasar with all the glass bangles he has and a sari shop owner with the saris in stock."

There was some running about. The name Sattu brought fear to their hearts. The man came with his bundle of saris, and the bangle seller with his tin trunk followed.

Sattu rapped on the door. "Open the door."

"Who is it?" the woman asked from inside.

"Sattyaba from Kumaj."

The name Sattyaba immediately brought her to the door. She drew the latch, opened the door and wiping her flour-covered hands on her sari, stood there staring at him. Sattu immediately prostrated before her. "This Sattya, for whom you daily pray and ask for a long life, he is bowing before you."

At Sattu's words, two teardrops of joy fell on his back. There was excitement in the market place. The lane woke up. Before you knew it, the whole village had gathered. The people made Sattu sit in the veranda. His new sister brought the oil lamp and performed an arati for him. "Today is the fourth day of Diwali, it is Bhaubeej," one villager said.

"And on this very auspicious day, a brother has found a sister," Sattu replied.

He presented his new sister with five saris. He had her wrists covered with bangles and then filled her pallu with Surati rupee coins. After that he stood up and declared, "Keep praying for my long life. I must go now."

The woman was too emotional to say anything. The lump in her throat was choking her. She felt as if it was her own brother who was going far away.

And Sattu left Nandgaon.

He reached Kumaj as the sun came up. His mother was very happy to see him. She served him and his friends special food prepared for the festival. Soon after, they finished eating he got ready to leave. He was in a hurry. At that moment, Banabai said in a, admonishing tone,

"For nothing you killed him."

"Whom?" asked Sattu.

"That Chaugulya."

"For no reason? And if the Mahar woman had died?" "The government would have punished him."

"Aga, but when? Only after she was dead, na?" Sattu interrupted his mother. "And not just one but two lives would have been lost needlessly. It is better that he was the one to die instead."

"But because of that you are fated to be in exile, na?" said his mother sadly. "He alone died, it is true, but . . ."

"I am not alone," said Sattu, "2000 people are ready to die for me. Let anyone oppose me. I will fight them. I will gather together an army and continue to fight. I have not done anything wrong. I haven't committed any crime."

Banabai said nothing. Sattu left Kumaj. He sent away his companions and taking only Gonda Gondhali along with him, he went to the barber, Baba Nhavi in Bahadurwadi to get some rest.

Sattu had many loyal friends and Baba the barber was one of them. He made arrangements for Sattu to sleep there that afternoon. Having been deprived of sleep the previous night, he slept soundly. Gonda Gondhali sat by him keeping watch. Baba went away to attend to his business.

Dada Patil's employees who had been on the look-out for Sattu for a very long time were excited to see him walk right into the tiger's den. They conveyed the news to Dada Patil. The news made Dada very happy. He immediately began to collect his men. By that time, Uma Chaugula who had also been tracking Sattu landed there. His presence emboldened Patil. With a gang of about fifty men, they surrounded the house in the stark afternoon. Uma instructed his people, "Get him dead or alive."

Seeing the commotion around the house, Gondhali was alarmed. He woke up Sattu. For a moment, Sattu was dismayed to hear that Dada Patil and Uma Chaugula had surrounded them, but then he immediately started planning the next course of action. Gonda Gondahli was looking utterly confused. Sattu said to him,

"What shall we do now?"

"Let's go out and finish off whoever comes forward to stop us."

Gondhali was ready for battle. He finished hammering the handle of his axe to the blade when Sattu said to him,

"We can't go out like that. How much fight can just the two of us offer?"

Gondhali immediately lost his urge to fight. Hastily he said, "So what shall we do? Tell me."

After some thought Sattu said, "Their attention is focussed on me. I will go out and surrender to them. You go out of the back door and get our men together. Surround Bahadurwadi. Tell Akaram and Anand not even a flea should escape from Bahadurwadi. Do you understand what I am saying?"

"Yes, yes," said Gonda.

"Thereafter you rush to Vategaon, catch hold of Fakira and tell him all that has happened." Sattu became grim as he spoke. Grabbing hold of his axe, he said, "Tell Fakira to come quickly. Tell him, 'Sattu needs a favour from you, come bestow it on him . . . and save Sattya of Kumaj'. Now go."

"So shall I go?" stammered Gondhali.

"Of course! You must. Make sure Fakira reaches here by midnight. I am going ahead."

Saying this, Sattu went straight out and stood in the courtyard. On seeing Sattu without his axe, all the axes raised for attack were lowered. But then fifty men rushed as one and caught hold of him. Uma was happy that he was caught alive. But Dada Patil was shocked to see this tiger of a man suddenly becoming so meek. His face swiftly turned pale.

They tied Sattu's hands and feet and thought of despatching him to the taluka office immediately. But it was not easy to take Sattu in broad daylight. Also, there was the danger of Sattu's men attacking them on the way. With this fear in mind, they decided to request for help from the taluka office. In the meantime, they would hold Sattu captive on the bank of the river until the forces arrived. And that's what they did. A messenger was sent to the government office while Dada Patil and Uma Chaugula sat with Sattu in a thickly wooded area of the river bank waiting for help. Many a man started calculating what his share of the huge reward amount would be!

The night was nearing its end. The cold on the bank of the river had turned harsh. The moonlight could not penetrate the thick foliage of the silk-cotton tree. In any case, the moon was now on the descent. The banks of the Warna River appeared to have become listless. The shadows of the kinjal, umbar and jambhal trees were adding to the darkness. The fish struggled in the water as it gurgled. In the distance, there was a loud sound and soon rocks and mud came crashing down. It was a landslide. Frightened by the sound, the fox waiting with its tail in the crab hole ran away. On one side, Dada Patil sat with his ghongadi wrapped around his head and his axe close to his chest. Uma had gone to the village to get some bhakri while Sattu lay motionless under the roof of a run-down hut.

How far would Gonda have gone by now? Where might he have reached? If everything has gone according to plan, that's fine. Otherwise death is certain. That's what Sattu was thinking. Then Uma came back with the bhakris and distributed them among his men. He went and sat down near Dada Patil and said,

"What are you thinking about, Dada?"

"Shall I tell you the truth? I'm beginning to think that by capturing Sattu, we are holding live coals in our shawls."

"But why?" asked Uma spiritedly. "If our messenger has reached the taluka office by now, then faujdar Babarkhan will certainly be here by morning. Why are you afraid?"

"How can you be certain that our man has gone to the office?" Dada Patil grunted. "Ever since we caught Sattu

I am filled with dread. Sattu is an army man. There's no telling what he will do. And why did he suddenly give himself up like this?"

Uma was a bit startled by this question. But to give courage to himself and Dada Patil, he said, "Patil, don't worry."

"What is the point of getting worried now?" said Dada Patil. "But this is the same Sattya who has been a headache even for the British sarkar. If he escapes, then he will not leave any of our progeny alive for sure."

These words of Dada angered Uma. He became surly. Cut off Sattu's head before sunrise and be done with it, he thought for a moment.

"Even if we kill Sattu, our lives will not be saved," Dada told Uma.

Wondering if his thoughts had somehow reached Dada, Uma hastily stood up. And Dada became fearful that Uma would go and do something to Sattya.

In the meantime, Fakira and Gondhali had gathered together their men and reached the outskirts of Bahadurwadi.

Fakira was riding his pure white horse; Sadhu, Savala, Pira, Mura, Bali and fifty such men rode with him. Fakira's horse was going at a trot. At the village boundary, one man came forward and asked, "Who goes there?"

"Is it Akaram?"

Recognizing Gonda's voice Akaram stopped, and Fakira halted his horse too.

Gonda asked, "How are things? Where is Sattu?"

"In the upper fields along the river. We captured Uma's messenger while he was on his way to the taluka office. We have surrounded the woodland now."

"Shabas!" exclaimed Fakira. "Come on." He spurred his horse along and all of them followed the mud path towards the wooded area. Fakira sniffed the air. He could smell rotting fish. The houses of fishermen were nearby. Their nets lay drying on the fences.

Fakira said to Savala, "Savalanana, pick up two of those nets and bring them along."

They reached the stream. Fakira tied his horse in the kinjal thicket and tightened his waist belt. Savala and Bali were to act like fishermen and come up to the river carrying lamps. The others would silently advance to where Sattu had been tied up. When Chaughula's men's attention was diverted to the lamps, they would attack. Having made all these plans, they moved forward.

Night was slackening her embrace and as she loosened her grip, Uma's impatience grew. He was looking around, listening nervously. Suddenly there was a disturbance in the river waters and Uma cried out,

"Kabira!"

"Ji!" Kabira ran forward.

"Can you see anything?"

"The embankment collapsed into the water."

"Ten of you remain near the hut. Go!"

Kabira went away. Sometime later, Savalya and Bali emerged out of the river. Seeing the lamps in their hands, Uma was startled. He woke the sleeping Dada. And just then, one person came crashing down near him.

"What ra, what happened?" Uma asked.

"I saw something," the man replied.

"What did you see?" asked Uma his voice shrill. The man said,

"Maybe a wild boar."

"Why are you running away like a wild boar?" Uma scolded him. That's when the lamps came close to them. Their sombre light flickered over the Warna River. The shadows of the trees started swaying in the glow. Uma asked in a menacing tone, "Who is that there?"

"We are fishermen." At that, all the men began to look at those lamps. And immediately, Fakira launched his attack. Axes clashed. Voices screamed, "Coming," "I'm dead," "Run!" There was a tumult. Men started falling to the ground, injured. Wielding his sword expertly, Fakira rushed forward. Uma spat on his hands and gripped his axe and started swinging it. He ran towards the hut and Gondhali shouted, "Daji, Umya is coming . . ."

"Let him come," said Fakira and lunged at Uma. Suddenly Sadhu cried out, "Force him down." Mura intercepted Uma. Fakira cut the ropes and freed Sattu. Akaram put an axe in his fist. Gripping the axe, Sattu shouted,

"Get back all of you. Where is that Uma Chaughula?"

Mura had injured Umya. Dada Patil had hurt his leg and was hobbling in retreat. When people realized that Sattu was free, there was a stampede. They began to run helter-skelter. Uma and Dada jumped into the river. Uma's men scattered through the forested area. Because one did not chase those who flee in the dark, Fakira summoned his men. The mob calmed down. Uma had escaped because he had to contend with both Fakira and Sattu. Everybody was aware of that. Otherwise, he would have wreaked havoc.

When everyone had gathered, Sattu dropped the axe in his hand and embraced Fakira. He said,

"Naik, this Sattu was saved because you arrived in time. Now you will be blessed by all the mothers and sisters. The entire population of the Warna valley will be grateful to you."

"Where is the need for gratitude?" said Fakira. "Even a stone needs another stone and here I am, a mere human being."

"People like you are rare," said Sattu. "You have raised a mountain of favours for me. Now I have one request for you."

"What is it?" asked Fakira. Sattu said, "Give me an opportunity to be of help to you in a similar manner. I will run to your aid . . ." He paused for a moment, then pointing towards the Warna River added, "I will change the course of this Warna River and bring it to you."

Fakira didn't say anything. They all started walking towards Nandgaon. As they reached the outskirts of Nandgaon, the cock crowed. They all stopped. Fakira's path branched out in another director from there. He was in a hurry to move on.

The two of them bid farewell to each other.

Fakira headed in the westerly direction and the sun started making inroads in the east. Stepping lightly on the clouds, he inched forward.

Sattu stood there, watching Fakira's retreating back, mounted on the pure white horse. Then he said to Gonda Gondhali, "One must have a sister who prays for one's long life and a brother like Fakira. Fortunately, I have both. Come on, let's go."

The song of the previous morning was echoing in Sattu's ears.

My grinding is done, I offer the last handful,
And pray to God, to give Sattyaba a long life.

Eight

Radha was being eaten away by the thought that treachery was bound to happen one day or another. Fakira's behaviour was adding more wounds to her already scarred heart. She wished Fakira would sit quietly at home. His enemies were waiting to ambush him . . . they could attack at any time, she feared. And she lived her days out with these thoughts.

Fakira freed Sattu and came back, and the very next day, Inspector Babarkhan came to the village and set up his camp there. But before the summons could come from the village office, a riot broke out in Mang wada. The Mangs began to fight each other and every single one of them was left wounded. The villagers were astonished to know that the Mangs who never even abused another Mang had suddenly taken up arms against each other. Babarkhan was furious. Uma Chaughula had accompanied him here to establish that Fakira himself had set Sattu free and that all of Fakira's men bore injuries from the skirmish by the river on that fateful night. Babarkhan had come specially to verify the "injuries" suffered by the men. He had made provisions to arrest all those who he found were injured.

But now his plans had gone haywire. All the Mangs had got hurt fighting each other! Babarkhan was very disappointed. Instead of summoning the Mangs that night, he ordered them all to come to the village office at daybreak. The Mangs divided themselves into two factions before they reached the village. One faction was led by Fakira, while the other was led by Savala. All of them bore injuries.

Babarkhan was sitting on the platform of the chavadi smoking a hookah. A guard armed with a gun stood behind him. Babar was drawing on the hookah slowly and blowing out the smoke through his widespread lips. His short body appeared broader since he was sitting down. With the thick eyebrows, bristly moustache, the long beard on his dark face and the spiky hair on his head, Babarkhan looked quite fierce.

Savala came forward quickly. He held up his injured right hand with his left and saluted the Inspector. Then he settled down on the ground nearby.

Vishnupanta Kulkarni, Shankarrao Patil and other elders were sitting in the village office with sombre faces. Babarkhan released a cloud of smoke and said angrily to Savala,

"What re, how do I appear to you? Tell me the truth."

"You look like a bear, sarkar."

The whole camp was shocked by his answer. They were worried what would happen after that.

"You are not afraid of me?"

"No, sarkar."

"And why not?"

"A dead sheep is not afraid of fire, saheb!"

"You are right," Babarkhan said. "Why did you get into a fight last night, re?"

"I had had a small amount of liquor, sarkar, so Fakira shouted at me. He hit me with a stick. That's how it started," Savala said in a single breath.

Babarkhan didn't utter a word thereafter. He did not make any further inquiries. He broke up the camp in the afternoon and left the village.

Later, Radha came to know that the fight was just a drama. Fakira had realized that he would be trapped because of the injuries he had sustained during the skirmish on the banks of the Warna, so he had deliberately started a fight. The memory of that incident continued to trouble Radha. The womenfolk of the village advised her, "Get Fakira married. That is the best solution. Once he is married, he will lead a straightforward life." But Radha was not convinced. She had not forgotten Fakira's father, Ranoji's history. Ranoji had given up his life, with the packet of sweets for his children tucked into his waist. This Fakira of hers was his son! Whether married or single, what difference would it make to him?

Fifteen days had gone by when Piraji from Chinchani came there. He said to Radha, "Akka, for twelve years you have not left this village and gone anywhere. Come to Chinchani now; spend a few days with us there."

"No, re baba! Atyabai, my mother-in-law is here, Aba can't do much work now. Besides, what about the devil that dances in this house? What shall I do with it?"

"You don't worry about that. Bring Atyabai with you. I will take care of Fakira. I will put a strong spell on the devil," said Piraji with a smile.

At Piraji's insistence, Radha, who was really quite fed up of the same routine and environment, decided to go to Chinchani. She took Rahibai with her.

Chinchani nestled in the crook of the Sahyadri Mountains and Parbati Mang's house was at the foot of a hill. The dense forest around, the high mountains behind and the pasture land beyond all appeared so different, so new for Radha. Parbati's family was also small and compact. There was sixty-year-old Parbati and his wife, Piraji, Piraji's wife and their small child, and Piraji's sister Sarubai, who had just come of age. The members of this family were like pearls bound together in a single string.

Within two days, Sarubai and Radha became good friends. Parbati treated Radha with respect as she was Fakira's mother. Once or twice he inadvertently mentioned to her,

"Bai, you are no ordinary woman. You are the mother of a real striped tiger!"

These words added a fistful of pride to Radha's body. She felt proud of Fakira.

When she saw Parbati's family, his home, Piraji's child, a new thought took root in Radha's mind. If she could get Fakira married, then he too would have a child . . . he would become a responsible family man . . . That was exactly what the womenfolk of her village had advised. People say that a wife is like a rein for her husband. So should she . . .

Radha liked Sarubai's looks, her sweet nature, her manner, in fact everything about her. She thought that if Sarubai became her daughter-in-law, she would be the best bride in the village. With this thought, she took Piraji aside one day and told him what was on her mind.

"Piraji, can I say something?"

"Akka, don't ask, simply demand," Piraji said. "I will cut off my head and lay it at your feet if you so wish."

"I don't want your head," said Radha. "Give me Sarubai. I'm planning to get my Fakira married."

"You like her as a daughter-in-law?"

"Yes, I like."

"Her looks, her qualities, her nature?"

"Yes, baba, everything."

"Then take her away immediately and get them married."

"And you will stay out of everything? Very clever. That won't do."

"Then tell me what you expect from me?"

"What will be your role in this marriage?"

"Whatever you want me to be. If you invite me, I will come and eat your puran polis."

"That means you'll only feast off my free food?"

"So tell me then exactly what I should do."

"How much of the marriage expenses will you bear?"

"All the expenses."

"But the marriage should take place in front of my house."

"Very well. I will come fully prepared and perform the marriage there."

"Good!" Radha was excited. "Ask your father in the evening."

"Why should I ask him?" Piraji retorted. "He will start beating the dholak drum with joy when he hears the news. Start the preparations here only. Load the cart with whatever you need. The bride is yours, the groom is yours, and this house too is yours."

Even the sky could not contain Radha's joy. When they told Parbati and the others that evening, their faces were flushed with happiness. Saru blushed shyly.

Having fixed Fakira's marriage, Radha returned home in haste. Both mother-in-law and daughter-in-law were thrilled with sweet visions of making a bridegroom of Fakira by tying the bashinga on his head very soon. The thought that she would have a daughter-in-law and a grand-daughter-in-law made Rahibai smile delightedly to herself. I am very fortunate, she thought.

Rahibai and Radha reached Karad at noon. Piraji had brought them there in his bullock cart and driven the bullocks really hard. When they reached the banks of the Krishna River, they stopped. Piraji unyoked the bullocks and the three of them settled down to eat their food. A number of travellers from far away places were resting in the shade of a mango grove on the banks of the Krishna. Some were having lunch, some had lit fires and were kneading dough, while others were resting after their meal. When Radha, Rahibai and Piraji finished their lunch in the shade, Radha overheard some travellers talking about a fever epidemic raging somewhere far away, because of which people were dying like ants. A chill shot through Radha's heart.

She was terrified to hear that people could die after a couple of days of fever. Her mind, which was elated at the thought of Fakira's marriage, was now overtaken by gloom. Her joyful face turned anxious and pale. She didn't want to stay in that mango grove any longer, so she asked Piraji to yoke the cart, and they made their way home.

At last Kartik Purnima—the full moon day in the month of Kartik—was upon them. The symbolic marriage ceremony of the tulasi plant was being performed everywhere. It heralded the start of the marriage season. Radha got Fakira married on the very first auspicious day. No other marriage had been celebrated as grandly as Fakira's in the twenty villages around. The whole village was at Radha's door to bless the couple. Savala was the chief manager of the event. He was helped by Ghamandi, Mura, Bali and Sadhu in making the arrangements. Vishnupanta and Shankarrao Patil personally looked after the guests. Dodging the British army, Sattu attended the ceremony with 200 of his men. He presented the newlyweds with Surati rupee coins. Everyone felt they saw Ranoji galloping across the maidan, riding on his beloved Gabarya.

Daulati and Rahibai were accorded the honour due to the parents of the bridegroom. Radha, being a widow, did not participate in the rituals and it was Fakira's grandparents, Daulati and Rahibai, who performed them. That day, Radha was truly happy. She did not mourn for the loss of her kunku. She decided to keep the bashinga tied to Fakira's forehead for five days.

The newlywed couple went around touching the feet of all elders and taking their blessings. With that the ceremony came to an end.

Radha, Daulati and Rahibai felt as if a momentous task had been completed. Both Daulati and Rahibai declared, "Our eyes have seen Fakira's marriage; now they can close forever at any time."

Fakira did not leave the house for six months between Kartik and Vaishakh. Radha's heart swelled with joy. Sarubai had gone to her parents for four days and had promptly come back. Now she wouldn't allow Radha to do any chores. She managed everything herself. And Radha, Rahibai and Daulati began to feel that they were being rewarded with a comfortable life to make up for all the hardships they had undergone in the past. But then the thought of getting Sadhu married wouldn't leave them.

Suddenly there was talk that the fever epidemic which had broken out six months ago in some far off area was now nearby. People were afraid. Horrible thoughts of death danced in every mind of that valley. They were telling each other stories about whole families and entire villages that had been wiped out because of the epidemic.

And it was true. The disease had taken a very serious form and was advancing inch by inch to capture the whole region. As soon as the epidemic touched a village, the inhabitants would abandon their homes, leaving behind all their valuable possessions and flee. As if they were being chased by a terrible forest fire. He who did not run was sure to die. Only ten out of 100 managed somehow to survive. There were no men left to bury the dead. When all the members of a family succumbed to the fever, no one had the presence of mind to keep a lookout for those who were alive. Once again, the news of the epidemic filled Radha's heart with fear. Daulati was afraid too and Rahibai was terrified. The same question plagued all three of them—"We sowed a thorn and brought up a Meru mountain . . . Will this magical Meru survive the onslaught of the fever?" In spite of this, people went about their daily lives—only they carried the burden of fear on their backs.

And then yet another disaster was upon them.

The month of Jyeshtha was over; the Mriga star was in the ascent. Smartly, the farmers finished sowing their crops. In the sky, dark rain clouds began to create a huge ruckus. Ugly, misshapen, fearsome, they rolled around menacingly, but then blew away without letting a single drop fall to the earth. The Mriga went away, leaving everything completely dry. The men thought that if the Mriga had deceived them, the next star would not let them down. With this consolation, the men contained the feeling of despondency that was clouding their minds.

But the next nakshatra a fortnight later also did not oblige. This led to a full panic. Ashadh, the monsoon month went by without rain. Clouds of dust began to rise. The grass which had sprouted in the pre-monsoon showers shrivelled up and became one with the soil. Foraging birds dug out the seeds from the furrows and a terrible famine swept the land.

The beautiful region turned desolate, as if a fire had raged through it. Men started wailing. Cattle chewed on rags.

Disease, famine and death joined hands to crush the superior and supreme human race. Death danced its horrible way to the village of Vategaon. Starving people became easy prey for the disease. Entire families suffered. It became much easier for death to fell men whom the famine had reduced to skeletons.

People started dying in Vategaon, and there was a pall of gloom over the village. People had no dhani, no master, no saviour to turn to. Initially, some pyres burned in the cremation ground. But soon there was a scarcity of firewood, so people had no choice but to bury their dead. In a short while, even that became difficult. Those who were alive had no strength to dig graves for anyone. So then large pits were made and as many corpses as they would hold were thrown into them. Before long, jackals and foxes came down from the nearby mountains and parked themselves on the plains. The dogs in the village fattened on the carcasses of dead cattle. The whole Mang colony was in the grip of the disease. Those who were still standing were struggling to get food. Old people scoured the threshing yards in search of grains. Radha and Sarubai milled the grain in the house and supplied flour to the needy. They nursed the ailing. Both of them were determined to share whatever they had with the Mang–Mahar colonies and die with everyone else if it came to that.

Fakira, Savala, Sadhu and Mura were exhausted from digging graves. The responsibility of burying not just the Mangs and Mahars, but all the dead from the whole village, had fallen on them. Death had wiped out caste discrimination.

It was mid-afternoon. The heat was unbearable. Fakira had just arrived and was resting. Saru and Radha were also back. Daulati and Rahibai were sitting in the house, making enquiries about the latest deaths when Mokya appeared.

"Is Daji there?"

"Yes, come in," said Fakira.

"Why come in now? Old Chinga, she is dead."

"Let's go then." Fakira stood up.

They buried the old woman and were on their way back when Mura said,

"Daji, this old woman could have survived."

"Why was she unwilling to live then?" asked Savala sarcastically.

Mura replied, "People are dying of hunger."

"Meaning?" asked Fakira and Mura told him,

"There is a not a single grain left in the Mang settlement today. I can't bear to see this suffering anymore."

"So what should we do?" asked Fakira.

"We can't do anything," said Mura helplessly.

As they were talking, they reached the mud track and turned towards Mang wada. Suddenly, Fakira stopped. "You go to the settlement," he told them. "Get every single person together and wait. I will just go to the village and come."

Saying this, Fakira hurried along the track towards the village. His whole body was numb with tiredness. He did not know how he reached Vishnupanta Kulkarni's wada. He realised where he was only when he saw the wada in front of him.

The wada was enveloped in a shroud of darkness. There was not a sound to be heard. Every now and then, feeble cries emanated from somewhere. They didn't even have the strength to cry out loudly. Suddenly, a couple of loud wails were heard, then silence prevailed once more. Only to be was broken by the eerie howling of dogs. All this created a ghastly, ghostly atmosphere in the village.

Fakira reached the entrance to the courtyard of the wada. The light of the single oil lamp burning in the niche on the side flickered on Fakira's strong body. "Abasaheb!" Fakira called out.

"Is that you, Fakira?" Panta hurried out. He had now crossed the age of sixty but his well-built physique was still impressive. With the large bald head, thick neck, sharp piercing eyes and fierce white moustache, Panta exuded the power of a veritable tiger. His voice too was deep like a tiger's roar.

Fakira went up and stood right in front of Panta, his big strong hands clasped behind his back. His handsome face was wet with perspiration. He looked straight into Vishnupanta's eyes as he searched for words in his mind. Without waiting for him to say something, Panta spoke up. "What is going on in the Mang and Mahar colonies?" he asked. There was a look of concern in his steadfast gaze.

Fakira looked at the oil lamp burning in the niche and said, "The Mang–Mahar race will not survive, Aba."

"How many people have succumbed so far?"

"In the last four days, about twenty, including young and old," Fakira muttered. His words sounded harsh in the darkness.

"So what do you want to say?" Panta asked.

Running his tongue over his dry lips, Fakira said, "I can't bear to hear children crying for bhakri and dying for want of food. My heart becomes a clod of mud in water."

The glow of the lamp shone on Fakira's wet eyelashes. He quickly turned his head away to hide his tears.

"No, don't, Fakira," Panta said comforting him. "You must face this bravely."

"Aba . . ." the words came out of the depths of Fakira's heart. "We Mangs and Mahars are eating pumpkin and kardu leaves to survive. But we can't any longer. Had it been mere hunger, we could have managed somehow, but this fever has pushed us to the edge of the hill." Fakira swallowed the rest of his words and looked at Panta.

Panta repeated, "So what next?"

Panta's grim voice echoed through the wada and in a low voice Fakira replied, "You tell us . . ."

"I? What can I say? I have informed the government that the village is in the jaws of a famine. But the government has not sent even a chit of paper in reply. I am reduced to a mere record keeper of deaths."

"So who is our saviour, our dhani, then?" Fakira sounded slightly irritated.

"No one is anyone's dhani," Panta said quickly. "I too have a lot of wailing around me, I am in deep trouble. But it is my firm opinion that you all must live. Today, it is more important to live than to die."

"But Aba, how do we do it?" asked Fakira, his voice sharp.

"In whatever way you can," Panta declared, "Do whatever you can, but live. Survive."

He quickly reached out and raised the wick of the oil lamp. The sudden brightness pierced the darkness and the darkness shuddered.

"So what should we do next?" asked Fakira, confused and hurt. Panta's face hardened and his voice had a bitter edge to it.

"That I do not know," he said, twisting the sacred thread around his chest tighter. "One thing is certain. You must not die like dogs . . . These days too will pass . . ."

Glowing embers seemed to have spilled out of Panta's mouth instead of words and they gave rise to an upsurge of confidence in Fakira's heart. He bowed before Panta and rising up, he said,

"Aba, I will go now."

"Go. Even the garbage heap can be redeemed, and you are human beings . . . human beings." Panta bid Fakira farewell. Just as a lamp flame burns brighter when the soot is removed, Fakira's mind became clear. He found enormous power taking birth within him. Courage spread through his young legs like an electric current. He set off for Mang wada at a wild pace, stamping out the darkness as if he was tramping through slush.

Panta's words, "You must survive!" hammered on his brain and accompanied him as he rushed ahead. The words had created a storm in Fakira's mind and this storm was driving him.

The 200 families of Mahars and Mangs sat in the clearing amid the cactus ring in grim silence, looking bewildered. The wind was making the thorny nivdunga crackle as if the atmosphere was crunching corn. In between, the hooting of an owl awakened fear. The very existence of human beings and their words, which were crawling amidst the thorns, was endangered. As many people as could shelter under the neem tree in front of Fakira's house, waited anxiously for him to come back. They were eager to hear what Panta had to say in this crisis situation.

Those who had become very weak and bent with hunger were saying to themselves,

"Let God enter Panta's mind and advise him to give to these poor souls, whatever he has in his house."

Some were staring into the darkness, hoping that Fakira would bring back twenty-five sacks of jowar. Others felt that Fakira had a good standing with Panta. So Panta won't let Fakira's words fall to the ground. He would definitely not let the Mangs and Mahars die. Making all such conjectures, they waited. Their eyes were on high alert. All hardships were forgotten and their wounded hearts were hopeful that Panta would come up with some solution. Giving up all thoughts of their bloodlines coming to an end, they awaited the sacks of grain that were going to come to them.

Suddenly, they all saw a large figure wrapped in a ghongadi, carrying a huge staff in his hand approaching them.

They perked up saying, "It's Fakira! He's come!" they straightened up. But in the very next moment they were disappointed. It was not Fakira.

"Who is it?" someone called out.

"I am Tayanu Mahar, ga."

There was a squirming in the darkness. Once again, the voices became mournful.

"So Tayanuba, how are you?"

"I have come after laying out all my people in a row," he said grimly.

Bhairu asked, "Has the old man's fever come down?"

"There is no medicine for this fever," snapped a frustrated Savala.

To which Tayanu said,

"There is only one medicine for this fever . . ."

"What? What is that?" almost everyone asked in a chorus.

"Bhakri!"

Hearing the word bhakri, all faces fell and hearts sank. Their life and living depended upon bhakri and that's what they were unable to get. Forget getting it, they were not even able to lay their eyes on it. These men yearned for just a piece of dry bhakri.

Just then Fakira arrived. Immediately everyone became attentive, their faces solemn. Some dusted themselves and inched forward. Everybody waited with bated breath, their eyes fixed on Fakira. He settled down on a root of the neem tree and said,

"So, tell me, ga . . ."

Tayanu Mahar came forward and asked calmly, "What did Panta say?"

"He told us to live."

"But how can we live on dry words?" said Savala and stood up, then sat down again.

"It is true. Kulkarni and we are walking the same road. Only difference, we will reach first, he will get there a little later. There means death. Understood?"

"So what is our way out?" Mura exclaimed.

"It means we have to die," cried out Kiwada Hari Mahar.

"No! We must survive," Fakira growled.

"Arra, but how?" asked Savala, his head cocked. Kondi Mahar stood up. With folded hands he pleaded to God,

"O Panduranga Vitthala! Almighty god, my two young sons are on their deathbed. For the last two days, they did not get even a sip of rice water. What shall I do now?"

"You must do what I tell you!" Fakira leapt to his feet and thundered.

"What shall we do, Daji, just tell us . . ." the words emerged out of all throats in a chorus. Silencing the voices, Fakira said, "Panta has applied to the government but the government has not responded. Looking at their red, Maruti-like faces, we had believed that the progeny of Maruti himself is ruling over us. But now I think they are the descendants of the long-slumbering demon Kumbhakarna himself. It is time to draw our swords and dance on their chests."

These ominous words of Fakira, "draw our swords and dance on their chests," sliced the darkness and reached far and wide. Briskly, Fakira went into his house. Radha, Sarubai, Daulati and Rahibai followed him. He was in a temper. He sprang to the devhara where the gods and the sword lay and picked up the weapon. It was the very sword which Ranoji had carried to the Shigaon jatra and had become fearless. The same sword with which Fakira had cut off Khot's hand.

Fakira then placed his forehead at his mother's feet. He clasped Rahibai and Daulati's thin feet and said in an emotional voice, "Aai, big Aai, Aba . . . I will die to allow these dying people to live. Don't stop me." Then he placed his hand on Sarubai's back and said to her, "Don't panic. Take care of everything."

When they saw the naked sword in Fakira's hands, the strength of an elephant surged into all hearts. There was some shuffling. Fakira started calling out names, "Sadhu, Bali, Mura, Keru, Savalunana, Ghamandi, Tayanu Mahar, Kesu Mahar, Sukana, Bhana . . . and all those who have the strength in their legs and valour in their hearts, step to one side."

His commanding voice penetrated every heart, and every heart responded its assent.

Like angry bees disturbed from their hive, 150 men stepped aside. Wild with rage, Savala jerked the ghongadi off his head and threw it in the air, slapped his thigh like a wrestler in readiness and yelled,

"Don't just stand there. Pick up your weapons. They have been starving for so long . . ."

Fakira repeated, "Yes, pick them up."

For a few moments, there was intense activity. Handles were hammered firmly into the axes, and swords unsheathed. Then Fakira addressed the old and infirm, "You give water to the dying and take care of them till we return. Tomorrow you will have a heap of grain here. Don't be afraid."

Only two stars twinkled in the dark skies. Their soft light fell on Fakira's sword and the sword looked fearsome. Fakira looked up at the sky to gauge the time of the night and then started walking; 150 gleaming weapons followed him. The rest of them returned to their homes.

"At least take Gabarya," said Radhabai hardening her heart. Fakira stood still then replied, "No, he will not be able to endure this ride. He is tired . . ." At that instant, Gabarya neighed in his stable. The sound echoed through the nivadunga thicket. Radha felt reassured. As if Gabarya was saying to her, "Don't be afraid. Fakira will return victorious."

As they went out of the village and started along the mountain, Savala increased his pace and matched his step with Fakira's. Leaning close to Fakira, he whispered, "Daji, where are we going?"

"We are going to loot the Malawadi Mathkari, the official of the matth." Fakira then broke into a run like an oncoming storm. Everybody followed.

Malawadi nestled in the valley of the neighbouring mountain just like an old man sitting cosily in his hut. All was quiet in Malawadi at that time. The village was unaware that the darkest night was dancing above its head. The massive stone-walled wada stood at one end of the village as if it was an outcaste.

Once a long time ago, a raja had bestowed upon a priest the ownership of fourteen villages in return for taking care of the ancient matth. Since then, the expenses of this monastery were met by the income from these fourteen villages. However, there was an ugly battle for control of the land and wealth of the matth and much blood had been shed. One person would murder another and stake his claim for the ownership of the matth. Even today, five "owners" are living out their widowhood in that immense building. The place is infested with people as a granary is with insects.

Every pillar of that four-courtyard wada had a large grain bin attached to it. Grain was rotting in some of the bins. These bins had been stacked outside and then dragged towards the pillars. Several hunting dogs lay curled up all across the courtyard. Next to every dog lay an armed guard. In the central courtyard of that wide wada, the matthkari slept peacefully on a cot. A 100 or more cattle, tethered under the roof of the outer veranda stood there, ruminating. The night insects had been frightened off by the snores of those who slept in there, unafraid. Holding the produce and the lives of the fourteen villages in its embrace, the mighty wada sighed in peace.

And at that very moment, Fakira's hands gripped the stones of that mansion. His 150 men had surrounded it and created a barricade between it and the village. Savala, Mura, Bali were to overcome the first hurdle by removing the door latch. Sadhu had seized control of the main thoroughfare of the village. Fakira was impatient to barge into the wada with the sword in his hands.

Silence prevailed, like the calm before the storm.

Nine

The official caretaker of the Malawadi matth lay snoring on his cot. Every now and then his mouth moved as if chewing something. He had absolutely no idea that a great calamity was about to grab hold of him.

Outside, Savala was working hard to prise open the door stopper. He had to do it without making any noise. If the sound led to a commotion before they stormed into the wada, it would mean certain defeat for them. That's why he was carrying out his task speedily but carefully.

Fakira was stomping around restlessly, impatient to enter the wada. He wanted to complete this mission and return home before sunrise. Therefore he was repeatedly exhorting Savala to hurry. "Savalunana, quick. Otherwise it will all go wrong."

Savala had finished his job. The door stopper was removed. "Hmm . . . it's ready," he said.

"I'm also ready. Push the door in," said Fakira, and Savala pushed open the enormous door with a loud crack. In the still of the night, the sound shook the massive wada itself. Burning torches and naked swords swarmed the matthkari's courtyard. The cattle in the outer veranda struggled to their feet. The dogs brought the roof down. The matthkari woke up in fright. He kicked his servants awake and started shouting loudly,

"Run . . . run . . ."

Fakira moved forward and warned,

"Don't shout, or I'll take off your head. Don't let a sound escape your mouth you all. Otherwise you will lose your life."

Everything went back to as it had been earlier. The servants lay down quietly. The dogs however did not understand what Fakira had said so they kept on barking. The matth official lay back on his cot and watched the proceedings.

Axes hacked the bins fastened to the pillars and a river of grain flowed out of them towards Fakira's feet. A 100 sturdy men began to hastily fill sacks with the spilt corn and drag them outside.

Sadhu and Ghamandi silenced the villagers who had been awakened by the matthakari's first clamour. At places, fifty or so men were loading their slingshots and stopping anyone from moving forward. Tayanu Mahar had singlehandedly prevented one stream from coming towards them. His imposing figure appeared like a demon to the villagers. And the valley shook with the fury of his cries.

Fakira's men were trying to run away into the darkness with the grain sacks. But the villagers had blocked the main pathway in the front so not a single sack was able to cross the village border as yet. When Fakira realized this, he signalled his men to move aside. Then he cut off the tethers of all the cattle and herded them on to the path outside the wada. Immediately, a barrage of stones was unleashed on the rumps of the cattle. Bewildered and frightened, the cattle created havoc in the narrow lane. Afraid of being trampled or gored, the villagers had to retreat. Fakira then carved out a path under the cover of a concerted slingshot attack.

Dawn was breaking in the east. The land, ravaged by drought, appeared desolate. The trees were somehow still standing. The thicket of withered karavanda bushes looked like beggars with dirty straggly hair. But the eastern sky still had the same lustre. Colourful clouds had begun to move slowly. Everything appeared calm. The land was scorched but the sky was full of vitality.

The thorns on the cactus hands crackled as they rubbed against each other. Birds twittered, the loudspeaker outside the temple in the village blared. Under the neem tree in the middle of the ring of nivadunga lay a large heap of pearly grain. Little children were sitting in a row with baskets and bags. The older ones jumped up and down excitedly. After a long time, they were going to feel the grain with their hands. Some were satiated by just the sweet smell of the grain! It was as if amrut, the heavenly nectar, had made its appearance there.

Mura, Sadhu, Tayanu Mahar were responsible for distributing the grains equally. Baskets were running around. Joy filled the homes of the Mangs and Mahars. The grinding stones that had lain inert for so long came to life and started going round and round. Cooking fires were stoked once more, and after ages the tavas warmed up to the heat.

After most of the grain was shared by everyone, a small heap remained.

"Daji, what do we do with this?" Mura asked Fakira.

"Not one grain must be unfairly given," Fakira told him. "Take a ladle and measure it out. Don't forget, on a single grain a man can survive for a day."

The sun had settled on the nivadunga by the time all the grain was distributed. It was a golden day in the lives of the Mangs and Mahars. Their children sat in the doorways eating, not the warm sunshine but fresh hot bhakris.

Once everything was settled, Fakira undid his sash, removed the sword from it and placed it back in the devhara beside the family gods.

The next day, the collector himself landed up in the village with his army. The first thing Inspector Babarkhan's men did was to surround Fakira and arrest him. Only after they had taken all the Mahars and Mangs into custody did they return to the village office. There, they first handcuffed the young and the notorious. Some were tied to each other like cattle, bound with a single rope. Then began the enquiry to find out who was responsible for looting the Malawadi matthkari. For the first time in his life, Fakira was standing with his hands behind his back. Mura, Bali, Bhairu, Tayanu, Ghamandi, Savala had also been handcuffed. The police had brought all the baskets of bhakri they had found during their search of the houses and had heaped them up in the chavadi. The yard in front of the village office swelled with prisoners and villagers.

The police had blocked all the entrance gates to the village. Bayonets glinted everywhere. Babarkhan moved around through the crowd, holding up his large belly. The matth official of Malawadi had a victorious grin on his face. He twisted his moustache as he looked arrogantly at the captive Mangs and Mahars.

As soon as Vishnupanta heard of Fakira's arrest, he rushed to the chavadi. The crowd parted to make way for him. A sudden hush fell on the scene. But Panta stood at the bottom of the steps leading up to the chavadi. He was trembling with rage. He did not speak, rather he shouted. People looked at the collector.

Panta said, "Saheb, what is going on here?"

"We have taken into custody the criminals," said the collector seriously, enumerating the names of all those arrested. Panta placed one foot on the step and asked,

"Do you accept that we are government-appointed servants of this village?"

"Yes, I do."

"Then why did you make these arrests without informing us?" Vishnupanta quoted the rules governing the role of the village officials. He raised his voice and his tone angered the collector. He growled,

"We have the right to do that. Besides, these fellows have openly looted the Malawadi matthakari."

"What proof do you have?" Panta asked his eyes fixed on the collector's face. "The matth official's grains have left a trail till the borders of this village and, besides, a large quantity of bhakri has been found in these peoples' homes," said the collector waving his hand at the people in front of him.

Though the collector uttered these words in a clear and civil fashion, Panta roared,

"Then why don't you arrest me? Because the trail has touched my village, and at this very moment, you will find a lot of bhakris in my house as well."

Panta looked around, fidgeting as if his palms and feet were on fire. All eyes were trained on him.

"What exactly do you want to say?" said the collector, his brow creased in a frown. "Please speak clearly, Panta."

"Then listen." Panta spoke frankly, as if addressing all the people present,

"Saheb, this village of mine has been devastated by the famine and my people are surviving by eating mud. On the top of it, the epidemic has attacked almost every home and destroyed whole families. The Mangs and the Mahars are dying a dog's death. I had informed you about all this, isn't it?"

"That is true. Go on . . ."

"So why did you not reply?" demanded Panta.

"It doesn't mean that just because I did not reply these people can create anarchy, take the law in their hands and loot someone. All this is not acceptable to us." The collector's face was flushed as he spoke.

"Then what is acceptable to you?" said Panta with an equally red face. "That people should die a dog's death? That they should eat the mud of three streets? That they should bury twenty bodies instead of ten in a single grave? I cannot put up with this, sarkar."

"So what can you accept then?" barked the collector stamping his foot. He shook the village office up with his tantrums. Pointing to Vishnupanta he asked,

"You think looting is fine? Anarchy is acceptable?"

"To that question, the answer is—yes," Panta declared gravely.

"All right. Carry on with the thievery. We will go to Satara right now and take the prisoners with us," said the collector narrowing his eyes. Panta replied in the same tone,

"Very well, do go. But be back soon."

"Why? What for?" asked the surprised collector.

"To arrest me, Vishnupanta," said Panta with finality.

"You mean . . . you mean you yourself will indulge in looting?" asked the collector rather startled.

Panta took the uparna from his shoulders, tied it firmly around his waist, gave the collector a scathing look and with his head held high, replied,

"Saheb, if some solution is not found for the famine and the epidemic, everyone will either have to die a dog's death or become a thief or dacoit to live for a few more days. And I am certainly not one to die a dog's death."

Hearing these words, the collector was frustrated. His voice softened slightly and he said,

"What is your advice? What should we do now?"

"You are the government. Provide us some relief from hunger," said Panta fearlessly. "Rescue the people from the jaws of death. Or else this Maratha gent will die but he will take you with him. Remember that."

Panta was talking. The people were listening. Each one felt it was he himself who was talking to the saheb. When Panta noticed that the collector had nothing to say, he started taunting him again.

"Saheb, what you see before you are real people, not corpses. They know that if coaxing won't make a reluctant bullock move, then poking it with a pointed stick will certainly make it run. A sword can't subdue them because they have tamed many with it."

Instead of being angered by this, the collector smiled and politely said,

"Please do not get offended because we did not take into consideration your age and your status. We will do our best to provide relief from the famine. We will also release all prisoners."

Barely had the collector spoken that the policemen came forward and all the handcuffs clattered to the floor. Within minutes, the courtyard in front of the village office was filled with laughter and jubilation. Panta then climbed the steps of the village office and sat down calmly beside the collector. As soon as Fakira's hands were free, he went and lay his head in reverence at Panta's feet. Shankarrao Patil twirled his moustache unthinkingly. "If one must be a man, one must be like Panta," thought the entire village as they looked at him with admiration. In a short while, the collector's party left for Satara and people went home saying, "Look you fellows, it was Panta who freed the Mangs and Mahars."

But eight days later, there was consternation in the village. Two orders from Satara had landed in the chavadi. By one order, Shankarrao Patil was dismissed from the post of Patil of the village. The second order declared that Raosaheb Patil was appointed in his place.

The whole village was alarmed and distressed. They were also angry because the government had shown disrespect to a capable, kind and magnanimous person by removing him from his post. Everyone started saying that Khot of Shigaon must have had a hand in this matter. They suspected that Khot had interceded with the government on his son-in-law's behalf and gotten him Shankarrao Patil's post as the Patil of this village. From the day Raosaheb took charge as Patil, the village office became like a tiger's den. The atmosphere was very tense. Vishnupanta, not at all pleased with this appointment, was waiting for an opportunity to pounce on Raosaheb Patil. He had held the new Patil on a knife's edge from day one. Panta was well aware that Shankarrao's dismissal was a ploy by the government.

Everyone was apprehensive that a new calamity would befall the Mahar and the Mang communities very soon.

And they were right. The first thing Raosaheb Patil did after he took over was to change the angle of the pagoti on his head, symbolically and literally. He took to carrying an axe, and accompanied by a band of young ruffians from his lane, he went around terrorizing the villagers. He told them, "Forget Shankarrao's times. It is Raosaheb Patil's regime now. You better behave yourselves." He maintained a strict watch on Fakira and some others.

One month had passed since Raosaheb Patil became the police Patil of the village. The sun was high but was on the way down. The heat was losing its edge. Raosaheb was sitting in the village office, and Panta was sitting on the other side, opposite him, doing his work silently. Patil had his cronies around him and they were all whiling away their time, giggling and gossiping. Janya Jadhav, who had smoked too much ganja, was high. Every now and then, he would put two fingers to his lips and through them, spit a stream of pan juice out on-to the street. Between these squirts, he was describing the qualities and the looks of his wife who had recently come to live with him.

Word had gone around the village that Jadhav's wife was very beautiful. Patil too had heard about it. That's why he was all ears as Janya Jadhav described her. Casting a sideways glance at Panta, he added in a hushed tone,

"Patil, I had never imagined that I would have such a good-looking wife. But God himself has given me one as beautiful as a banana stem."

"It so happened," said Patil, getting into the mood, "that God also had smoked ganja at the time. That's why he tied a banana stem to a thorny babhli tree." Saying this, Patil guffawed loudly. All those with him laughed loudly. The chavadi echoed the raucous sounds. The vein in Panta's forehead throbbed and he looked up. "Patil, this is the village office, not a gossip corner," he admonished the young man.

Patil immediately stopped laughing. His face fell, but he quickly controlled himself. He scowled at Panta. "Remember Panta, I am the Patil of the village and not a dombari, a street performer."

"So stop behaving like one," flashed Panta. That sent Patil flying into a rage.

Lifting his head high, he said to Panta, "We will behave as we please. You need not advise us."

"Do whatever you want in your own house," said Pant as he continued with his work. "He who can't tell the difference between a temple, a chavadi and a dharmashala should not aspire to the role of a Patil, nor treat it lightly."

"Don't preach to me! I haven't become a Patil for fun. I have come to it because it is my right. I have been appointed to this post."

"Then behave like a Patil," Panta growled.

"But who are you to check me?" said the Patil in desperation.

"I am Vishnupanta Kulkarni. You better behave yourself otherwise within four days, I will straighten you out. Don't let the Patil's post go to your head."

Hearing sounds of this altercation, a mob gathered in front of the village office. "What's going on Patil?" they asked.

"Ask that Panta . . ." saying this, Patil nodded in Panta's direction.

"This Patil is trying to convert the village office into a brothel," Panta retorted.

Just then, a special messenger arrived from Satara with a new government order. Therefore, the earlier argument was pushed aside. Panta read the order and threw the paper at Patil.

By that order, the Patil and Kulkarni were given the authority to compel all Mang and Mahar youth and other noted criminals in the village to report to the office three times a day.

Raosaheb literally jumped up when he got the order in his hands. He looked at Ramoshi who had been leaning against a pillar of the chavadi and listening all this while and barked, "Ai you fellow, you Ramoshya, don't sit there dozing. Go round up all the Mangs and bring them here . . . Go, run."

Ramoshi adjusted the patka on his head and went to the Mang settlement. Raosaheb looked at Panta with a victorious smile. He noticed that Panta was looking slightly crestfallen. He yelled again, "Ai Ramushya, bring that Tanya Mahar also with you!"

Ten

It was midnight. Every inch of nature was in dense darkness. There was not a sound anywhere. Only the crickets chirped in the cactus thickets. But even their intense chirping did not split the ominous silence. On the contrary, it only emphasised the harsh and cruel night.

It was time for reporting to the police. Fakira was lying on his bed, unable to sleep. For the last fifteen days, he had stayed awake all night thinking of the day when he was forced into reporting at the village office, and the arrogance which Raosaheb Patil had displayed.

Fakira was distraught. What an injustice perpetrated on a human being. To have to get his hajiri, his attendance, recorded in the chavadi by the Patil, three times a day. If he wanted to go to some other place, he had to take written permission from the Patil and it was up to him to grant it or not. Even if he did, then one would have to hand over the permission letter to the Patil of that place and get him also to record his presence three times a day. If something went wrong, then he would have to undergo three months of rigorous imprisonment. Fakira was sure that Khot and the government had colluded to inflict this humiliation on him. It was an act of vengeance, he believed. Fakira felt suffocated. He couldn't go wherever he wanted to. His limbs were no longer his own but tied to Raosaheb Patil's yoke. The law had put a ring through his nose, like a bullock, and handed the reins to an enemy. What was the next step forward? Would he have to live like this all his life?

In this agitated state, he lay with, his eyes closed, talking to himself. His strong mind was giving him advice.

"Till yesterday, you were like any other person. But now you are a prisoner of the government. Patil is now your master. Shankarrao Patil or Vishnupanta Kulkarni cannot come to your aid. The law has overridden them and their decline has begun. That's why, for the last fifteen days, this scoundrel Patil has been marking your attendance at midnight. In the morning and evening you are expected to go and record it yourself in the Patil's presence."

"So what should I do?" Fakira was crying out within himself. "For how many days and why? The government can come and behead us or put us behind bars, but why this kind of oppression? I am not a slave. I am an officially appointed guardian, a protector of my village. My father was cut down on the maidan for the sake of our village. And I have to report to the chavadi three times a day? I will not do it."

"What? You won't do it? Then go to jail for three months. You'll come out and will have to go back to the attendance marking routine. If you say no again, then it will be imprisonment again . . . the cycle will continue."

A huge storm brewed in Fakira's head. It charged him up. The heat radiated into his bed and he felt he was on fire. Fakira could no longer bear the tension in the air. He quickly got up. Saru was fast asleep next to him. Her even breathing showed her sense of security in his presence. On the other side, Radha lay motionless. No movement was seen from old Daulati and Rahibai. Sadhu slept under the trellis in front of the door. Gabarya slept on his legs. Like a true horse, he would not let his back touch the ground only for sleeping. For some reason, Fakira felt extremely nervous. After a while, he calmed down and lay back on the bed, his hands locked under his head. Like ghosts, his thoughts began to dance in front of him. Again, that fateful day when the Ramoshi came to summon them all to the village office floated before his closed eyes. All the Mangs were standing in a row in front of the village office and the Patil was glaring at them with an axe in his hands. Fakira was also one of the crowd. Patil recorded all their names and then warned them,

"Today onwards, all Mangs and those Mahars who follow the Mangs must come here twice a day and mark their attendance. I will come every night, wake you up and register your names. If anyone is absent, then it will be handcuffs and hard labour."

Recalling that incident made Fakira anxious once more. Suddenly all the dogs in the Mahar settlement woke up and started barking furiously. Immediately, Fakira lay back and muttered, "Attendance register is here."

He pricked up his ears and started listening intently. His head was again spinning in anger at the thought that the scoundrel Patil would now come from the Mahar to the Mang settlement.

The youthful Patil was walking in the lead taking smart steps, holding an axe in his hand. He had set out with Ganya Koli, Janya Jadhav, Ekoba Parit, the washerman, two Ramoshis, Tatya Mang and another eight men from his brotherhood. They had four–five lanterns with them. A naked sword glinted from under Janya's arm. And several spears were tasting blood.

Patil's scream, "Ai Tayanu Mahar" in the Mahar settlement was heard in the Mang colony. Then all the dogs in the Mang wada woke up, and within minutes, started barking crazily. There was chaos and confusion. Amidst all this, the Patil was advancing, calling out names on the way . . . "Bahiru Mahar," "Aaaai Kisha Mahar," "Ai Dadya . . ." and cries of "Hajir" responded to him. The dogs were barking. Since these dogs were barking, all the other dogs in the village also got excited and joined in the cacophony. As a result, the whole village was woken up. This had been going on for the last fifteen days. The sleepy villagers cursed the Patil under their breaths and tried to go back to sleep.

In a short while, this procession reached Fakira's door. Patil stopped abruptly and called out, "Sadhu, Ranu."

"Ji, I am here," said Sadhu from where he lay and immediately the Patil roared, "Fakira Ranu."

"Present," answered Fakira. But Patil was not satisfied. He called out again, "Fakira . . ."

"What?" responded Fakira angrily from inside the house. The Patil got enraged. Stepping forward a bit, he hollered "Fakira, come outside and mark your attendance."

"I won't come out," Fakira's voice was raised. Sadhu woke up and he sat up. He was wondering why the Patil was being aggressive, when the next order came.

"You will have to come and stand in front of me to mark your attendance."

'No, I will reply from inside the house. Just like this." Fakira was now angrier and Patil also lost control. He gripped the handle of the axe tighter and flaring his nostrils, he cried out,

"No, marking attendance from your wife's side will not do. Come out here."

At that, the door crashed open and Fakira stood in the doorway. The yellowish red glow of the lantern settled on his face. He looked exceedingly fierce. His red eyes were emitting fire. There was a rush of blood in his strong muscular wrists. That one sentence had made him wild. Sadhu stood up quickly. Daulati had woken up. Sarubai, Radha, Rahi were all looking on, astounded.

Fakira stepped out of the door frame and looking intently at Patil said, "What did you say?"

"Come outside to mark attendance."

"And what else?" Fakira yelled. At that Patil turned to look at him when he felt a resounding slap from Fakira's hand on his left cheek. The power of that blow sent his pagota flying, and Raosaheb himself lost his balance and fell down. But he immediately recovered and flung his axe. But Fakira wasn't there. He had run in to get his sword. So Patil's axe lodged itself in the wood of the door frame.

Radha stopped Fakira from reaching for the sword. Daulati also blocked his way. Saru held his hand. They knew that if Fakira laid hands on the sword, there would be a massacre. That is why they prevented him from getting to the devhara. When Fakira realized that his mother was blocking his way, he turned back. Then like a flash of lightning, he went straight for Patil.

In the first swoop, he pulled Patil down. Patil reeled on the ground like a rat being mauled by a cat. A hard kick sent a sharp pain through Patil's body. Straightening his legs and holding his stomach in pain, he began to groan and look pleadingly at his companions. After a while he cried out,

"Arra . . . I am dead ra."

Daulati came out and grabbed Fakira. Radha also joined him and both of them held him in a tight embrace. Suddenly, Janya came forward to attack with his sword. Sadhu hit him in the back with a stick. Janya dropped the sword and fell in the darkness. Fakira bent down quickly and picked up the sword.

"Don't kill him. He is the Patil of the village," said Sadhu.

By then, Patil got up and turning towards the village, began to howl. In a moment, the whole village woke up. The Mangs took out their arms. The Mahars ran to the Mang settlement. A mob of villagers started moving towards the Mang settlement. Nobody knew what had happened and who exactly was howling.

It was truly an unusual situation. For a second, Fakira was confused. But he quickly collected himself and signalled to Sadhu to be prepared.

In a short while, the whole village gathered in the Mang settlement. There was a crowd at Daulati Mang's doorstep.

Fakira had tightened his sash and taken a sword in his hands. Savala, Mura, Bali and all the Mangs were ready, waiting in the darkness. They had tied up their head gear in readiness to fight.

Tayanu Mahar cried out, "Arra, who is this howling?"

At once people realised it was Raosaheb Patil.

So then they turned to him. Someone asked him, "Patil! What is the matter?"

By that time, Patil's family members had also joined the crowd. Patil glanced at his people and started, "The Mang kicked me. Fakira beat me!"

Many people were shocked to learn that the Patil was thrashed by a Mang. A Mang beating a Patil? That was an outrage, an insult to the whole village, some thought and got very angry. About twenty-five of them waved their axes and shouted, "Where is he? Where is that Fakira?"

Savala said in a stern voice, "Fakira is here. Anyone who wants to die may come here."

Thinking that this was going to lead to a big fight, some people started running away. In the stampede, many fell in the cactus thicket. The villagers were afraid that if the Mangs attacked them in their neighbourhood, there would be a carnage. So one by one, they all fled towards the village and reassembled outside the chavadi.

Here in the Mang wada, the Mangs had come together and were sitting at Fakira's doorstep, thinking over all this. How had this catastrophe struck so suddenly?

Adversities sometimes walk towards you of their own accord. That's what had happened here. Fakira was distraught. Patil had deliberately been provocative. Now the villagers and the government would join together. And Khot would fuel the fire.

Suddenly, Vishnupanta arrived with a lantern in his hand. When he saw Vishnupanta, Fakira had tears in his eyes. He fell at Panta's feet.

"Get up. Tell me, what exactly happened," said Panta quietly.

"Patil started the aggression," said Fakira. He narrated the whole incident to Panta. Then he said, "He has deliberately escalated the matter."

"Yes, he was bound to do it," said Panta smiling wryly.

Savala took off his pagota, placed it in front of him and asked, "Do we have any dhani, a protector or not? Can anyone just come and beat us as they please?"

"It is like this," said Panta in a conciliatory tone. "These keys are now being turned from Shigaon. The influence lies there. However, while hitting the scorpion, God Mahadeo himself has been struck. The feelings of the villagers have been hurt. So . . ."

"So what should we do then?" interrupted Fakira.

"The villagers will become aggressive. The wheels of the government will start turning. Saying that the village Patil was assaulted, the government, Patil, some villagers and Khot will come together to attack you."

"What is the way out?" Daulati asked.

"You must leave the village," said Panta gravely. "It is sometimes wise to dodge the trouble. Besides, Khot has kept a strict watch on all those who are required to mark their attendance."

"I feel the same way," said Fakira. 'I will immediately leave the village."

"Do that," said Panta. "Later on, I will slowly change this situation. I will also go to Satara and plead on your behalf. But in the meanwhile, if the villagers attack you, do not fight them. I will leave now."

The Mangs went up to the main path to see Panta off. When Panta turned back to take leave of them, all the Mangs bent down low to salute him. Panta's eyes widened.

"Go!" he exhorted them. "Don't become weak. Days don't build houses and settle down. These too will pass." In the pitch darkness, the lantern in Panta's hands was swinging as he walked, and the light was pushing the darkness away. As he went past the Mahar settlement, he saw a large crowd in front of the village office. Many a lantern was burning, many a torch was flaring. Panta turned towards the crowd. When they saw him, everyone fell silent and began to stare at him.

Raosaheb Patil was sitting with his legs spread. Since all his front teeth had broken, he kept spitting blood. As soon as he saw Panta, he straightened up and howled pathetically,

"Look what has happened to me. I was beaten up."

"I am aware of everything that happened," said Panta. "Keep calm right now. We will see what can be done about it tomorrow."

"Tomorrow?" shouted Patil and jumped up, "My teeth have fallen out, are they going to grow back tomorrow? And what's the point of us keeping quiet? No, we are not going to take this. Right now, we are going to slaughter the Mangs and burn down their huts. Let the bastards die."

"Listen to me, Patil," said Panta in a very firm tone. "You are very impulsive. While taking attendance, you deliberately instigated Fakira by saying, not from inside the house, come outside to answer. And now you are talking of burning their huts? Go then, go right now and set fire to their dwellings. No one will stop you because Fakira left the village long ago."

"You mean he has run away?" someone asked.

"That I don't know." Panta's voice was harsher. He turned to Patil and said, "Not a single male head of the family of the Mangs is at home. Their horses must be far away by now. Go and burn their huts. But don't think that those who have died on the hillside for the sake of this village are weaklings. Fakira will not remain silent for long. You burn down his hut and then be ready with water to douse the fire in your own wada later on. Go . . ."

The atmosphere became tense with Panta's words. The torches appeared to be burning more fiercely. The listeners were appalled. However, with false bravado, Patil said,

"Let me see him come and burn down my wada."

"Very well, then. I am not responsible for anything anymore," said Panta covering his ears with his hands.

"You face the consequences of whatever happens after this. Fakira has taken his men to the mountains. Right now, his horses must have reached there or they may be climbing up the mountains."

Eleven

A high cliff had stuck its head into the clouds. These enormous clouds meandering over the mighty Sahyadris had to change course every time they collided with the mountain faces. The wild winds blowing across the forests were subduing the vegetation into meekness, forcing them to make way for the gusts to cut through. Tall and sturdy trees like the babhli, pimparan, jambhul, sagvan and pangira as well as the dense bushes of karavanda and bori were forced to bow down to the wind, while dry leaves and broken twigs were made to prostrate before it. In the heart of the mountains, in a thickly wooded area Fakira had set up his camp. Eight work horses were tied under the thicket of a karavanda bush, while Gabarya stood with the saddle still on his back. It seemed as if he too was aware of the difficult situation they were in. The atmosphere was tense and Fakira's men hid in the crevices and crannies of the mountain sides, covering all the main access routes. The presence of armed men had made the tangled karavanda thickets look ferocious and given them the air of a military camp. Bold and fearless men like Piraji from Chinchani, Nilu from Sajur, Sadhu, Murari, Bhairu, Savala, Tayanu Mahar, Bahiroji Mahar and Ghamandi were gathered there.

During the last one month, many brave Mangs from remote areas had come and joined hands with Fakira. They had taken a collective decision that it was better to fight and perish than to report three times a day at the police station like criminals. Fakira had made all preparations and allotted specific tasks to his men.

In one month, Fakira had covered many miles on the shoulders of the Sahyadris and made many domineering and oppressive forces bite the dust. He had vanquished those who had become rebellious in their regions. Most people trembled at the mere mention of his name. And Raosaheb Patil, who had heard of Fakira's dreaded reputation, was trying to secure his own last days.

Fakira could not forget the day he had left home. His mother Radha had helplessly slapped her forehead to mourn her loss. Old Rahibai was beating her breast. And Daulati had saddled Gabarya through his tears. Saru had held back her sobs. Because Sadhu and he had become absconders, these four hapless souls were in this pathetic condition. When would they be together again? When would they all meet?

Everybody had been intensely anguished since this traumatic situation had come upon them unexpectedly. Fakira and Sadhu, the mainstays of the family had to go into hiding. When would they be back? Or will the Government, Patil and Khot finish them off? These and many such scorpions were stinging the minds of Radha, Daulati and Rahi.

Not only Daulati's home, but every household in the Mang settlement had wept that night. Because at least one man from each family had fled with Fakira.

When they were leaving in the middle of the night, all the people, young and old, had gathered in their doorways to see them off. Images of their thin, gnarled hands and emaciated bodies kept flashing before Fakira's mind. The experiences of the last few days had completely changed him. He recollected that incident as he lay sheltered in a thicket.

Eight days had passed and Fakira had not received any news from home. Saru was constantly in his thoughts. He was also concerned for the other members of his family. His mother must be sitting mournfully with her back against the wall, Aba must be fretting and big Aai agitated. My home, my yard, my plants and bushes, my village, they are all distanced from me now. For how long, he wondered.

The night was silent. The world of the mountains had become one with the darkness and gone quiet a long time back. Even the mighty Sahyadri appeared docile. Every now and then, a night bird flew past calling shrilly. Or a wild boar punctured the darkness with its grunts. Little foxes, afraid of that deadly boar snout would run for their lives. Fear gripped the hares too as in the high and inaccessible crevices, the hyenas laughed harshly.

Ghamandi had gone home around sunset. He was supposed to inform their families about their welfare and bring back news from them. Therefore, everyone was waiting for his return. Fakira too was alert for signs of his arrival.

Pira and Baloba from Ghonchi were sleeping in the adjoining thicket, snoring loudly. Because of that none of the others could rest. Attracted by their snores, a huge wild boar was slowly approaching the thicket, puzzled by the strange sound, its ears pricked up. But nobody had anticipated the boar's attack on those two men since they were all absorbed in their own concerns. They could neither sleep nor stop worrying about their own fate and the fate of their wives and children. Savala was sitting under a thicket, wrapped in a blanket. He had smoked a lot of ganja and was under its influence. He was muttering something and Tayanu was listening to him from where he lay. He had folded his ghongadi over a hollow and was lying with his huge axe next to him, and responding to Savala's story with a "hmm" or "hann". Savala insisted that he should hear Tayanu's response to every statement of his. In case Tayanu failed to do so, he would nudge him and ask loudly, "Are you awake?"

"Yes, yes, carry on," Tayanu would reply, pulling the blanket over himself. Satisfied, Savalya would proceed.

"These white people are the descendants of Hanuman. When Hanuman burned down Ravan's Lanka, Ram granted him a boon. 'One day you will be a king.' That's why they have become our rulers. But alas, this boon of Ram's is proving costly for us. They have put us on call three times a day . . ."

"Wait," said Tayanu pushing the ghongadi off his face, "Ram was a god. If this is a reign of his devotees, then who are you? Why do you have enmity for them? Explain to me . . ."

"Awha," said Savala addressing Tayanu. "That's what I don't understand," he said sheepishly. "We are poor people, why do we alone have to face this?"

"And listen further," Tayanu added, "if the white men are the progeny of Hanuman, why don't they have tails like him?"

"Who knows, ba!" said Savalya and pursing his lips, fell silent. He thought for a while and then whispered, "Maybe the sahebs do have tails, but they are hidden by their ijars, inside their pants."

Tayanu burst out laughing at this remark. The entire hill-side was awakened by their loud laughter. It appeared as if the whole Sahyadri range was laughing too.

"Daji . . ." Fakira called out from the adjoining thicket. Savala controlled his laughter and looked in his direction.

"Shall I come there?" Savala asked.

"Ghamandi is not here?"

"No."

"Why hasn't he come yet?"

"Who knows?"

"Has he lost his way?"

"Don't know."

"He should have been here by now."

"True. Who knows, he must be stuck somewhere."

"The night is almost gone . . ." A tremor crept into Fakira's voice.

Looking up at the stars, Savala said, "The Goat hasn't set and the Thieves haven't reached it yet. He will come soon. You go to sleep."

"I think Ghamandi has lost the way," repeated Fakira.

"So what shall I do, then?" asked Savala.

Fakira replied, "Try giving him a bird call."

Savala came out of the thicket and went to the edge of the cliff. Standing there and looking down, he let out a cry like, peacock's. His call reached far into the night. Everyone listened intently for a response.

After several moments, a responding call was heard from below. Savala jumped with joy. "Ghamya is here!" he yelled. The wild boar approaching the thicket where Baloba lay snoring, panicked and ran into the bushes below.

After some time, Ghamandi came up the hillside. He was accompanied by Bhiva Mang of Bedasgaon. When Fakira saw Bhiva, he was a little happy. This Bhiva was quite stoutly built. Besides, he was a relative of Savala. So there was absolutely no possibility of any betrayal. In any case, Fakira needed additional men. Everyone was happy to see the man from Bedasgaon. They all patted Ghamandi's back for bringing news from home and also a bold man to their group. Ghamandi gave them all news from their respective families and the special messages they had sent. Finally, he reported that Khot from Shigaon had been staying in the village since one week. "Every night Patil comes to the Mang settlement and searches all the houses. He abuses the women and children. It seems yesterday, the very big saheb from Satara had come on a visit. He said that he would give a reward to anyone who captures Fakiradaji. So Daulu Aba and Radha Aai have asked you to be more careful. Ganu Ramoshi from Shigaon is expected to come and . . ."

"Don't let him climb the mountain," Khandu yelled. "Khot must have bribed him and sent him here. There's bound to be treachery."

"Naik is right," said Fakira. "We should not trust anyone henceforth. Every person must be properly scrutinized. Otherwise we all will be dead in one go." Then he turned to Ghamandi and asked, "What else did Aba say?"

"Aba?" said Ghamandi. "Ganya also has to present himself in front of the police periodically. So he went and asked Aba to send him to Fakira."

Tayanu was listening silently until now. He interrupted. "All lies. Now the government will deliberately charge men to report periodically. They will be told to ask Daulu Aba to send them to us here. Then they will betray us . . ."

"That's why we should be careful," Mura said.

Everyone was dismayed by the thought of such a betrayal. They also realized that their enemies were not sitting idle. Rather, they were making plans to attack them from all sides.

But they were hugely pleased that a strong and sturdy person from Bedasgaon had joined their fold. When Bhiva had seen the fierce side of Fakira, he had been surprised. Fakira, a man from his own community, had led a rebellion against an oppressive regime and had inspired him. Fakira appeared as a god to him. And he was determined to join in the fight and fight till his last breath.

Tayanu was the happiest to see Bhiva. Bhiva's thick grey whiskers had spread themselves across his wide jaw.

Under bushy grey eyebrows, his large red eyes looked menacing. He seemed to be perpetually angry. Tayanu liked such men.

It was past midnight. The wind was up and was blowing recklessly along the cliff wall. A fire of mountain logs burned softly. Savala, Tayanu and Bhiva were warming themselves around it. Bhiva stuffed the chillum with embers and pushing his moustache aside, took deep long drags on the pipe. Ghamandi had returned. He had brought news from the homes of all the men and hearing that all was well there, they felt a big burden was lifted off their chests. Many had fallen asleep, snoring among the thickets. Gabarya was pawing the ground restlessly, while Fakira was lying nearby, wide awake. Sleep just wouldn't come to him. After some time, he jumped up and came out of the thicket. He felt better when the breeze blew across him. He went towards the fire. As soon as Bhiva saw him, he said, "Come, sit . . ."

"Hmm . . . so tell me how are things in your valley?" asked Fakira sitting down by the fire.

To which Bhiva replied, "The government treasury is in Bedasgaon. So the amaldar, the police officer, has moved the whole village way outside. And then we have to give this hajiri at the police station three times a day . . . We have no time to even shake our heads."

"Treasury?" asked Fakira narrowing his eyes. "Why there?"

"Government collection from that region first comes to Bedasgaon. From there, it is despatched to Kolhapur," said Bhiva.

"How many persons guard the treasury?" he asked.

"What guards?" mocked Bhiva, "At the most, three or four men come by. There is one bahman alone guarding it."

"A Brahmin?"

"Yes, a bahman."

"Is the government not afraid that someone will try to loot the treasury?" asked Fakira in surprise.

"Who will dare to loot it?" said Bhiva, "This sarkar is not afraid of anyone. That's why they have kept it in the bahman's wada. When the treasury is full, they take it to Kolhapur. At that time, seven or eight gunmen accompany it."

"How much cash does the treasury contain?"

"Who knows how much there is," said Bhiva, and the cash from the treasury started jangling in Fakira's mind. He quickly returned to his thicket and called out for Mura, Bali and Sadhu. The three men jumped up and ran towards him. Taking them into confidence, Fakira said, "The treasury of the Britishers in Bedasgaon is overflowing." His head turned towards the east.

The sky was turning crimson. Multiple hues were splashed across the sky. Treading on a velvet carpet, the new sun was stepping onto the earth. Looking at this charming picture, the birds began to sing to each other,

The shesh cobra has swallowed the eighteen hours!
The east has lit up its face!
On its forehead the red kumkum glows, declaring
It is morning!

"So what do you plan to do, Daji?" asked the three. Looking towards Bedasgaon, Fakira said seriously,

"Get ready. Let's loot that treasury. The white saheb should feel as if a dormant tiger has awakened. Let us see how they make our attendance compulsory in the police station and rule over here."

"So for when should we plan it?" asked Sadhu.

"Immediately. That wealth is trapped in the bahman's wada in Bedasgaon," said Fakira, his voice rising, "Let's set it free. But first let me go and meet Aai, Baba, big Aai. You get organized here. Gather at least a 100 staunch men and start."

Bhiva had overheard this conversation. He came forward and said, "But that bahman has a gun. A man's valour is useless against a gun. It will be a tough fight . . ."

"My courage will face any cannon, it won't be useless," declared Fakira. "He has a gun? Let him have it. How many bullets will it fire? We will take ten bullets each. A dead sheep is not afraid of the fire. Rather than die tomorrow, let's die today. But with dignity and courage, like true human beings. Panta used to tell us a story. There used to be a king here. I forget his name. He used to say, 'Rather than live like a goat for a 100 years, it is better to live like a tiger for one day.' And that is true. Let's be like a tiger and die like one. Come on, gather the men and get ready to start moving. In the meantime, let me go visit my home and meet my Aai."

As Fakira, Sadhu, Mura and Bali were discussing this, the lord of the skies, Ravinarayan, made his way serenely and appeared above the horizon. He too seemed impressed by Fakira's words. The whole world was flooded with the sun's rays. They spread over the mountains and bathed the forest in a golden yellow light.

Small wild flowers nodded their heads in the breeze as they bowed to the sun. The world was awake and ready for action. Fakira's men went and bathed. Some prayed, and some performed sun salutations as they dried their dhotis. Mura, Bali and Sadhu went about their chores with the Bedasgaon treasury on their minds.

The whole forest seemed to be whispering the words "Bedasgaon cha khajina." It was the topic of discussion in every thicket. The whole day passed discussing the treasure.

Fakira was impatient to set out. Ghamandi loaded the saddle onto Gabarya and said, "Don't go alone, Daji. Raosaheb Patil has appointed guards to keep watch."

"All right, I will take Savalunana with me," said Fakira. "Tell Savalunana and Tayanuaba to go with me. Don't worry, I will be careful. You also better be alert here."

The sun rolled slowly down behind the mountain to the west and Fakira started riding Gabarya towards the east. Both were going home but the sun was alone while Savala and Tayanu walked with Fakira like executioners.

All was quiet by the time they reached the outskirts of the village. The lanes were deserted as the farm labourers had returned home a long time back. Someone was speaking in the village and in the silence of the night, his voice carried over a long distance. Fakira, Tayanu and Savala reached Patil's veranda and stopped because Fakira was faced with a dilemma. It was regarding Gabarya. If Gabarya was taken inside the village, he would whinny and neigh and wake up the whole village. People would recognize his sounds. Gabarya, who had been a faithful friend and who Fakira loved dearly, had suddenly become a problem. Fakira was deep in thought when Savala asked him,

"What are you thinking about, daji?"

"About Gabarya."

"Means?" said Tayanu.

"As soon as we reach our neighbourhood, he will neigh and announce our arrival and then . . ."

"That is true," said Tayanu. After a moment he added, "So let us do one thing. I will wait here with Gabarya while you and Savalya go home."

"But what about you? When will you go to your family?" asked Fakira, surprised at this suggestion.

"I? I will go when Savalya comes back." He turned to Savala and said, "Listen Savalya, you come back soon . . ." Fakira felt unhappy as he handed over Gabarya's reins to Tayanu. Then he started walking into the dark with Savala. When Savala turned towards his own house, Fakira said, "Nana, Tayanuaba also wants to visit his house. Come back quickly and let him meet his family."

A dim lamp was burning in the house. Daulati had finished eating his bhakri and was sitting there picking his teeth. Rahibai was getting ready to lie down. Radha was feeling very uneasy. Saru was restless. She had not seen Fakira for almost a month now. A fire was burning inside her and she could do nothing to put it out. Pain becomes less when it is shared, she knew, but who could she tell about her feelings in this house? So she suffered in silence and alone. As if this was not enough, every day there were new rumours in the village. Some said an arrest warrant was going to be drawn in Fakira's name.

Some others spoke about soldiers from Satara having surrounded Fakira. Yet others said that Khot from Shigaon was keeping vigil and he would catch Fakira himself. Once or twice, Saru had seen some strange men loitering about their yard. This kind of news struck her ears and grieved her heart.

For some reason, Radha was very angry that day. Looking out into the darkness, she was muttering to herself, "Shouldn't he have come to meet his wife at least? Forget about us . . ."

Daulati heard Radha and his eyes flew open. In a hushed voice, he said,

"How can he come? The enemy is keeping a close watch."

"That's true," said Rahibai. "It's better that he doesn't come. Deva re, don't let him come here!"

Suddenly, Fakira barged into the house. Exclamations of surprise and joy that rose in their stomachs got stuck in their throats. Radha, Saru and Rahibai held back their sobs with great effort. Daulati embraced Fakira. His hands were shaking. Placing his sword in his mother's hands, Fakira lay his forehead at her feet and Saru was lost in the moment. The occasion was such . . . one could forget everything. But clever Daulati quickly went and stood in the doorway keeping watch. Their sorrowing hearts had suddenly found cheer. Pearls of adulation flowed in the form of tears. Agitated hearts calmed down. But at the same time, they missed Sadhu desperately.

Tayanu came to the door very early in the morning with a cheerful countenance after having met his wife and children. Fakira set out with him. Before he left, Saru handed him his sword and for no reason, she blushed and looked coy. Radha, Daulati and Saru accompanied him till the mud path and saw him off. Rahibai gave him her blessings from the doorway itself. When they saw Savalya and Gabarya by the track, they were all happy. Daulati patted Gabarya's mane and kissed his forehead. Placing his cheek against Gabarya's face, he whispered, "You fellow, take care of my babu."

After Fakira finished taking leave of them all, Radha said, "Now we must let you go. Don't worry about us. Take care of yourself. Soon we will have another Fakira in our house!"

Saru blushed furiously to hear Radha say this. Fakira quickly looked at Saru but in the dim light, he couldn't see her flushed face. Suddenly, he felt a surge of energy course through his body as he leapt onto Gabarya's back. Fakira was riding towards the mountains. Radha was standing there, staring at his retreating back.

In the east, a thin red line was slowly becoming clearer and bolder as it slit through a dark cloud. A chink of light was making its way out of a crack in the wall of darkness.

Twelve

Fakira and his band of men were walking towards Bedasgaon along the ridge of the pride of Maharashtra, the high and mighty Sahyadri. At that moment, they too appeared as imposing as the mountain. Circumstances had transformed them into the taut arch of a bow.

They were walking one behind the other along a narrow foot path. Nobody hurried because the sun was still high in the sky. It was also moving placidly over the top of Vishalgad fort. The banks of Warna shimmered in its rays and the dense forest seemed to be splashed with a silver sheen.

The mountain was alive with the surrounding sounds. Some birds were swooping and circling as they made their way home to their nests. There was a clamour in some nests. And some birds were making sweet music from their perches in the trees. Fakira, wearing an ashtee dhoti firmly wound around his waist, was sitting still on Gabarya, looking into the distance. His face was extremely grave. He was thinking about what could happen in Bedasgaon. Like dry leaves in a gusty wind, his thoughts stirred up his mind. Fakira knew that the government would make heaven and hell one when they learnt that the treasury had been looted. Then what will become of me? Who will Aai, big Aai, Saru and Daulati Aba have after me? I didn't tell Aai what we were planning before I took their leave. It was a mistake. Yes! A serious mistake not to tell her that I was going to loot the treasury at Bedasgaon.

This thought kept pricking Fakira's mind. But Gabarya was carrying him fearlessly forward every minute. Bali was leaping ahead with a stout staff like a huge pestle in his hand. His nostrils flared as he inhaled and exhaled deeply. Ghonchikar Bali rode his horse, holding on to his flowing beard which the wind was trying to dishevel. Mura kept pressing down his moustache to give them a neat shape. He resembled a ferocious tiger. On the whole, every one of them was free from fear. Though they were aware that they would be encountering death that day, they were all not at all dispirited. But they were entangled in thoughts of their families as they marched towards Bedasgaon.

They reached the outskirts of Bedasgaon as the sun had set and dusk had fallen. Fakira divided his men into teams and instructed them to go to the sandy banks of the Warna to the west of the village. They wanted to get some rest by the river bank. Besides, it was not possible to make a move until the village had gone to sleep. Accordingly, they dispersed and Fakira prepared to enter the village with Savala, Tayanu, Pira, Sadhu and Khandu Ramoshi. When he reached the village centre, he noticed a number of people sitting and talking on a platform under a tree. They saw Fakira's team with their instruments, the trumpet-like sheeng, the halagi drums, their torches, swords, spears and axes and their curiosity was aroused. One of them couldn't contain himself.

"What village from, pavana?" he asked.

Savala spontaneously responded,

"Bukkalpur."

"We are a Tamasha troupe," added Tayanu Mahar, "Have our people passed by here?"

"No, ba," said a young villager. "But where is your nachya, the dancer?"

"He is the one who went ahead," said Tayanu, "You will see him this evening anyway."

"You're saying you will perform your tamasha here in our village?" asked a villager excitedly; and Savala said, "Yes, in front of the bahman's wada we will put on our act today."

"Oh great, it will be fun," said all the villagers, and seeing Fakira they thought he must the sardar, the leader of the group. Fakira slipped out of the village.

Faces had become unrecognizable in the dark. The Warna valley was still and at rest like the weary hardworking villagers. Silence prevailed. Darkness had drawn a thick cover over everything. In the twinkling starlight, only the surface of the Warna shimmered like the blade of a sword. The grave silence was broken intermittently by the strange call of an odd bird somewhere in the distance. When all of Fakira's men had assembled, they gargled their mouths and unwrapped their bhakris. "Let us eat this bhakri as if it is the last bhakri of our life," Fakira said, "Who knows who will live and who will die today. For we are going to break the government's treasury—actually break the door and drag Yamaraj, the god of death, out." He paused and then continued, "The government will go mad when they hear of the loot and we will have to fight it out with them once again." Fakira's companions were listening to him, their bhakris in their hands. Bhiva stood up and said, "Let's loot the treasure even as we die, so that our children will eat happily at least for some days. Who knows what the future will be!" Saying this, he put a piece of the bhakri into his mouth.

"But we slipped up a little while ago! Now the whole village will gather to see the tamasha outside the bahman's door. It will be our 'tamasha', our disgrace they will witness," Tayanu said.

"That won't happen. We will just attack," said Pira. "All the spectators will flee into the lanes. Wait and see what tamasha takes place!"

Everybody finished their meal. Some of them smoked ganja. Mildly intoxicated, they started their preparations. It was quite late by this time. The whole village appeared to be sound asleep. Taking that into consideration, Fakira said, "All right, light the mashaals." They all got up at once and began to light the torches. In the glare of the mashaals, the peaceful Warna River woke up. The flowing water appeared turbulent. Axe blades were hammered onto their handles and spears polished. Ghamandi warmed the halagi drum. These brave men were going to conduct a dacoity to the accompaniment of the sheeng horn and halagi drum. They were preparing to pawn their lives. They were not cowards who would attack stealthily and kill. Rather they were the gallants who would play loud music to wake up death and thereafter embrace it. Fakira hurried ahead.

Someone called out, "Hmm . . . let's go." They all started walking. On reaching the village, the halagi drum was struck, the horn blown loudly. The entire region shuddered. Bedasgaon startled awake and listened intently.

"Why the sheeng now?" the villagers asked themselves and also replied to themselves, "Must be a marriage procession."

The lanes of the village vibrated with the sound of the halagi, and the shrill cries of the sheeng created an atmosphere of dread. Like a whirlwind, Fakira stormed to the gates of the Brahmin Raghunath's wada. The wada was now awake. It was sitting fearlessly with the treasure worth one and a half lakh tucked inside it. The huge and strong old main door was shut tight, and from a lookout window in the arch above the door, Brahmin Raghunath was watching and wondering whether it was a wedding or an attack. For a little while, this doubt troubled him. But he soon knew it was no wedding. It was a dacoity, the men were there to loot. Raghunath got his gun ready.

Fakira was grappling with the door, his chest pressed against it so that the gun in the window above couldn't get him in its sight. Naked axes and swords were flashing. A sudden rush of energy strengthened their resolve. "Charge the wada!" was the thought that propelled them forward. Raghu had waited for something to happen but soon lost his patience. He fired a bullet in the dark. The village knew what was happening. A dacoity. The news travelled fast and soon the brave amongst them rushed to the wada with whatever weapons or implements they could find.

As soon as Fakira heard the first gunshot, he yelled, "Put out the mashaals, douse the torches."

Within a minute, it became pitch dark and Mura cried out, "Prepare your catapults to attack! The villagers are rushing here . . ."

The smooth pebbles carried by the horses from the Warna riverbed started clattering in the lanes. Many of the advancing party fell to the ground. But before long, Kakira's men ran out of stones. Pira said to Fakira, "Daji, the stones are finished but the villagers are not retreating. The lanes are packed with people."

"Take out your arms then," said Fakira, "and show no mercy. Cut your way through whoever stops you and head for the river. Do not disperse. Fight as one and keep moving." Hearing these words, the brave men like Savalya, Pira from Chinchani, Nilu from Sajur, Tayanu, Bhima, Mura lost control and slashed their way out. They overpowerd those in the lanes and made for the river.

Raghunath the bahman came down with his gun. The villagers believed that they had repelled the attack and prevented a dacoity. They sighed in relief. Many patted themselves on the back. Others began dreaming of the reward the government would give them for their bravery. Slowly some went back to bed. And once more silence took over.

But by the river bank, Fakira was mad with rage. The humiliation of failure was burning his heart. Everyone was fuming. Fakira snapped at them.

"Speak up . . . what shall we do? Even after reaching the door, we retreated to save ourselves and ran away. All our lives, we have been running and death has been chasing us. How long must we run? Better that we go forward and embrace death. Facing death is bravery, but running away takes a man to hell. Everyone dies, we all have to die. But even in death, there is noble and evil. For someone who dies a dog's death, whether he lives or dies, it doesn't matter. If we are going to run away, let's burn these weapons right here on the banks of our Warna mai, smear the ash on our foreheads, surrender to the government and live. We have no right to carry these weapons."

"What could we have done?" asked Mura, "The villagers were unrelenting. Luckily, we forced a way out and reached here safely."

"Safely?" Fakira snarled, "When were we ever safe? Ever since we came out of our mother's womb—no, even when we were in it—we have been tasting blood. Fighting." His voice turned shrill. "We were never safe. My father was killed on Sanjirba's hillside. Ever since then, I have not had a day's peace, not a little bit of happiness . . . The enemy did not allow it. Ask that Savalanana."

Fakira's voice was the only sound in the surrounding silence. He was not talking, rather he was showering live coals on these valiant men and they were slowly burning up. The cool waters of the Warna were once again warmed from their heat.

After a while, they drank the cool water of the Warna, and were refreshed. They shed the tiredness. They were inspired to resume the fight.

"All right, let's go back," said Tayanu Mahar standing up. "We will break down that door or get broken ourselves!"

"Come on, come on," they all cried out. Wielding his axe, Pirya shouted, "Get up, warm up the halagi!"

"Now if I show my back to Bedasgaon, I will not take my father's name," growled Savalya. All were motivated anew. A fresh wave of determination coursed through them. The halagi was warmed. Stones were collected and loaded into sacks. Swords were drawn.

Soon the halagi sounded and the sheeng cried out, twice as loudly. There was much discussion among the villagers. "The dacoits who had run away are back for the final assault. Perhaps they are back with twice the number of men . . . they won't back off now. Why should we die for the sake of the government?" they said. "The treasury is the government's, the guard is an upper caste Brahmin, the men looting are dacoits. What for should we die?" they thought wisely and did nothing. A few spirited men rose up but when they saw no one else was with them, they also sat down.

Fakira came to Raghu bahman's door. Posting his men outside the range of the gun, he had all the paths and lanes blocked. Then, with Pira, Mura, Tayanu, Ghama and Sadhu, he started his assault on the door. The brahmin's gun was firing bullet after bullet over their heads and Fakira continued his battle with the door. Suddenly, Pira got it into his head to pick up some heavy stone slabs lying there. He used them to ram into the door. His madness infected Bali as well. Soon, the others joined in. With a resounding crash, the door fell open.

Before the head that was firing the gun could turn around, the courtyard of the wada was filled with people. Mura, Bali and Ghamandi had entered and broken the inner door and grabbed the gun from Raghu. As soon as he lost his weapon, Raghu the brahmin fled inside the dark wada. An agitated Mura went looking for him.

Fakira came out into the courtyard. Torches were brought in and peace was restored. Just then, they spotted Raghu the brahmin standing in front of a closed door, a sword in hand. He had locked his womenfolk and children in the room and was standing outside it alone to guard their honour. Looking at him, Fakira asked,

"Who are you?"

"The owner of the wada," said Raghu Brahmin sharply, "Raghunath Brahmin."

"That's very arrogant of you!" said Fakira, "I am the owner of this wada today. Get out of my way," he said advancing towards Raghu. "Where is the safe? The treasure?"

Raghu Brahmin screamed hysterically, "I will not allow anyone to advance further," and started waving his sword around. The steel blade quivered.

This brahmin is trying to intimidate me by brandishing the sword, Fakira thought, overcome with rage. He leapt forward and drew out the sword at his waist.

"I will not be frightened by the sword, and I will not leave without taking the khajina. Move out of my way! I want the safe. I don't want your life . . ."

"But he wants to give it up," taunted Tayanu, but Fakira stopped him and demanded again, "Where is the treasure?"

"In that room. Behind you."

Fakira was a little puzzled. If the treasure is behind me, why is he standing on the opposite side? There must be something valuable in that room, Fakira thought. "Why are you standing there, then?" he asked.

"My women and children are here, inside." Fakira moved two steps forward and said,

"You bahman you think only you have a family and we are heads of cattle? Come on, open that door."

Fakira's voice rang through the wada. The door opened.

Four women, Raghu Brahmin's wife, his sister-in-law and two young girls came out and stood before him. With folded hands, Raghu's wife said, "Baba, clean out this wada if you wish, but these two girls are yet unmarried. I beg of you, our honour, our dignity . . ."

Saying this, the women started taking off the ornaments they were wearing. Fakira was overcome by what he saw. "Aai, wait!" he said remorsefully. "I have come only to loot the khajina. Not to loot your honour. Your honour will not feed my hungry people. Go, get back into your house."

At that moment, Pira emerged from the room behind Fakira.

"It is an iron safe; there's no key." Fakira looked at Raghu who quickly said, "The key is kept in Kolhapur."

"I see," said Fakira, "Well then, just pick up the safe as it is and go."

"It's a monster," said Savala, "very heavy."

Fakira thought for a moment. "Get your men to fetch the village ironsmith. Tell the wadar to bring his hammer with him."

Savala, Mura and Bali went to the village and returned with the wadar. With heavy blows of his powerful hammer, the wadar broke the iron safe and a pile of Rs 50,000 lay before them.

Fakira had broken the safe in Raghu Brahmin's own wada in his presence! He paid the wadar for his effort, then left Bedasgaon with the Rs 50,000 stuffed into a sack.

After paying his respects to the Warna River, the party was on its way along the hillside. After walking a fair distance, Fakira stopped. He distributed the cash among all his men. But before that he kept aside two shares for the poor and destitute Mangs and Mahars. The rest was divided equally among the men.

All of them secured their cash in their waistbands and started towards Vategaon. Instead of wondering what would happen next, they were thinking that their families would now see some good days. Gabarya, with his peacock-like gait, was proudly bearing Fakira on his back.

At the same time, Raghu Brahmin was galloping towards Kolhapur on his horse. He was impatient to report to the government that the treasury had been looted. He was breathing hard through his flaring nostrils and goading his horse to move faster.

Thirteen

"We must catch Fakira at the earliest, otherwise we will not get even one pai out of Rs 50,000" Bapu Khot was saying, "I don't understand how such a large army fails to catch him even after fifteen days."

"It is simple," said the district collector, "The one fleeing has one path, those chasing him have a 1000. There is no trace of them. So the efforts of our men are wasted. Besides, we can't believe that this Mang would show such audacity."

"Wait, sarkar," Raosaheb Patil interrupted the collector. "We don't understand your last sentence."

"The meaning is clear. Listen," said the collector, "if Fakira only wanted money, he would have robbed your house. What need did he have to create enmity with the all-powerful regime? So I feel that those who looted the government treasury must be terrible people. Carrying away government treasure after breaking the safe with a hammer is . . ."

The collector paused. His face became grim as a shadow of worry fell over it.

A military camp had been set up on the Nerle hill-side. All the senior officers from Satara had landed there. The white army had packed its guns and from the white tents pitched there, armed white men strolled around the camp, as if someone had declared war on them.

All the official machinery was moving with the single-minded motivation to capture the miscreants and crush them.

The government had adopted the policy of "set a thief to catch a thief." Towards that end they had befriended the notorious criminals from that valley. They had been provided with everything, including arms, food and aid. In short, the Britishers had tried to unite the sky and the earth in this venture.

Today, a select band of the shrewdest men like Bapu Khot, Raosaheb Patil, Kabira from Kumaj, Dhondi Chaugula, Ganya Mang of Satara were present at the camp site. The senior officers were watching their faces keenly and trying to sort out the truth from the lies and make sense of their words.

After a long thought, Bapu Khot said once again,

"The government must keep in mind the fact that a Mang attacked Patil, the headman of his village and ran away. Ask Raosaheb here, his teeth were broken by that absconder." Everybody looked at Raosaheb, thinking, "Oh, so this was the person who was attacked."

Right in the centre sat the senior-most officer. He was an Englishman. He couldn't understand Marathi so an interpreter stood to attention next to him. When he heard an important sounding word or a change in the expressions on the faces of the elders in the room, the officer would signal to his interpreter. The man would quickly bend down and respectfully whisper the gist of the Marathi sentences in English. Everyone called the officer John Michael. He was here now to wipe out the men who had looted the treasury. When he noticed everyone staring at Raosaheb Patil, John Michael asked the interpreter, "Who is this man?"

"He is the police Patil of a village. He claims that a Mang called Fakira from his own village must have looted the treasure."

Hearing this, the officer turned red and his blue eyes flashed as he asked,

"What is this Fakira like?"

The officer's question left the men flabbergasted. They waited to see who would reply first. The arrogant Khot held out his handless arm and said, servilely, "Mai-baap, Fakira is a very formidable man. He looks like a lion but has the strength of an elephant. As for the sword, he wields it like lightning."

"Yes, yes," interrupted Raosaheb Patil, "He chopped off my uncle, this mama's hand."

The officer's face became grim and the worried look intensified. "So where is he now?" he muttered.

"Absconding!" Everyone said in unison and the officer became grimmer. This incited Kabira. He signalled to Khot and Khot said softly, "This Fakira gets assistance from Vishnupanta Kulkarni. In fact, that bahman is his main support. Fakira is the one who looted the treasury. If I am proven wrong, I will cut out my tongue."

"So get hold of him," exploded the officer and glancing at everyone said, "Do whatever it takes to nab Fakira."

The atmosphere in the camp became tense. The officers tightened their belts, checked their arms and listened carefully for further orders. Drawing lines on the table top with his fingers, the officer said,

"Requisition the special force and have him surrounded. At the same time, keep up the pressure on this Sattu who is with him! Question him, harass him. Go on, get started."

There was a heightened flurry of activity. All energy was concentrated on Fakira. All thoughts started chasing Fakira. Thousands of arms followed Fakira's trail. Hundreds of horses started to gallop. On all lips was one word, F-A-K-I-R-A! And then . . .

The sun rose slowly. Its rays entered Mang wada, dispelling the thin veil of darkness. The Mangs woke up and panicked. The children were frightened. Grabbing their little ones and holding them to their bosoms, the women started running. But . . .

Under the cover of darkness, the British soldiers had surrounded the Mang settlement. They had blocked all paths. Their weapons carried the message of death. Everywhere, the white soldiers lay in wait like hunters.

Seeing the chaos amongst the people in the Mang settlement, an officer issued an order, "Nobody should run. Those who run will die. Everyone remain in your own houses."

A wave of fear rippled through the settlement. The Mangs sat outside their hutments meekly, waiting to see what would happen next. Just then Raosaheb Patil shouted, "Don't enter your houses." Turning to the officer, he said, "Sir, we must seal their doors."

"Seal their doors?" said the officer glancing at the Mang dwellings. "Their huts have no doors, so where's the question of sealing them? I don't get it. Seal the doors, the man says. Seal doorless doors!" The officer couldn't stop laughing at this.

"Why are you laughing?" said the Patil angrily.

"So should I cry instead?" the officer retorted.

"I will show you how to seal the doors," said Patil.

"Then go ahead and do it," said the officer, his eyes flashing. Patil went forward and announced, "Block the entrances with the nivadung cactus and the thorny babhli branches."

"I agree, that works," the officer nodded approvingly.

In a short while, all the entrances to the Mang dwellings were blocked. Denied entry into their own homes, the Mangs sat helpless and homeless outside their doors. The army kept a close watch on them.

With the Mangs and Mahars confined outside their homes, they began to be treated like animals. Why is this injustice being done to us, they wondered. They have surrounded us to catch Fakira. All right, since Fakira is one of us, they have decided to punish us. But how can they catch Fakira by sealing our doors? What does this mean?

At that time, Babarkhan was in hot pursuit of Fakira with a select band of soldiers and strong horses as Fakira rode through the Sahyadris, dodging the army. He had his chosen companions Sadhu, Bali, Mura, Savala, Tayanu

Mahar, Nilu and Chinchanikars Pira and Bhiva with him. Gabarya seemed to have understood the urgency. His hooves hardly touched the ground. Through dense kir forests, over jagged peaks and across the plains, he galloped with Fakira astride him. The army horses chasing him were soon exhausted. Many riders changed their mounts, while many soldiers abandoned the chase.

Capturing Fakira was not easy. The soldiers had by now understood the difference between chasing him and arresting him. Everyone was afraid that if this Fakira suddenly turned around to confront them, their efforts would be go in vain. They too were worried about losing their lives.

Fakira had also considered turning around and confronting the enemy with a surprise attack and crushing them. After a flight of eight long days, he had reached the top of a mountain, after misleading his pursuers. Today, he was sitting wearily under a tree, deep in thought. Only if they turned back and routed the enemy quickly would they be able to breathe freely, he thought.

His companions had all finished eating and were ready to go ahead. As they were about to saddle their horses, Fakira said,

"How much longer should we flee? We don't know where the rest of our people are. There's no news of them. Right now, we urgently need more strong men with powerful wrists, but that's what we don't have."

"What's on your mind, then?" asked Savala.

"Nothing," said Fakira, "I am wondering if we should teach our pursuers a lesson before going further ahead."

"Make up your mind," said Mura.

"We must decide only once we come to know what the government is up to," said Fakira. "If they are complacent, we shall collect our men, turn on the enemy and finish off the devils."

Everyone became serious at the thought of turning back and crushing Babarkhan. Savala said, "Have a little patience. If there is a direct threat to our lives, we will kill or get killed. Right now, let's just wait."

Fakira had chosen to wait on that mountain top till sunset because Ghamandi was expected with news from home that evening. Fakira's family and his home were uppermost in his mind that day. After having received their share of the cash, most men had gone back to their respective villages. What must have happened to them? Was any one of them arrested? What if one of our group gets arrested? If he is found with the booty, the white army will not rest and will not let us rest. This Babarkhan leading the chase is after the treasure only. But what if one of our men is captured and he confesses to the crime?

Fakira was drenched in such worrisome thoughts. He was thinking what the final action should be.

It was evening. The sun was on the descent and shadows were lengthening. A veil of darkness was slowly creeping over the world. The sun's rays had lost their energy and were now struggling against the dark. The wild wind was rushing through the grass, flattening it and making the tall trees shudder. The birds had returned and were sitting in front of their nests. They were creating a racket with their chirping and twittering. Wild cats with their sharp nails withdrawn into their paws were trailing the birds. The fertile plains below were hazy in the fading light, and the green farms looked like black spots dotting the landscape. The villages looked like piles of houses clustered together with a cloud of smoke drifting over them.

Imperceptibly, today merged with tomorrow and the evening dozed off in the lap of the night. The range of vision became limited and the whole world became invisible. It was pitch dark all around.

Fakira had eaten and now lay in the bushes. He was waiting for Ghamandi to arrive. Mura, Pira, Savala, Bali, Sadhu too waited nearby, watchful and alert. They wished he would hurry up. They were worried. There was no telling what the soldiers would do. It was possible that they were climbing the mountain too. And that venomous cobra, Subedar Babarkhan could strike anywhere at any time.

Suddenly, there was a commotion at the base of the mountain and Fakira leapt up. He listened intently. Then Tayanu piped up, "Perhaps a wolf has snatched a sheep from a shepherd's flock." After a while, they saw a man approaching them. Savala stepped forward and cried out, "Who is it?"

"It's me, Ghamandi."

Everyone was overjoyed to see Ghamandi. They embraced him one by one and then sat around on a rock. Fakira asked, "What was that commotion at the base?"

"Babarkhan has turned back," said Ghamandi.

Hearing this, everyone let out a sigh of relief. It was as if a burden was lifted from their chests, and immediately relaxed hearts began to smile. But Fakira was still very serious.

"Why did that Babarkhan turn back?"

"Why? Because man fears the snake and the snake is fearful of man."

Then they turned to Ghamandi for the news he had brought.

"Babarkhan, Bapu Khot, Chaughula, Kabira and the government have combed the whole forest. They arrested all our people this morning and took them away to Nerle. Even Panta has received a summons to the camp. He was to go . . ."

"Who was arrested?" Fakira was quick to ask.

"Every single one of them—Daulu Aba, Radha Aai, old Aai, Saru kaki . . . not a soul was left behind in Mang wada."

"You mean everyone, every single one?" Bali asked in surprise.

"Not one human being in Mang wada," Ghamandi reiterated, "They have blocked all doors with branches of prickly babhli. The cattle are starving."

"That's a disaster," Bhura cried in anguish.

"Disaster?" said Ghamandi, almost tearfully, "Government soldiers are crawling around like ants. They are arresting anyone in sight. Everyone says that it was Fakira who looted the treasury."

They were dismayed by this remark. Fakira was deeply grieved. Morosely he said,

"My nest is broken and I have fallen into the bed of the scorpion! What next?"

Suddenly the atmosphere in the bush became tense. Images of Radha, Daulati, Rahibai, Saru being arrested floated in front of Fakira's eyes. How would the aged and the infirm, the women and children manage?

This action by the government enraged Fakira. Despondently, he sighed.

"Now we must do something," he declared.

"Well what do you want us to do?" asked Mura, and Fakira replied,

"Anna, you must go right now to Kumaj, catch hold of Sattu and tell him all this. The camp at Nerle must be destroyed."

"All right, and what else?" asked Mura.

"And," Fakira replied, "confirm the day and time when Sattu will reach the camp so that we can also gather our men and attack at the same time. There is no alternative now. Death is staring us in the face. If it must, then let it come quickly."

"But where should I return to?"

"Ride through the night. Meet Sattu. Finalize everything and reach Saatdarya by tomorrow night. In the meantime, I will get everything ready here and wait for you," saying this, Fakira turned his gaze towards the sky.

Stars twinkled in the clear skies. The silver starlight flowed over the dense kir forest. It was silent and the rebel soul of Maharashtra, the mighty Sahyadri Mountain sat there motionless. For millennia, it had proffered invaluable help to many a mutineer in this steadfast position. It seemed as if this chief of all patriots, the inspiration of balladeers was listening to each word of Fakira and smiling to himself. It was he who had provided a safe haven to many a patriot and taught many a heartless oppressor and ruthless invader a lesson. This Sahyadri, the presiding deity of Maharashtra, appeared solemn and silent today.

Having made the decision to attack the Nerle camp with the help of Sattu, Fakira stood up. Mura embraced him. It was a deeply emotional moment for both. Soon after, Mura mounted his horse.

"Ride away . . ." said Fakira, "The right opportunity rarely comes and if it does, it doesn't stay. Let us not delay the attack on the camp. I will also not sit idle. If Babarkhan starts pursuing me again, then tomorrow itself I will turn around to punish him. Go now. Tomorrow is not far away. Take care."

Mura quickly pulled the reins and his horse reared. He then went beyond the bushes and galloped away. The forest awoke to his thundering hooves. It was as if the Sahyadri's huge heart itself was thudding. For a long time, Fakira kept listening to the sound and gradually Mura was lost to the night . . .

. . . and Fakira jumped on Gabarya's back and Gabarya began to trot. Everyone followed him. Nobody knew where they were going.

Halfway down the mountain, Khandu Ramoshi asked, "Where are we going?"

"Naik, don't ask me that question again," said Fakira sharply."I am like a dry leaf floating in the wind . . ."

"Don't ever say that," the Ramoshi quickly responded, his voice shrills. "He who marches with head held high cannot afford to be a dry leaf . . ."

"You are right, Naik!" Fakira dismounted and putting his hand on Khandu's shoulder, said, "I was a little rattled."

"Don't be," said Naik, "Let's dig in our heels and fight, and die on our feet."

"Shabaash!" exclaimed Fakira.

"Let's die as we destroy those who shackled us, shackled our honour, our offspring, our mother the Krishna River . . . This Nerle camp, we will destroy it. We may die but this land, this mountain, these trees, there is no death for them . . ."

With these words of Fakira's, they all rode down the mountain.

Fourteen

The sun was about to set. Vishnupanta walked out of the camp towards his horse, looking grim. Bhairu Ramoshi was waiting for him with his horse under a tree. Panta turned and looked back when he heard someone calling out to him.

"Gavkar, it's Daulati. I am here."

Without a thought, Panta approached Daulati and stood still in front of him. Daulati was tied up along with a 1000 other people. Seeing Daulati, Radha, old Rahibai, young Saru and other Mangs of his village bound like that, Panta became extremely emotional. In a choked voice, he quoted an aphorism, "'What fate offers, man must accept.' I tried to reason with the officers but they say that they are holding you as hostages and will not release you till Fakira surrenders. Daulati, you are a noble soul. I salute to you! How many blows will you keep enduring? You are a vajra-dehi, a diamond of a man."

"Aba," said Daulati, his voice shaking, "This grand-daughter-in-law of mine is in captivity . . . she is pregnant . . . that infant within her is also a captive.

What sin have I committed that these old people, these children must see this day?"

"Don't cry, Daulati-Aba. I will meet Fakira and tell him this."

"No, no," said Radha pitifully, "We will die like this, but he must not surrender. Tell him that."

"Yes, yes, he must not," said Daulati, "We have not many days left in this world. But Babu should not give up. Tell him not to worry about us."

Daulati and Radha were talking; Rahibai was crying softly with her head down. Saru's eyes were swollen from weeping. This was a new experience for her. As Panta was leaving, Saru bent down and touched his feet, and Panta wiped his tears with his uparna.

"Carry on, it will soon be dark," Daulati called out in a loud and firm voice.

Panta returned home but he was very restless. He felt extremely uneasy. He didn't even eat his dinner that night. He was feeling miserable after having seen the pathetic condition of the people on the hillside at Nerle, their hardships and the sheer injustice of it all. He just could not bear the fact that such awful atrocities were taking place under his tenure as the gavkar of the village. He felt as if he had visited the real, heartless hell.

The lantern hanging by the beam was burning steadily. Everything was quiet. Half the night had passed. Panta was sad. He was sitting alone in the veranda, his upper body bare. His long grey moustaches were untidy. He knew that sleep would not come to him that night.

How could he meet Fakira? The question was tormenting him.

Suddenly, he heard footsteps in the yard. Panta looked up and saw Bapu Khot and his son-in-law Raosaheb Patil enter the veranda. Panta was surprised to see them. "How are you here, so late in the night?" he asked.

"To meet you," said Khot. "We understand that you had gone to intercede on behalf of the Mangs . . ."

"Not true," said Panta vehemently, "I was summoned as a public servant of the village. I had gone in that capacity."

"How it can be?" said Khot, "All right, listen to this. You will not plead for them. You will not help them henceforth. That's all we have to say."

"I don't listen to anyone," Panta thundered, "You may request me. You are no one to order me. And whether I intercede or not, and on behalf of whom, is my business."

"Listen Panta," Raosaheb Patil growled, "Don't argue. This village, this pandhari is mine. If you want to survive here, then live in peace. Otherwise . . ."

"Otherwise? What will you do?" Panta shouted.

"Otherwise we will straighten you out," was Patil's reply.

"Really?" said Panta calmly, "Then first get off the veranda. Go. Now!"

"Ahwa, but listen . . ." said Khot softening slightly, and again Panta shouted, "First, get out of here."

Bapu Khot and Patil left and Panta's mind was inflamed. This situation was new for him. He realized that even his life was not safe anymore. He muttered to himself, "Man should not be so wicked and so foolish."

It was well past midnight. Panta got up and not knowing what to do, he decided to lie down when suddenly Fakira appeared in the veranda. Seeing Fakira, Panta's dejection vanished. Raising his bushy eyebrows he exclaimed, "Fakira, how are you here? And alone?"

"Why?" said Fakira, "I have come with my whole army."

"Really?" said Panta, looking out. Khandu, Sadhu, Pira, Ghamandi were standing there. Fakira had formed groups of men and installed them at various places around the village limits. He had entered the village with a select few.

Looking at the five–six men in the courtyard, Panta said, "Fakira, your enemies are lying in wait for you everywhere. You shouldn't roam around like this. It is dangerous."

"Actually, I have come with fifty men. Give me your last blessings."

"Wait," said Panta, putting the mandil on his head, "Let's go far out into the forest. We must talk. Just today, I had gone to the camp. I will tell you everything." So saying, he stepped out into the courtyard and started walking. Fakira followed him. After they were outside the village boundary, Panta sat down under a mango tree. Fakira sat down in front of him. In a worried tone, Panta began to speak. And Fakira began to listen carefully.

"The government has reached the end of its patience. They are determined not to rest until they catch you. To this end, they have they have made heaven and hell one. They have captured thousands of innocent people and kept them on the hill as hostages. The people are desperate and are fearing death. My hair stood on end when I saw their plight."

"That's what I don't understand," said Fakira, "Why are they holding the whole region to ransom just to arrest me?"

"I asked this question in the camp," said Panta gravely. "To that, John saheb quipped 'A mouth will open only when the nose is pinched.' 'You mean apply the branding iron where the pain is? I asked."

"So what did he say?" Bali's response was instantaneous. Panta answered,

"He said, 'For a disease that is not cured by divine medicine, surgery is the only solution.' That's why they have taken all your people prisoner and are holding them as hostages. Not one of them will be released until you are in their hands. That decision is carved in stone."

"Did you see any of our people in the camp?" asked Fakira.

"I not only saw, I also met all of them," said Panta.

"My mother?"

"Yes."

"Aba?"

"He too."

"Old Naru?"

"Yes, yes, all of them," said Panta impatiently, "I don't want to remember that incident. There is no other example of human beings treated so cruelly. Young, old, children, all are tied up with a single rope like cattle. It is not a camp, Fakira! Narka, hell itself has descended upon that hill. I met Daulati, Radha and talked with them. The sight of our Saru's hands tied up burned a hole in my heart."

Panta suddenly paused. As if he didn't know what to say. No one spoke for a long time. The horrors of the camp were recreated before every eye.

"What did Aai say?" Fakira asked.

"They are all of the opinion that you should not surrender. They have come to terms with the pain . . . but . . ."

"But what?"

"But," Panta repeated hesitantly, "the officer insists that you should surrender. There is no guarantee that these people will still be alive by the time you surrender."

"So what should I do?"

"You should surrender."

"I alone?"

"Not alone."

"Then who all?"

"Fakira, Pira, Mura, Bali, Tayanu, Savala, Hari, Khandu, Bhiva," said Panta and added, after a pause, "the tenth one, Bali from Ghonchi was arrested this morning."

"He was arrested?" they exclaimed, shocked.

"Yes. Captured and tortured. He had a skirmish with the army on the Krishna Bridge at Karad. After he was taken prisoner, the soldiers and Khot kept pulling out all the hairs of his beard throughout the eleven miles to the camp. I didn't recognize him when I saw him. He is also injured . . ."

"It's over then. Not much point in staying alive now. Only death will make life meaningful!" Fakira turned to look in the direction of Nerle and called out, "Bali!" Then quickly getting to his feet, he said, "Aba, tomorrow, I am going to destroy the camp."

"But destroying the camp is beyond your capacity," said Panta, "How can you fight the army? There is a battalion of armed men there."

"May be," said Fakira, "I will get killed while killing the rulers. It will be better to die against the enemy than to surrender to them."

"But what after that?" said Panta, "Eight people dying in a fight and 800 people being slaughtered . . . you decide what is right. But decide quickly and save the lives of those poor innocent people. Khot, Kabira and that Patil now are bent upon vengeance. Even my life is in danger, Fakira. Just now, Khot came and threatened me."

"Let me think over it," said Fakira, "I will consult everyone as to what should be done and once we decide, I will come and meet you."

"Do that." Panta stood up and started towards his wada. Fakira walked off into the woods. He decided to gather all his scattered men together, consult them and then take the final decision.

Starlight was streaming down like milk. All of nature was bathed in a silver sheen. The air was fragrant with the scent of the kanheri, the oleander flowers, by the well; and in the cremation ground adjoining the farm, the ghaneri, the lantana bushes were blooming in full profusion. Between the farm and the cremation ground, were seated Savala and Bhima and their ten men. The others were lying down, bundled up in their ghongadis.

Savala and Bhima had been smoking ganja and under its influence were saying whatever came to their minds. The wind heightened their intoxication. Bhiva was completely high. He whispered, "Pavana, now let us do . . ."

"What should we do?" grunted Savala, and Bhiva said, "Fakira will be late in coming. Till then, you tell me a story, and I will sing a lavani."

"What? A lavani?" exclaimed a surprised Savalya, "You will sing the traditional lavani?"

"Why? Why not?" said Bhiva angrily, "There is no other singer like me in our village."

"That may be true, but," said Savala, "the farm is nearby and we are sitting in the Patil's village."

"But you first tell a tale," growled Bhiva, "Then you listen to this Sarjya's lavani song."

"All right, baba," said Savala, "I will start the story . . . Listen . . ."

"A potter had a donkey. Every day, it would get very tired after working hard. So the potter used to let him loose to graze at night. This donkey would eat up all standing crops. And feasting on wheat, green gram, sugar cane and carrots, it became very fat. Nice and round like a pumpkin."

"So it used to thieve through the night and return home during the day?" interrupted Bhiva and Savala said,

"Yes. One day, the donkey met a fox. The fox was also a thief. The two became friends. They would go around stealing and eating through the night. Nobody could catch them."

"Then?" Bhiva asked. And Savala continued,

"It was a starlit night like this. The donkey and the fox had entered a farm and were gorging on the greens. After eating their fill, the donkey said to the fox, 'Ay friend, shall I sing a song?' The fox got alarmed. 'Mama,' the fox said, 'you have a coarse voice, how can you sing?' The donkey got angry. 'You bhadavya, you wretch, what you think, I cannot sing?'

"So what did the fox say?" asked Bhiva and Savala said,

"What could he say? He said, 'Donkey mama, you sing here. I will go and keep watch from the bund there in case the farm labourers wake up and come.' The fox went a good distance away. He settled down on a bund, and the donkey started singing in its tuneless raucous voice. That awakened the farmhands. They came with their sticks and beat the donkey till it fell down. Then they brought a heavy grinding stone and hung it around the donkey's neck, so that it wouldn't run away when it came back to its senses."

"And then what happened?"

"When the donkey became conscious, it tried to run with the stone round its neck. The fox saw him and said, 'Mama, your song was so good that you got this award!' That is the end. My story is over. Now you sing your lavani."

Bhiva appreciated the story. Suddenly, he started laughing loudly. Listening to his ugly laughter, the farm workers woke up with a start and thinking that a ghost had come to life in the cremation ground, took to their heels.

Still laughing, Bhiva said, "Forget my song. Otherwise I too may get a grinding stone around my neck, ra baba . . ."

At that moment, Fakira arrived. They all gathered around him. Fakira told them what Panta had said.

"Till eight men surrender, the government will not release our people," he said.

"Which eight men?" They asked in unison.

"These," said Fakira, "Fakira, Pira, Mura, Bali, Tayanu, Savala, Bhiva and . . ."

"So what is your opinion?" they asked.

"How can I say that just now?" said Fakira. "I only told you what Panta said to me. What we should do next we will decide once Mura is back. Only if we get Sattu's backing can we attack the Nerle camp and raze it to the ground. Otherwise . . ." Fakira paused.

"Otherwise, we must cut our own necks. Only on receipt of eight heads will the government release the hostages who Khot has kept on the hillside. And if the eight of us do not give up, every single one of them will die a dog's death." After a long sigh, he said, "But the biggest blow was the arrest of Baliba Ghonchikar this morning."

"What? Bali was caught?" All exclaimed in surprise. In a pained voice Fakira said,

"Bali was held in Karad and Khot pulled out his beard all the way—eleven miles—to the camp. The Khot who shackled him and tortured him is still alive. But we are also alive. The Patil who sealed our houses with thorns is still standing on his feet and here we are, deciding whether we should surrender or not . . ."

"Listen," said Khandu Ramoshi, "Khot is here, with his son-in-law. Sitting here, he is turning the keys, manipulating . . ."

"What are we waiting for?" said Savala frenziedly, "Let's get hold of Khot in return for Bali! Come on!"

"Yes, right," said Bhiva, "and that Patil too. Blow for blow, come on, let's go!"

"Let's show them our might," said Tayanu and everyone got up.

"Wait," ordered Fakira, "If we want to capture Khot, then it should be done as cleanly as a cat knocking off a hen. And we will drag that Raosaheb also on the way. After that let whatever happens happen."

"You wait here," said Bali, "We will come back quickly. Don't worry. Even his wife will not know what happened . . ."

"I will go to the house," said Fakira, "You come quickly to the Mang settlement." Bali, Pira, Savala, Sadhu hastened to the village with fifty trusted and motivated men. Once they crossed into the village, they moved with bated breath. Lightly gripping the weapons in their hands, they dashed to Raosaheb's wada and latched on to the walls like lizards.

People were still awake in the wada. Khot and Patil were making plans for the next day. Many people like Ganu Naik, Ganya Mang were sitting around. Ganu Ramoshi had presented many of the absconders before Khot. It was decided that they would help in arresting Fakira and in return, the government would give them amnesty for their crimes.

The men left after quite some time. Khot came out into the courtyard. Some men were sitting on the veranda. Lanterns were burning. Khot hooked his sacred thread around his ear, climbed down from the veranda and went to ease himself behind a wall when . . .

Savalya grabbed him in a fierce embrace. There was a little struggle but soon Khot's feet were lifted off the ground and his mouth clamped shut. Khot didn't know what had happened. All he could tell was that he was being taken far away.

When his uncle didn't come back for a long time, Raosaheb Patil was alarmed. He stared into the darkness and quietly came to the door. He thought that perhaps Khot was talking to someone. He went to the veranda, looked around and called out,

"Mama?"

There was no answer. Only silence all round. Where could Mama have gone, he wondered and stepped off the veranda when . . . he was engulfed in another frightful hug. First he felt his mouth being gagged, and then he felt as if he was flying in the air. Then he realized that he was embraced by, or rather, in the deadly jaws of death. Cruel death was carrying him away. Mama too must have been taken on the same path, he thought and cursed himself for falling so easily into the trap.

When they put Patil down in the Mang settlement, he looked around, his eyes wide in anger and bewilderment. Fakira was standing in front of him. Pira, Savala, Bali, the swords, the axes, the big huge men and their incredible deeds . . . thinking of them all, Patil was petrified. When he looked down, he saw his noble uncle, Bapu Khot lying there by his feet all trussed up.

"Shabaas!" said Fakira, "My brave warriors! Now let death come at any time; I am prepared. Had these two remained behind and I had died, they wouldn't have left even a sign or trace of our community."

"Fakira, you better let us go," said Patil threateningly. Immediately, with one kick, Khandu felled him to the ground.

"Forget your Patil-ki, your position as Patil now," Khandu yelled.

Fakira pulled the Patil to his feet and dragged him to the door. "Why did you seal our doorways?" he snarled, "Why did you bear enmity against me for no reason? You took my poor people to Nerle and confined them there . . . Why, what for did you do all this? Speak!"

"He will not open his mouth now. Come on, let's take the two of them away," said Sadhu. And so they set off for the mountains with their two captives.

Savalya was walking beside Khot and he whispered in his ear, "You held my people at Nerle, now I will hold you up on the mountain."

Early in the morning, they reached Saatdarya. The sharp wind was stinging and the pale moon waning. Darkness was slowly spreading over the woods. A streak of light had defined itself on the eastern horizon and a huge black cloud stood erect and motionless, bisecting that line. But the energetic wind was pushing the cloud away and rays of light were escaping from under it and hurrying towards the earth. These rays had cast a new hue on the southern sky. Silky clouds floated about like boats with broken sails. The woods were waking up. The birds were mesmerized by the exquisite southern sky.

One of the peaks of the Sahyadri Mountains had touched the sky. On top of that peak stood a huge banyan tree. It looked like an erect shendi, a tuft atop a huge head, and its innumerable aerial roots had clasped the mountain in a tight grip. The ruins of an ancient temple lay nestled amidst the web of those roots. To the west of the temple was a containing wall overlooking the cliff. Two miles below the sheer slope lay the flat ground. Looking down made the head feel dizzy and the eyes roll.

Fakira had based his camp at this location. As soon as they reached the temple, Fakira tied down Khot and Patil and parked their horses along the wall. He appointed men to guard them.

The question uppermost in all their minds as they reached the top was what should be done with these two men. They sat around in groups discussing the matter. These two men are the root of all our hardships. Come what may, we should not let them go. Even if we die, we must not let them live. If they are freed, they will wipe out our entire bloodline. These are monsters. We must get rid of them. But how? What kind of death should we give them? Why shouldn't we push them off the cliff?

The war-like spirit of brave men does not get intimidated by adversity. Because fighting is in their nature. The mind is not naturally devoid of fear. It becomes fearless after undergoing relentless hardships. Just like steel is tempered by fire, their minds had toughened after a lifetime of suffering.

Fifteen

"How is it Mura has not yet come?" asked Fakira.

"It is a difficult climb," Sadhu replied.

"He is late."

"He'll come when the moon rises."

"What phase of the moon is it?"

"The moon will rise at midnight today."

Fakira didn't say anything more. He became thoughtful once again. Mura ought to be back soon. Once we get news of Sattu from him, we should take a final decision, he was thinking and waiting impatiently for Mura. It was much after the sun had set. Darkness had announced its presence in the kir forest on the mountain top. They were all sitting under the banyan tree talking amongst themselves, but their eyes were focussed on the path Mura would take. With his coming, their future would be decided. The two captives taken the previous night were lying behind the temple wall and listening intently to the conversation between their captors. Their hands and feet were bound and they were greatly agitated. They were sure that they wouldn't get away with their lives, since the whole gameplan had been turned upside down. They were cursing god for having played such a cruel joke on them. These berads, whom they had oppressed for ages, were going to have their revenge at one go, they thought. Now they had no alternative but to face whatever came their way. The father-in-law and son-in-law were groaning and moaning their fate. Their feet were bound at the ankles, their hands had been tied behind their backs, and a large stone was secured to their waists to keep them apart. They had been left in two opposite corners of the temple yard. They had lain there all day, unable to do anything, from the time they were brought to that place the previous night. They had absolutely no idea what their surroundings were like. As the night progressed, they felt that death was inevitable.

But Khot had not lost his spirit. He was fighting to survive. He had been continuously tugging at the very rock to which he had been bound. The minute he heard movements outside, he would lie still and moan. Hearing his father-in-law's moaning, Patil began to count the hours to certain death. A little after midnight, Khot managed to dislodge the rock. To prevent it from falling and making a loud noise, he cushioned the fall with his back. He then slowly dragged it along as he crept towards Patil. Like a rat, he started gnawing at the rope on Patil's wrists. He worked really fast. Once he had cut through the rope, he rested. Death was moving away from them, he thought. Then he put his mouth close to Patil's ear and whispered, "Now hurry up and free my hands!"

The moon had climbed up the mountain. The surroundings were bathed in moonlight. The huge shadow of the banyan tree had stretched right across the west, enveloping the cliff and the area beyond it. Under the cover of that shadow, Khot and Patil were busy trying to release themselves from the ropes that bound them.

Patil had just straightened up and was freeing Khot's hand when a horse's hoofs clattered in the temple yard.

Alarmed by the sound, Khot muttered, "Who could have come now?"

"Let anyone come . . . but how do we go from here?" Raosaheb Patil whispered and Khot said,

"The moon is overhead. Let's go through the shadows in the back."

When they saw Mura, all the men were relieved. Fakira patted him on his back and the men sat around him in a circle, eager for news from Sattu. In a low dejected tone, Mura said,

"Kabira, Chaughula and Inspector Pawar have surrounded Sattu. He doesn't have time even to scratch his head. He's struggling to move towards the camp but hasn't been able to. So Gondhalya passed on Sattu's message to me, 'You go ahead. I will dodge Pawar somehow and attack the camp. You be prepared.'"

"But when?" interrupted Fakira and Mura muttered,

"That's what's not decided . . ."

"Just drop that plan then," said Fakira disappointed. "We have to hand ourselves over."

After telling Mura the events of the previous night—the meeting with Panta, the arrest of all their people and the capture of Patil and Khot—Fakira added, "The government has issued an order that only when we ten people present ourselves at the camp will our women and children be set free."

"Ten people?" asked Mura "Which ones?"

Fakira replied, "Me, Fakira, you, Bali, Hari, Pira, Savala, Tayanu, Bhiva, Khandu and the tenth—Bali from Ghonchi! But Bali is already under arrest."

"What? Bali arrested!" Mura was shaken. Fakira urged them, "Let's get down to work. We must give ourselves up at the camp tomorrow morning. Also decide what is to be done about that Khot. Let's go."

At the mention of Patil and Khot, they all got up and went inside the temple. But neither of the two men were there. When they realized that their captives had escaped, they were stunned. Savala cried out,

"Daji, they've run away! Escaped!"

"How can they?" said Fakira, "We were in the front and there is no way in the back. Run, cover all paths. Don't let them get away alive."

Within minutes, there was a flurry of activity. People started running about in the moonlight. Fakira became even more worried. The fact that his sworn enemy whom they had captured should escape from under his nose was like a thorn pricking his heart. The thought of killing Khot first and then surrendering started taking root in his mind.

After quite some time, Ghamandi came running and declared, "They both fell down the cliff behind the temple and died . . ."

"They died?" said Fakira with a sigh, "Good thing, I suppose . . . Ask everyone to come back."

"Should we bring up their bodies?" asked Ghamandi.

"No!" exclaimed Fakira.

Fakira did not sleep a wink that night. He made preparations to surrender at the camp the next day. He finished his bath early in the morning, put on the cleanest clothes and tied an ashti dhoti around his waist. Savala, Mura, Tayanu, Pira, Bali and Bhiva also got ready. Savala polished his sheeng to a shiny gloss. He had decided that they would present themselves to the sahebs to the sound of the sheeng. They all were sad that their days of rebelling were coming to an end. Who had won and who had lost this battle, they wondered. The thought that in the end they had to give up, hurt them deeply. But the fact that they were surrendering of their own free will and not because they were crushed and humiliated in battle, was greatly satisfying.

A little while before sunrise, Fakira called Sadhu and gave him instructions on what to do next. "When we surrender, there will not be such a careful watch on the others. Slowly they should all return to their homes." With those words, Fakira mounted his horse. Everybody, including Sadhu, accompanied him till the outskirts of the village. There they dismounted and embraced each other once more, knowing in their hearts that this would probably be their last meeting.

Fakira entered the village and went straight to Vishnupanta's wada. He put his head on Panta's feet and paying obeisance to him said,

"I am going to surrender. Take care of my community. Sadhu is here . . . after this."

Panta didn't utter a word. His throat was choked, full of unspoken emotions. He also started out to see them off till the village boundary.

Then Fakira went to Shankarrao Patil. Shankarrao came running out and embraced Fakira.

The news reached the village that Fakira had come and those villagers who had escaped arrest, gathered to see him off.

On reaching the outskirts Fakira stopped, turned towards the villagers and joined his hands in a namaskar. Shankarrao said,

"Go on, do not be afraid. The village will never forget you. Your father fell on the Sanjirba hill and now the son on the hill at Nerle. Panta and I will follow you to Kolhapur. Give my name as a guarantor for your bail."

Hearing this, Fakira was doubly invigorated. He quickly mounted Gabarya, and Savala's sheeng made a huge sound.

The nine horses galloped to Nerle, Gabarya leading them all.

When they were near the campsite, the sheeng blared once more and the whole camp shook with the reverberations. People came out of their tents to see what was happening. Fakira entered the camp, dismounted in front of John saheb's tent and went straight in. The officer was taken by surprise and was slightly unnerved. Sharply, he exclaimed,

"Who are you?"

"Fakira Ranoji Mang."

The saheb didn't say anything for a long time and kept staring at Fakira. There was a clamour outside—

"Fakira has come," "Fakira has arrived!" That brought the saheb to the present and he said,

"Fakira? Do sit down."

Placing the splendid sword he was holding onto the table, Fakira said,

"I have come to give myself up. These are the other men—eight of them."

"I understand," said the saheb with a smile, "You have shown wisdom by surrendering. All right, why don't you take a seat?"

"But saheb," said Fakira, still on his feet, "You haven't shown good sense in arresting my innocent village folk and holding them as hostages."

"What else could I do?" said the officer, "What would you have done if you were in our place?"

"We?" said Fakira, "We would never have tied up your women and children to nab you. We would have dismantled you first and trampled you under our horses' hooves."

John saheb turned grave hearing this. He picked up the sword and tested its sharpness. Shrugging, he changed the subject, "Where did you get this sword?"

"It was given to my ancestors by the mighty king Shivajiraje. My father fought against Khot with it and I fought you with it."

"And you were defeated in the end," said the saheb with a laugh. Babarkhan, the collector and all other senior officers had arrived and were standing behind Officer John Michael. The interpreter had been listening carefully and translating adeptly as the saheb was speaking animatedly. The saheb was immeasurably impressed by Fakira's resolute face. But his words "And you were defeated in the end" had hurt Fakira grievously. He retorted, "Sir, of what use is a sword that has lost its sharpness? A sword without its edge and a rebellion without backing are bound to fail. My support was not adequate, that's why I am giving the sword to you."

"Very well. Now return the money from the treasury," said the saheb with a hearty laugh.

"I did not loot it with the promise to return it!" said Fakira.

"That is all right. But return at least a part of it. Only 15,000"

"You first give us that," interjected Savala, "then we will return it to you."

"So that makes it Rs 70,000 in all, isn't it?" John Saheb turned to Savala as he spoke, "A dacoity of Rs 55,000 and this additional 15,000! You are a bear, man . . ."

The officer thought for some time and then said something. The interpreter turned to Fakira.

"The saheb says you had planned to attack the camp?"

"Yes, it's true!" said Fakira, "But it was not in my fate to attack the camp and it was not in yours to see it happen."

"All right. So what next?" said the officer.

"Release all the innocent villagers."

"Agreed," said the officer and turning to Babarkhan ordered, "Release all the people Fakira points out to."

Babarkhan nodded and Fakira came out of the tent. Seeing him, the crowd on the hill started crying out. Fakira ran straight to Radha and embraced her. He touched Daulati's feet, and then he took Saru in his arms and held her close. The waters of the Krishna and Koyna rivers gushed forth from the eyes of these five people. Radha was struggling to speak out, but no words would come out.

"Why did you come? You should not have . . ." said Daulati, wiping his tears.

"No, no. I have caused you grief all my life. Now to see you held like this and be alive myself . . . it was not . . ." He didn't say anything more.

Radha finally spoke.

"Where is Sadhu?"

"He is safe," said Fakira, "Aba, Aai, big Aai, Saru, you don't worry. Go home now. Sadhu is there, he will take care of everything."

Radha stared silently at Fakira as if she was in a trance. Rahibai, controlling the trembles in her neck, was dabbing her eyes. Daulati was bewildered. Then Fakira said to Babarkhan,

"Cut all these ropes . . . set these innocent people free. Come on! Hurry up!"

Hearing this, Babarkhan turned and looked towards the camp where John saheb was standing. He conveyed Fakira's wish to the saheb and the saheb ordered everyone to be freed. Within minutes, they were all out and running in ten directions. Fakira's family did not move. Radha and Saru were looking at Fakira with their very souls reflected in their eyes.

"And one last request, saheb," said Fakira, going up to John saheb, "This sword and my horse should go to my Ajja. We worship the sword every year."

"All right!" said the officer and Fakira was very happy. He took the sword and handed it over to Radha and once more he touched her feet. Then he went and stood beside the officer.

Savala, Mura, Tayanu, Hari, Bali and Bhiva were all talking to their families. They were meeting them for the last time.

The sun was moving towards the west. The atmosphere on the hill was one of gloom. Two hundred people, young and old stood together. Fakira, Mura, Hari, Pira and Tayanu joined their hands in reverence and took their leave. They then moved into the camp.

These two hundred people were returning to their village. They had no energy in their bodies; their hearts were left behind in the camp. They kept turning back every now and then, mournfully. Their tears flowed unchecked. The unceasing struggle, the fight, the battle for the sake of the villagers—they remembered it all and each of them said,

"They gave a good fight."

Rahibai had been seated on Gabarya's back and Daulati was leading him. Radha held the sword close to her and walked, wiping her tears. Saru was constantly looking back.

"Sarubai, what are you looking at?" said Daulati sadly, "Babu will not come back now."

"No, no, don't say that," exclaimed Radha, as she felt a sharp pain in her chest. In a heavy voice she said,

"What sin did I commit that I had to see all this? On the maidan his father fought and died, the packet of pedhas still tucked into his belt . . . now the son is entering the jaws of death on the Nerle hill for the sake of his mother. To whom shall I tell this wonder?"

"To our own minds," said Daulati, "Tell your woes to yourself and your joys to the world . . . come on, let's go."

As Radha came up the bank of a small stream, she suddenly stopped. An old memory was revived. Distraught, she closed her eyes and recalled that incident. The others stopped and looked at her.

Fakira was a boy then. A British military camp had been set up at Nerle. Many of the children had gone to see what the sahebs were like. Radha had looked for Fakira everywhere but couldn't find him. She had started crying. Then Attar had told her that Fakira had gone to the hillside. Radha started walking towards Nerle. She followed Fakira's footprints which she saw on the hot sand. When she had reached this very spot, she saw young Fakira running towards home.

She had been overjoyed. Seeing his face drenched in perspiration and the urgency to get home, she had been overcome. She had quickly knelt down, and in a flash, Fakira had rushed into her arms. Radha had risen holding him close to her chest. With her sari, she had dusted the sand off his feet.

Experiencing this old incident in a new form made Radha's mind go numb. She lost all her vitality, her energy. But suddenly she spun around and stared in the direction of Nerle. And she saw little Fakira, Ghamandi, Mura and Bali coming towards her. Quickly she knelt down and held her arms wide. Fakira rushed into her open arms.

And suddenly Radha came back to the present. She had been hugging Fakira's sword! Saru helped her get up. Feeling utterly helpless, Radha looked far into the vacant landscape and let out a heartrending cry, "Fakiraaaaa . . ."

Anna Bhau Sathe's Preface to the Marathi Edition

Painful Expression

Along with my novel '*Fakira*' I am also presenting you with a brief statement. It has been my aim to continue writing, regardless of the commendations or condemnations my work elicits. It is best not to get into any discussion or debate here.

I am writing this piece just to say a few things about the novel *Fakira*. The novel *Fakira* is not purely the creation of my imagination. It's my belief and personal experience that if any creative act does not reflect universal truths and life experiences, then words like creativity and perceptivity become meaningless. For if truth is not supported by life experiences, then creativity is as useless as a mirror in the darkness. If no reflection is seen no matter how hard one tries, then all skill and ingenuity is ineffectual. Like a wingless bird, creativity cannot fly. I am too weighty to take off on such flights of imagination.

Just as creativity needs to be rooted in reality, imagination also needs the wings of life experiences. If experience is not coupled with empathy then we would never be able to understand why we write.

That is why I always try to write with empathy and compassion. Because those who I write about are my own people. Their concerns are my chief concern. There is no other way I can write.

Even this *Fakira* is mine. I am not equipped to 'make real' what does not exist. I have written what I saw, heard and experienced. *Fakira* has emerged from that experience. I have gathered together all of Fakira's exploits in the backdrop of the mountains and their foothills and constructed this mansion. That is all. And there is a reason for it. When Fakira was galloping all over I was relaxing in the cradle. That midnight when Fakira charged into my home, he had looted the British government treasury. He called for Appa from the courtyard. Appa wasn't at home so my atya, (Akka, his sister) went to the door and conveyed to Fakira the news of my birth. Hearing this, he took from the pouch at his waist, two handfuls of Surati rupee coins, handed them over to Akka and said, "Take care of the baby and its mother." Akka had heard the pounding of his horse's hooves. I came to know about Fakira's heroic surrender much later. Even the magnificent sword with which he had challenged and defied Babarkhan on several occasions, I saw after a long time. Many years later my mother told me that the first guti (dry fruit paste) of my life came from the money plundered from the British treasury! Later, I stored all the stories narrated to me by Akka, Appa, that village, those mountain ranges, those valleys and plains, and I held on to them in silence. Fakira had done me a favour. How could I ever forget the two handfuls of Surati rupees looted from the British treasury he had showered on me at my birth? My first solid food was on account of his benevolence. And I kept wondering how I could repay the debt I owed him. Finally, after exploring the profound depths of Marathi, the language of saint poets Dnyaneshwar and Tukaram, and thirty billion Maharashtrians, I lavished it on Fakira, hoping to recompense the two handfuls of silver coins.

My only intention was to bring to light that which had been ignored, to illumine that which was in darkness so that it stood forever enshrined in Maharashtra's temple of knowledge and learning.

Maharashtra has a tradition of tireless and unceasing efforts towards bringing into the forefront, those who have been in the shadows. One of the first names that come to mind in this regard is Mahatma Phule. The other name is late Shri M. Mate. Because he dared to venture into the realm of the marginalized and he was immediately condemned with the derogatory epithet 'Mahar Mate'. Yes, people such as these critics have also taken birth here. But Mate's greatness will never diminish. I will take it forward. Though Fakira was one of the marginalized, he was not a stranger to me. He was one of my own. I have written this novel by collating the entire gamut of his deeds. How worthy is this novel, Maharashtra will decide. For Maharashtra! You are great, you are wise, you are the initiator and the executor, and I . . .I am nothing!

Anna Bhau Sathe
01 March 1959
Chira Nagar
Ghatkopar
Mumbai 39

Two words

Foreword to the Marathi Edition by V. S. Khandekar (Acclaimed Marathi Writer)

The man: (from the courtyard): What's going on? Can I come in?

I: Of course, do come.

Visitor: (Entering) No no, if some important work is going on then . . .

I: Work is going on, yes, it's important but you can come in. Perhaps you can help me with it.

Visitor: (sitting in front) And how is that?

I: You see, in some kinds of work, the more the members involved, the greater the pleasure! Literary aesthetic pleasure is one such. If there is no one to share that joy with, it begins to taste insipid sometimes. Unless you are part of a group slurping basundi with great relish, the true taste of the sweet dish is lost. It is something like that.

Visitor: You are writing something new, it seems?

I: Unh hun . . . No! I have to write a preface. Am pondering over it.

Visitor: You've been writing quite a few prefaces and forewords of late!

I: Look, this is what happens. When a man becomes old, young people come to do namaskar and seek his blessings. Obviously you are bound to bless them. When cricketers retire, they have to guide younger players, na, its similar to that. The youngsters keep playing, hitting the ball, but as a senior, you must be there to appreciate, encourage and sometimes advise them on how not to play a shot or how to make stroke . . .

Visitor: For whose book are you writing a foreword?

I: Anna Bhau Sathe's.

Visitor: Shahir Anna Bhau Sathe? He was here the other day! Aho, but he composes ballads, scripts, tamashas. Are you writing a foreword for one of his tamashas or what??

I: If I knew enough about it I would definitely done so. But today the book I am writing a foreword for happens to be a novel. It's his third novel. He also writes short stories, does Anna Bhau. They are quite absorbing! Have you read 'Khulwadi'?

Visitor: (Smiles) Khulwadi? Is it a collection of some humorous stories?

I: Not that there is an absence of humour in Anna Bhau's stories, but he is predominantly a serious writer by nature. He has the soul of an author who writes with intense social commitment, as one who has encountered great ordeals, not from behind seven veils, but face to face, one who has witnessed the harsh truths of life most comprehensively. Naturally, his stories are unique about humanism though there is protest in it. You must have heard of well-known writers of 'grameen' (rural) literature like Dighe, Mate, Thokal, Bhosale, Vyankatesh Madgulkar, Mirasdar, Shankar Patil, down to Ranjit Desai and many others, but his Khulwadi has a very different manner to it.

Visitor: And how is that?

I: You know what a pungent spicy pithla loaded with onion tastes like? Anna Bhau's stories leave you with that kind of taste. (Hearing that visitor giggles. Seeing him laugh) If you don't like this simile from the kitchen I can bring in another from the sky. Anna Bhau's stories are like the brilliantly hued western sky at sunset . . . But let it go! Anna Bhau has lived and experienced the life and experiences of the lowest strata of society. And he has internalized it all in his writings. His literature is different from that of the white collar, upper class / caste authors. Anna Bhau is not like writers like me . . . who write about what they see from their windows or experience the outside world from the comfort of the armchairs on their terraces. He was born into that home. Just as blotting paper instantly absorbs extra ink from paper, Anna Bhau's creative and sensitive mind absorbed the tears of peasants, Dalits and the downtrodden in the villages, right from his childhood. Not just the tears but their dreams, aspirations, their loves and hates. All that he has assimilated into himself completely. His stories have emerged from all these experiences.

Visitor: Then I must read this new novel of his!

I: I was about to tell you that! Your palate, bored of the tasteless, sensual, erotic stories of Pune-Mumbai will find this an exciting change. This novel is set in the Varna valley and its surrounding areas, and the main characters are from the Mang and Mahar communities.

Visitor: Oh! Is it a 'social reform' novel or what? Harijan Welfare and all that . . .

I: It is not a novel of today. It intersects the past and the present. A historical novel, but not one set in the times of Shivaji Maharaj and Tanaji, or Emperor Ashoka or Chandra Gupta. The novel talks about the plight of the villages of south Maharashtra after the British established themselves as rulers in our country in the early nineteenth century. But it is specifically about the Mang community from the Varana valley and describes the exploits of a valorous father son duo in that village. That Anna Bhau should write this novel is natural. His childhood was spent in this valley. And the community he has graphically portrayed as it existed fifty or sixty years ago is one he was born into. Every creative writer knowingly or unknowingly dips into his own personal life.in his writings. Anna Bhau

Sathe is not an exception to the rule that every writer is influenced by the events witnessed, things heard and the cultural traditions imbibed, which become deeply etched in his consciousness and reflected in his writing.

Visitor: But what is the plot/ storyline of this novel?

I: Look, a summarized version of the novel will not give you the true flavour of it. I believe that one should never give a brief outline of the plot of any novel. Aho. Tell me by looking at a photograph of a dance can you tell the range and variety of her talent? Hence we should not discuss the summary of any novel. Look, here are some pamphlets and some flyers of a program lying here. Can one really gauge the broad range of skills by merely looking at the picture of a dancer? Some pages of the manuscript are lying here. Read the first chapter and see for yourself.

I read it, and I felt as if a film was unfolding before my eyes. The first chapter of this book describes how Ranoji, the head of a Mang family is late returning home that night, the anxiety his mother, father, wife, and children go through as they wait for him, how the idea of capturing the Jogani from the neighbouring village and bringing it to his village thus bestowing glory on it takes birth in brave Ranoji's mind. It also shows how the young Fakira's words galvanize Ranoji's desire and on the second day how this invincible fighter gallantly wins the Jogani for his village and in such inimical conditions he still remembers to bring his beloved sons a packet of pedhas (a sweet box) and eventually as he successfully enters his village bounds with the Jogani, is treacherously killed by his enemy who breaks tradition and enters Ranoji's village. All this has been presented in a most vivid and graphic manner by Anna Bhau Sathe.

Visitor: The incident you just described must be gripping. But if the author has structured the plot of the whole novel around the Jogani, then wouldn't it be an account of faith and old fashioned beliefs of a time gone by, and a depiction of the influence they have on the rural society of that period?

I: Look, the novel is not set in today's time. It takes place about fifty-sixty years ago. Even those middle class novels of Haribhau of today depict blind faith and superstition. Where is the rebellion and protest against blind religious practices?

Visitor: Besides the intense rivalry that exists between the two villages because of the Jogani, what else is there in this novel?

I: The author has constructed the rest of the narrative from this very rivalry. Attempts are made to retrieve the Jogani that Ranoji had brought home. His son, now a young man, valiantly fights to hold on to the Jogani in his village. This Fakira is the protagonist of the novel. His courage, his daring, his refusal to tolerate any kind of injustice, and his rebellious personality dominate the subsequent action of the story. I just told you how interesting opening of the novel is. The end of the story is much more captivating and heartrending! Fakira and his supporters continue their revolt against the British from their hideouts in the rivers valleys and mountain caves.

Visitor: But what is the purpose of their revolt?

I: The same usual one. The stiff competition between the two villages results in the Government becoming suspicious of all Mangs and Mahars. Compulsory reporting to the police is imposed on them. This utterly humiliating practice of branding Mang and Mahar communities as criminals in order to control them eventually becomes intolerable to Fakira. It sparks off more clashes. Fakira and his band steal food grains for their starving Mahar and Mang community members.

Visitor: You just mentioned that the conclusion of the novel was heartrending. Is Fakira hanged or what?

I: Oh! You have slowly extracted the entire plot of the novel from me! But never mind. I found the last scene very effective. Fakira and all his followers repeatedly disobey the police, but then their family members are arrested and held hostage. There is no possibility of getting help from a trusted friend like Sattyappa, and there is absolutely no hope of victory. When he sees this, Fakira presents himself to the authorities and manages to get the release of his community members. Anna Bhau has portrayed his surrender in a most elegant and dignified manner.

Visitor: Even this incident you are describing fits perfectly into a movie sequence!

I: These are the salient features of Anna Bhau's novel. It is true that it is full of harsh but intensely moving events but what is special about all the incidents is their credibility. The reader is able to visualize them all, as if they were taking place before their very eyes.

Visitor: But do the series of dramatic and heart touching events make it a good novel?

I: Absolutely not! Without realistic characterisation, it will only be a crackling series of incidents, a mere cord of crackers! Three characters in this novel will easily grip the reader's mind. The first is Fakira. His amiable, heroic, and compassionate personality pervades the novel like a dazzling light! But more than him I liked the characterization of Fakira's mother Radha and the Kulkarni, the head of that village, Vishnupanta. Radha figures in the novel very briefly. Throughout the story she has to experience the pain and pleasure of being the wife of a fearless fighter and the mother of a mighty son. Though the author has only touched upon the intense feelings of a mother and the deep emotions of a wife they touch a chord in the reader's heart. The character of Panta has laso been portrayed in an eloquent manner. Pant who is magnanimous, loveable, compassionate yet firm and humanitarian, ages as time passes and the reader's respect for him grows stronger.

Visitor: The language of the novel must be the grameen or rural kind?

I: The language of this novel too has a uniqueness of its own. Anna Bhau writes, effortlessly, the white collar/ standard city prose. As for the idiom of the rural folk, he knows it like the back of his hand. He has grown up listening to it, and yet it has a special stylistic quality. There is not a false note in it. The author's descriptions of nature or his manner of presenting everyday incidents in a new light add a most elegant and poetic flourish to the language. For example look at these sentences: ". . . uncontrolled Gabrya started with the speed of lightning', 'those words had built permanent home in his heart,' 'courage is honed on the whetstone of poverty, he believed' Mother you are no ordinary woman, you are the mother of a tiger!' 'Here humans lived like weevils and insects in a grain cellar.'

Visitor: I must say, I had come for a casual visit, and what a good thing it was!'

I: This writer is gifted with creativity. He has experienced all those elements which fuel the miseries in life. There is a kind of anguish in him. He is a staunch supporter of the rebellious temperament, and celebrates the spirit fighting against injustice! All this you will easily notice while reading this novel. However there are certain things Anna Bhau should pay greater attention to, I feel. His novel sometimes seems to be a series of incidents. Only when situations, characterisation,

> atmosphere, thematic unity and style come together in an organic manner do we have an aesthetically pleasing work of art. Anna Bhau not yet managed to effect that construction. Besides, the most inspiring part of his novel, no matter how good it is as a portrayal of that period, after Independence, historical fiction or tales of adventure and bravery have very little appeal. But Anna Bhau is one of those writers who believe that aesthetics and social relevance are pivotal to their writing. Such writers cannot cling to the past when they protest about justice or injustice in their work. Today the very nature of all protest in our society had changed. If Anna Bhau took into account the villages of today, the lives of their downtrodden communities, and the perennial problems that haunt them, it is likely to be more enlightening. An author with a social conscience and temperament should always be inspired bearing in mind the advice of the poet Keshavsut who said, "The contemporary period is a vast land, carve beautiful caves there."

Even though I feel Anna Bhau should do something like this, I am fully aware that every author has his / her own strengths and limitations. Does the river flow according to the wishes of the people on its banks? Whatever zigzag turns it takes, it does make the soil along it fertile doesn't it? Artists too are like that. Keeping this in mind lets us wait for Anna Bhau Sathe's fourth novel.

Kolhapur:5/3/1959
V.S.Khandekar

Acknowledgements

It has been my privilege to translate Anna Bhau Sathe's iconic novel *Fakira* from the Marathi to English. Translating this novel has been a tough task and for a number of reasons it took two years to complete. The prime challenge was to deal with the dialectic Marathi language extensively used in the novel *Fakira*. This dialect is spoken primarily in Sangli and Satara districts of Western Maharashtra which is very different from the formal Marathi language of Maharashtra. Translating *Fakira* into English without losing its context, holding the essence and retaining the cultural connotations in the original text was an arduous task. Though I have endeavoured to achieve this to the best of my capacity, I have maintained, to a large extent, the essence of the original text. If anything is lost, it may be the limitations of the translator.

I had the rare honour of collaborating with Dr. Faye V. Harrison, my supervisor at the University of Florida-United States of America. Dr. Faye always encouraged me in all my academic strivings. Regarding this translation project Dr. Faye gave many pointed suggestions such as the writing of the proposal to the publishers, selection of the publisher, reviewers and other related processes. In spite of the globally difficult times due to the corona pandemic and her own busy schedule at the University of Illinois, Dr. Faye edited the proposal repeatedly and gave invaluable support in making this project a reality and happily agreed to write foreword to *Fakira*. My words cannot adequately–express my gratitude to her for the unstinting support.

I am immensely grateful to Professor Suhas Pednekar-Vice Chancellor of University of Mumbai and Professor Ravindra Kulkarni- Pro Vice Chancellor of University of Mumbai for their encouragement to come out with this translation.

I am indebted to a large number of colleagues, friends and relatives without whom I could not have completed this book of translation. Dr. Milind Awhad-Department of English- Jawaharlal Nehru University-Delhi, Prof. Dr. Shivaji Sargar- University of Mumbai and Dr. Rajesh Karankal- Head, Dept of English-University of Mumbai invigorated me from time to time. In my endeavour Dr. B. S. Waghmare- Centre for the Study of Law and Governance, Jawaharlal Nehru University Delhi- guided me on the structure of the book, linguistic nuances and related technicalities. I am deeply indebted to him. Thank you very much for your keen interest in my work Dr. Waghmare sir. Dr. Bhimrao Bhosle from The Centre for Applied Linguistics and Translation Studies (CALTS), University of Hyderabad, called me several times and exhorted me to take up this translation project. I know for sure that Dr. Bhosle would be happier to see the completion of the English translation of *Fakira*.

I would like to acknowledge the support from CTES President Advocate Leeladharji Dake, General Secretary Mr. Ramesh Mhapankar, Joint Secretary Mr. Sharad Acharya, Treasurer Mr. Deepakji Chauhan, all Management members, the Principal of N. G. Acharya and D. K. Marathe college Dr. Vidyaguari Lele for their support in this literary venture.

My mother Jijabai and father Namdev have also been great motivating forces behind this work. Being unlettered, they didn't understand what exactly I was doing but my mother's moist eyes would always indicate I am making them proud. I must also thank my amazing wife, Kranti. Her involvement in this work has been two folded. From the beginning she eagerly followed the progress in the translation, reading and editing the early drafts. Her valuable support in taking care of all the house hold responsibilities, our kids, their schooling and more importantly tolerating me seating in front of laptop for long hours and for many months only made this book possible. In getting this book done she was as important as I was. Thank you so much dear Kranti." I am also thankful to Aditi and Abhinav that they could see their father available on all Sundays and public holidays but would only prioritize the translation work and miss out his duties towards them. Aditi could also be called as the first reader of this translation work. She would curiously read the translated pages and question on certain words which brought in more clarity in the work.

During the course of this translation I have received help from many quarters, I would especially like to thank my Uncle Mr. Anandrao Gaikwad who incessantly talks to people about me and always is proud of my accomplishments. My teachers Prof. S. N. Pandit, Prof. Subhash Dongre, my friend Dr. Uttam Ambhore - Head Dept of English- Dr. Babasaheb Ambedkar Marathwada University Aurnagabad and Prof. Mrinalaini Chavhan have always charged me with additional energy and perseverance to achieve this work. Dr. Sanjay Deshpande-University of Mumbai, Dr. Sonu Saini- JNU, Delhi have also been truly anxious to see this work completed at the earliest.

The biggest hurdle in the translation process was to capture the essence of dialectic words into Marathi. Hailing from Western Maharashtra, Mr. Sunil Ware (IRAS), Mr. Tukaram Sathe, and an international scholar Mr. Kabir Das were the ready reckoners to get the precise meanings of all the words I stumbled upon. I thank you all three for your invaluable support in this initiative. I can write extensively on Mr. Kabir Das about his tireless efforts getting this book published. From getting NOC for publication to find the publisher and an apt introduction for the book, in all such demanding tasks Mr. Kabir was involved untiringly. I am sincerely thankful to him for being there with me. My friends Prof. Madhu Bala and Prof. Radhika Mukharjee with eagle's eye suggested possible improvements in the translation.

I'm very glad that I got to work on this manuscript with Mrs. Keerti Ramchandra. We have never met, but in our conversations her passion for translation and her understanding of both regional dialects of Marathi and English came through clearly. With her conscientious, diligent and sensitive editing and our dialogues about the cultural and linguistic nuances pertaining to the land of *Fakira* we have tried to capture the power, the spirit and the poignancy of this novel. Between us we hope we have been able to fulfil the author›s objective to ‹bring to the fore that which had been ignored, to illumine that which was in darkness so that it stood forever enshrined in the temple of Indian literature. I wish that my new 74 year old friend and I will get more opportunities to discuss translation and work together on other such projects.

At Penguin Random House India, Ms. Manasi Subramanium, Executive Editor, Ms. Ananya Bhatiya, Associate Commissioning Editor and renowned linguist and accomplished scholar Dr. Ganesh Devi have been the true pillars of the publication of *Fakira*. Without their keen interest and highest professionalism, this publication would not have been possible. Many thanks to you all three. I find myself short of words in thanking sufficiently to Dr. Ganesh Devi for his immense contribution in this translation project. I must also underscore Dr. Devi had personal loss at home yet he agreed to write the Introduction to *Fakira* which speaks volumes of his commitment and contribution.

And last, but certainly not the least, I thank Penguin India and all its readers.

understanding of both the languages of Marathi and English, and through [illegible] with the text [illegible] difficult and [illegible] and [illegible] about [illegible] understanding the text [illegible] to the land [illegible] we have tried [illegible] as possible [illegible] [illegible] of this novel [illegible] hope we have been able to [illegible] the author's [illegible] [illegible] that which [illegible] [illegible] to the [illegible]. I wish that [illegible] [illegible] will [illegible] [illegible] such [illegible]

[illegible] Radhika [illegible] [illegible] and renowned linguist and [illegible] scholar Dr Ganesh Devy [illegible] the [illegible] of the publication of [illegible]. Without their [illegible] this publication would not have been possible. My thanks to you all [illegible] words [illegible] to Dr Ganesh Devy for his [illegible] contribution [illegible] this translation project. I [illegible] Dr [illegible] [illegible] contribution.

Last, but certainly not the least, I thank Penguin [illegible] editors.